I0549892

BLACK OPS & LINGERIE

A NASH MYSTERY
BOOK 2

VELLA DAY

Erotic Reads Publishing

Black Ops & Lingerie
Nash Mystery Series
Book 2

Copyright © 2017 by Vella Day

www.velladay.com

velladayauthor@gmail.com

Edited by Rebecca Cartee and Carol Adcock-Bezzo

E-book ISBN: 978-1-941835-44-9

Print book ISBN: 978-1-941835-45-6

ALL RIGHTS RESERVED. No part of this book may be used or reproduced in any manner whatsoever without written permission of the author except in the case of brief questions embodied in critical articles or reviews.

This is a work of fiction. Names, characters, places, and incidents either are the product of the author's imagination or are used fictitiously, and any resemblance to actual persons living or dead, business establishments, events or locales, is entirely coincidental.

ABOUT THE BOOK

Mystery or man? Why not both?

This was not Kane Cornell's lucky day. It was supposed to be a simple protection detail, but when the senator is nowhere to be found, Kane has no choice but to turn to the sexy yet guarded deputy of Savory, Arizona for help.

All Sky Nash wants is to be promoted to detective. When she finds her first dead body, she's determined to find the killer. She certainly doesn't need the overly macho and hotter-than-sin private eye taking up her time. She's the first to admit that Kane's presence makes it too hard to keep her wits about her. But her determination to solve the case forces her to stick her nose where the US Government doesn't want her, putting both of their lives in danger.

Can Kane's love and Special Forces talents save them from a horrible fate?

CHAPTER ONE

For those who believe, no proof is necessary. For those who don't believe, no proof is possible.

---Stuart Chase

Officer Sky Nash might enjoy supervising the Navajo Open Market, a place where the local tribes sold their silver jewelry, woven blankets, and pottery to the public on the third Wednesday of every month, but it wouldn't earn her any points toward becoming a detective. Neither would checking Earl Chee's story about a UFO sighting last night, but at least it would give her a chance to check up on the old man.

Sky turned off Arizona's route 98, a few miles past Savory's town limits, onto the rutted dirt driveway to his farm. Rocks pinged off the undercarriage, and dust coated the newly washed cruiser.

Sky skidded to a stop in front of Earl's house, sending a huge dust cloud into the air. Cutting the engine, she scanned the area to see if the reported UFO was in plain sight, though she didn't expect to see anything.

As she waited for the air to clear, the front door opened, and Earl rolled his wheelchair down the wooden incline to the driveway and sent her a toothless grin. Sky eased out, trying not to sink too far into the powdery dirt.

While Earl had an open and imaginative mind, she wouldn't call him a crackpot like her boss did. She believed in the possibility that life could exist elsewhere, but she wasn't ready to say there were aliens walking around on the face of the earth.

Earl stopped in front of her. "Thanks for coming out so quickly."

"No problem. I've been meaning to come by this week anyway. You need anything? Want me to pick up some feed for the animals?" Being handicapped made his life extra hard, especially since his wife's death six months ago.

"Nah. I'm doin' okay, considering."

She pulled out her pad to show him she would take his report seriously. "So tell me what happened." The sun beat down on her face, warming the chilly fifty-degree air.

He rubbed his thigh above the amputation. "Last night, I was getting ready for bed when the sky lit up on the north side of the property."

"Uh-huh." She glanced in the direction of his finger, but the wooden house blocked her view. There had been a lightning storm a little before midnight, so perhaps that was what he'd seen. "Go on."

"When I seen this spacecraft, I got real excited thinking maybe my friends had come back for me."

He'd previously told her that his *friends*, lived forty-seven light years away, so she doubted they'd come for a visit. "But it wasn't them?" she asked.

Earl had also claimed he'd been to a faraway planet, in some kind of exchange program with the aliens back in 1975. The extra dose of radiation on the trip back from the Zeta Reticuli solar system had caused him to get cancer and lose his leg—or so he believed.

"Afraid not. Anyway, I was about to check out the craft, when this big eighteen-wheeler pulls up next to the ship. I waited a bit to see what they were going to do and then these two guys jump out of the truck."

"Were they human?" She could never tell when she spoke with Earl.

"Hell, yeah, they were human, and they had themselves some big rifles, so I decided it best to stay inside with the lights off."

Sky jotted this down. "Smart. You saw the craft land?"

"No, dammit, I didn't." He hung his head. "I was looking for my special binoculars."

"Could you tell what they were doing?" *They* could mean either the men or the supposed aliens.

"Not so good. They were probably waiting to see what the aliens would do before they made their move. Then someone else showed up. I didn't see no other car, so maybe this new guy had been hidin'."

She was surprised Earl didn't conclude the third person was a passenger on the spacecraft or had beamed down. She glanced at the house and noted the spotlights mounted on the corners of the roof. "Then what?"

"Once the men were done, the three of them got into a whoppin' shoutin' match."

"Could you hear what they said?" She almost forgot to take notes.

"They were too far away."

"How far is too far?" she asked, as she swatted at her flyaway hair from a sudden gust of wind.

"'Bout fifty yards."

Not close enough to hear but apparently near enough to see. "And then?"

"One of them knocked the newcomer down and leaned over him. The first guy grabs a shovel and starts digging a hole, but at the time I didn't know why. Not wanting them there, I grabbed my shotgun just in case they decided to come in and take me. I got to the back bedroom, opened the window, and fired a few shots at them. I mentioned that when I called it in."

"The Chief didn't tell me." No surprise there. She decided to refrain from saying it might not have been the smartest thing for Earl to draw attention to himself. She wasn't convinced Earl's eyes weren't playing tricks on him. *Two men fight with a third and start digging a hole,* she noted. *Earl fires shots.* "Did they return fire?" If they did, she'd need to find the casings.

"Nope. They got back in the truck and took off. They didn't seem to give a hog's butt I was trying to take 'em down." He shrugged. "Maybe they were wearing vests like on those crime shows."

"Probably. Can I see where the craft landed?"

"Sure, lemme pull up the cart."

As she turned to follow Earl, a burst of gunfire shattered the cruiser's windows and put holes in the side panel. Holy shit. The crack of glass and metal was louder than Fourth of July fireworks. She shoved his wheelchair behind the cruiser, away from the spray of fire. "Duck down," she shouted.

She did a tuck and roll to get out of the way, sucked in a breath, and dropped to all fours.

"Sky?"

She looked up. Flashes of light came from the rocky hills about five hundred yards away, and the sand in front of Earl's house rippled. Damn. She drew her gun and took cover at the back of the cruiser, her breath caught in her throat. Her Glock 23 didn't have the range to reach the attacker, but she needed to protect Earl somehow. Just as she leaned out into the open to take aim, a bullet grazed the back of her left arm. "Dammit." The sharp burn made her jolt upright.

"Sky!"

The stinging ebbed as blood dripped down the inside of her sleeve. She holstered her weapon and crouched next to him. "I'm good." An extra dose of adrenaline flooded her body and blocked some of the pain. "You okay?" she asked.

"Sure am. We need to get you inside." He nodded to her arm.

"Let's wait a minute." She had to make sure he was safe. No telling who they were after—her or Earl. When no more gunfire sounded, her breathing slowed. She covered her wound with her right hand to stem the flow. *Think.* "Whoever is out there might be waiting to see our next move." Her heart wouldn't stop racing, and her fingers shook. "I need to call for backup. You have any idea who's shooting at us?" Using her good arm, she fumbled for the cell phone in her top jacket pocket, and her bloody fingerprints smeared the screen. Crap.

"Could be the aliens," Earl mumbled, his head nearly between his legs.

"I don't think the aliens would have lasers on their guns. Only a sniper weapon could shoot that far with such accuracy."

He twisted his face toward her. "You're right. When I stayed on planet Serpo, I never saw a more peaceful civilization. They had no reason for guns."

She refrained from rolling her eyes. "It's clear our attacker or attackers are human. Keep low; I don't want you to be next." She called the office and got through—a rare event in this remote area of Arizona. "Hey, Harriet. It's me." She gritted her teeth against a quick blast of pain.

"Ask for medical help," Earl whispered. "My skills are a might rusty."

Sky covered the phone. She wouldn't ask what kind of medical skills Earl had. He'd most likely tell her he'd gotten a medical degree somewhere in Zeta Reticuli. "It's a scratch. I've had worse." She told Harriet about the shots fired, but not that the cruiser was damaged or that she'd been injured. If the Chief found out about his precious vehicle, he'd be here faster than a missile warhead, and he'd somehow believe she was responsible.

The dispatcher assured her she'd send the best, but since the only other officer on the day shift was Harvey, she wouldn't get any real help.

Sky disconnected but kept watch on the far hill where the

shots had come from. "You piss anyone off lately?" she asked. The natives around here would never shoot at the law.

Earl shrugged. "It could be the two men from last night who killed their partner. Maybe they don't want a witness."

"What? Someone's dead?" She stared at him.

"I told the Chief."

She slapped the bumper and cursed. She and the Chief needed to have a talk about him keeping her in the loop. She couldn't do her job properly if her boss didn't give her all the information and show her the same respect he showed his male officers.

"On second thought, the men could have found out the aliens were trying to contact *me*," Earl said.

"That must be it." She lifted her hand from the wound. The bleeding was down to a trickle.

Earl wheeled backward. "We need to get you fixed up right quick." He held up a finger and waved it. "And no arguing, young lady. I've seen enough infections in my time to kill a whole slew of pigs." He smiled. "The barn animals, not—"

"I got it." The distant rumble of an engine rolled over the mountains away from them. "Sounds like our snipers might be leaving." The telltale sign of billowing dust added to her conclusion. Earl kept a long-handled grabber in the side pocket of his wheelchair. "Hand me that metal claw." Sky slipped off her jacket, and using Earl's extension rod, she waved the material in the open to see if she could draw fire, but no more shots rang out. She nodded at the cruiser. "You realize the Chief is going to kill me for this."

"It's not too bad. I bet Morton's Garage can fix this up in no time. Come on inside. We'll worry about the cruiser later."

"Easy for you to say." She stepped behind his chair and pushed him to the door, keeping an eye on the hills in case she'd been wrong about their attackers' departure.

Inside, she checked her wound and the damage to her jacket while Earl located a small first aid kit. The hole ruined the wool coat, so she'd have to wear her slick leather coat to work for a few days until she ordered a new one.

He handed her a tin metal box. "Looks like you just got grazed."

Needle pricks pulsated along her arm, and she sucked in a breath. The morning had started out so well, and now she'd been shot. "Yeah."

Sky took out the iodine and cleaned the wound the best she could, but it stung like a bitch. Earl then helped her wrap the injury in gauze.

Gravel sounded on the driveway, and colored flashing lights speared the front window. "That was quick. Harvey must have been nearby." She stood up so fast her vision blurred. Holding onto the top of the chair, she waited until her balance returned to normal then slipped on her coat. "Let's hope we can get to the bottom of this."

They both headed outside. At six-three and three hundred plus pounds, one hundred of which spilled over his waistband, Harvey Bonner huffed as he ambled up to them.

"You okay?" he asked, raking a gaze along the cruiser's side.

At least his tone had been tinged with concern. "Better than my vehicle." She pulled out her notepad and listed the events that led up to the shooting, including the fact Earl had found a body.

Harvey's eyes widened. "Where is he?"

Earl moved toward them. "Out back. Let's take the golf cart. It's the only way I can get around out there with the stones and scrub brush. My wheelchair's not built for the rough terrain."

"I'll walk," Sky offered. The two-seater golf cart wouldn't fit all three of them.

Harvey didn't argue. She hurried behind them to make sure her coworker didn't do anything stupid when he arrived out back. She'd heard he'd once been a great officer, but his zest for the job evaporated after his son overdosed.

They all reached the site three minutes later. With her

mouth open, she stared at the corpse only half buried. "Dear God."

It sure wasn't what she'd expected. The person didn't have a head.

CHAPTER TWO

Security expert, Kane Cornell, pulled in front of the Savory, Arizona police station around two p.m. Thursday. The five-hour drive from Phoenix made his back stiff and his patience thin, but he'd come here to protect Senator Overton, not to be comfortable.

He polished off the bottle of warm water that had been baking on the front seat for the last two hours and eased out of his ten-year-old Jeep. Between Phoenix and Savory, he'd driven through a ton of small towns, all of which needed a financial boost. Savory could use more industry, but it didn't look depressed. It was clean and spruced up with flowers, looking like a community with a lot of pride.

A log cabin style bed and breakfast, called Rosalie's, situated to the south of the sheriff's department, was decorated with flags and sat across the street from something that belonged in a circus. Flashing pink neon lights bordered every window of the establishment, and a ten-foot metal mock-up of an alien space-ship, complete with little green men sticking out of the top, sat on the roof of EBE's café. It seemed out of place in the mostly conservative looking town.

Kane's former commanding officer, General Arnold Stent-field, claimed a government agency had invited Senator Overton to a research facility close to Page, Arizona. Stentfield had received intel that the trip might end badly, so when he failed to get a hold of the Senator, he called Kane for help. His last known stop was in Savory, about an hour south of Page. When Kane asked why the General didn't involve the FBI, he said he wanted to keep this on the QT. That was fine by him. The extra paycheck would come in handy.

Most likely, Overton wanted some peace and quiet and had turned off his cell. Regardless, Kane promised he'd remain by the Senator's side until the General sounded the all clear.

He glanced at the café again, debating whether to grab a bite to eat first or ask questions about the Senator. Two women ambled out of EBE's, arm in arm, one wearing a green sweatshirt with a gray alien on the front, and the second wearing a pink visor with a spaceship on the bill—tourists most likely, or so he hoped. The General had mentioned something about extra-terrestrials being the town's main focus, but Kane had blown him off. After seeing what the town had to offer, there might be something to his claim.

Kane climbed the three brick steps to the sheriff depart-ment's entrance and passed an inviting bench bordered by two rockers. Inside, the enticing smell of chocolate chip cookies caused his stomach to grumble.

The main area of the station appeared to be a little over a thousand square feet and was filled with lots of natural light. If he could see through walls, he bet he'd find an evidence locker, holding cells for prisoners, and an interrogation room. All in all, Savory was lucky to have such a nice facility.

An older woman, whose nameplate read Harriet, sat at a small wooden desk next to a slightly out of date dispatch system. Beside her was the coveted plate of cookies, still warm by their strong smell, but he resisted asking for one.

"May I help you?" Harriet had pretty, silver highlighted, blonde curls and a smile that crinkled her eyes.

"I need to deliver an urgent message to a visitor who's here—a Senator Paul Overton."

Her eyes widened at the mention of the name, and she sat up straighter, and then tugged on her brown uniform shirt. "I didn't know we had a dignitary in town. Oh, my."

"Perhaps someone else knows his whereabouts?" People in small towns knew the comings and goings of everyone.

"Well, Officer Harvey Bonner is out on a call and Elmer Peacemaker isn't feeling too good today even though he works nights. Doc said he might be coming down with the flu. It's been going around, and Detective Denison is recovering from bypass surgery." She waved a hand. "But you didn't come here to find out about our health, now did you? That just leaves Officer Nash to help you."

Since there was only one other person in the room besides Harriet, the woman seated at the desk toward the back of the office must be Nash. About thirty, she had pretty features and dark hair that fell past her shoulders, held back by sunglasses on top of her head.

Her short-sleeved beige uniform fit snugly, and the gauze bandage wrapped around her upper arm added to the mystery. Her head was bowed, as she examined a photograph. "She'll do."

"She's single, you know." He almost laughed at Harriet's boldness. "Are you married?" she asked.

A direct question deserved a direct response. "Used to be."

Her smile disappeared. "Did your wife leave you?"

The familiar rush of agony stabbed at his gut. "She died over two years ago from cancer."

Her face reddened as she averted her gaze. "I'm so sorry."

Kane nodded and maneuvered his way to Officer Nash's desk. In front of her, a photo lay face up, and his stomach tightened at the decapitated male.

Not wanting to invade her space by standing over her, he dragged a chair from an empty desk and placed the seat in front of her desk. She pulled what looked like a murder logbook toward her and began writing, apparently unaware of his presence.

He leaned forward. "Excuse me?"

Her head jerked up, and her eyes darted right then left as if she thought he'd materialized out of thin air. "How did you get here?"

"I drove?"

She rolled her eyes before a small smile caught her lips. "What I meant was, I didn't see you come in."

Had he not been here for serious business, he would have enjoyed the banter. "You were preoccupied with your body there."

"You're right. That's not a good trait for an officer, now is it?" She tossed him a smile and shoved the photo into a manila folder. "What can I do for you, Mr.—?"

He stuck out his hand. "Kane Cornell. I work security in Phoenix." She returned the handshake before leaning back in her chair.

"Sky Nash." She swiped an errant strand of hair off her face. "Phoenix, you say? You're a long way from home. How can I help you?"

He stared at her, surprised a white woman would be employed at the Reservation.

"To answer the question you're too polite to ask," she said, "I was adopted by a Navajo family after my parents were killed. I was twelve before I found out I had a grandmother back in West Virginia, but by then I was happily enjoying my life here."

"I see." That explained a lot. He placed his card on the desk. "I need to deliver a message to Senator Overton and hope your fellow there isn't him."

"A senator's in Savory?" She glanced at the closed folder. "For your sake, I hope so too, but from his body type, I'd say he's a tad too young to be our Congressman. This one was murdered two days ago. When was the last time anyone heard from the Senator?"

"He flew from Washington DC to his home in Phoenix yesterday, so your man, thankfully, isn't him. Overton planned to drive his RV to Page, meet his constituents, and then take a short vacation in Salt Lake City. His office has been trying to contact him since he left but has had no luck."

"He's missing?"

"I'm guessing he's just hiding from all the crazies back in DC." He chuckled. No lie there.

She steepled her hands, the tips of her fingers resting on her lips. "We're only fifty minutes southeast of Page, but he would have come up 89 from Flagstaff. Route 98 is out of his way. You sure he came through here?"

"According to a gas receipt he did."

"I trust you called him?" She tapped her fingernail against her lips, taking his mind to the wrong place. "Mind you, cell phone service around here can be spotty."

"I called several times. Twice, I got his voice mail, and the rest of the time, the call was dropped. I stopped by to let you know why I'm here, should anyone give you flak about me asking questions."

"I appreciate that, but you need to be careful. It's easy to get lost and driving can be quite tricky with all the soft sand and falling boulders."

"I'll keep that in mind." He stood and grabbed the back of the chair to return it to the empty desk.

The bell above the door rang and loud footsteps smacked the floor. Kane turned. A Navajo man, who was closer to sixty than fifty, marched toward them. From the decorated uniform, this man might be the one in charge.

When the imposing figure reached them, he nodded to Sky, and then faced Kane. "Heard someone new was in town. What can we do for you?" They shook hands. His nametag read, Chief Lapahe.

The town didn't need cell phones when news traveled this fast. Perhaps the receptionist had blown his cover. "I was just telling the officer here that I'm trying to locate Senator Paul Overton."

His brows rose. "Didn't know he was here. You might not be aware, but this is a Navajo Reservation."

"I am thank you."

His lips twisted. "There are places you shouldn't go; it can be dangerous for a white man to roam around alone asking questions, even today." He turned back to Officer Nash. "Take this young man around and help him with whatever he needs."

Her brows rose and her chin edged forward. Clearly, she wasn't happy with the command.

"I was about to run down one of my leads on the case *you* assigned me," she said.

"Don't tell me a UFO really did land on Earl's place?" Lapahe raised his brows in an exaggerated fashion.

"No, but the dead body you didn't tell me about was real."

He shrugged. "Thought Chee was making that part up."

"He wasn't. Can't someone else take Mr. Cornell around?"

Clearly, she didn't care he was standing next to her.

The chief looked around. "Like who?"

She took in a deep breath and exhaled slowly as if she was trying to decide how much to argue. "Fine, I'll take him." She waved a hand. "I guess my dead man will be just as dead later this afternoon."

Not wanting to inconvenience her, Kane took a step forward. "Sir, that's more than generous, but I'm good."

The Chief's eyes narrowed. "That wasn't a suggestion."

Kane needed to find the Senator fast to provide him the needed protection, so having a guide might speed up the process. "Then sure."

Too bad General Stentfield didn't know who had invited the

Senator to visit the research lab on the outskirts of Page or the location of the lab itself, or he could have asked them. Top-secret operations had a way of holding tight to that kind of information.

As they exited, Kane held the door open for Sky, and her eyes briefly widened. Maybe there weren't many gentlemen around Savory or else all five foot two of her had intimidated the lot of them with her long stride and gun.

She reached the bottom step and faced him. "If, as you said, the Senator didn't reach Page, maybe he decided to stay at one of our RV parks. We've got two nice ones."

"Great. Let's check them out." Perhaps the RV parks closer to Page had been booked.

"Could you drive? Someone decided to use our new cruiser for shooting practice."

"Ouch." He nodded to her injury, and she turned a pretty shade of pink. "Did you get in the way?"

"I'm hoping it was a ricochet."

"I'd have thought such a small town wouldn't have a lot of crime." He prayed those same criminals hadn't done something to the Senator.

She chuckled, and the sound came out pleasant. "Not a lot, but unexplained things happen here all the time. There's a large contingent who believe aliens are coming to attack the city, and they need to protect themselves at all cost."

He laughed. "Duly noted."

They reached his Jeep and Kane opened the door for her before walking around and sliding in on the driver's side. "Which way?"

"Head west on 98. We'll start with the Wildacres RV Park. It's the nicer of the two, and given that your subject is a senator, I'm betting he'd stay there."

"Works for me."

The drive west was rather desolate but still beautiful. Red rock hills were surrounded by miles of golden sand mounds striped with blues and browns against a brilliant azure sky. The landscape was interrupted only by a blazing sun. The quiet drive gave him time to think. To his surprise, the silence between him and the officer didn't bother him like it usually did when he was paired with someone. Then again, his occasional partners weren't this pretty. *Don't even go there.*

"Turn right at the next road," she said.

Make that a bumpy dirt road. He couldn't imagine the Senator staying at a trailer park, but if he'd driven the camper, he probably didn't have many choices. As Kane rounded the curve, an oasis appeared with pines, green grass, and a sign claiming there was a swimming pool with a Jacuzzi tub. It was all very impressive. Two tall stone pillars bordered the entrance leading into the campgrounds. "Who'd a thunk it? This place is nice."

"Told ya." She grinned, but he refused to address what that did to him, or how much he actually enjoyed the jolt of pleasure slicing through him.

Don't get sidetracked.

A small mobile office sat wedged between two doublewides. Off to the side was some kind of combination convenience store and Laundromat. According to the sign, showers and restrooms were behind and to the right. An expensive looking RV sat beneath a Piñon pine on the far side of the park, and no other trailer came close to matching the elegance of that vehicle. He nodded in its direction. "Looks like I've found what I came for."

"We need to check in at the office first. It's protocol and politeness."

He had no problem following the rules as long as it suited him. A thin woman with a slightly hunched back, no younger than seventy, came out of the office favoring her right leg and smoking a cigar. "Howdy, Sky. Who do you got here?" Her voice was so low, he wondered if she took steroids or had suffered from throat cancer.

Sky made the introductions and told her that Kane needed to speak with the Senator.

"Well, I'll be damned," the office manager said. "I knew he must have been some kind of celebrity given his fancy ride." Betty hacked up something into a tissue. "Sorry." She inhaled again and coughed.

He urgently needed to speak with the Senator, and ask him to call his aide. Kane knew he would have to stay for a few days until the tour concluded, ensuring that the Senator returned home safely. However, to hurry these two women from catching up might be a mistake. Finally, Sky must have taken sympathy on him and said her goodbyes to Betty.

Despite the cool breeze, the sun made standing in the open quite warm. They made their way over to the only ritzy set of wheels on the lot, and after a quick check of the license plate, relief rushed through him. He'd found the Senator. Kane knocked then stood back, but no one answered. Damn.

"Seems he took off," Kane said. Maybe he was already at the facility, which wasn't good.

"Did he trail a car behind the RV?"

It had been careless of him not to ask. "Don't know, but I can find out."

He dialed the Senator's office in Phoenix. After being forwarded three times, he received his answer. "Thanks." He faced Sky. "No car."

"I wonder how he planned to get around. Driving this big RV would waste a lot of gas."

"I agree." Kane knocked again in case the Senator was asleep or indisposed, and then jiggled the knob. "That's odd. It's open."

Sky smiled. "We trust people here."

"The Senator is from Phoenix and works in DC. He wouldn't change his habits that quickly." Kane stuck his head inside and called, "Senator?"

Once more, there was no answer.

Since Kane's job was to protect the man, he pushed protocol aside and entered.

"You can't go in without permission," she called from behind.

She was the protective kind. Good. "Ma'am, where the Senator is concerned, I do have permission." He wouldn't mention Overton's life could be in danger. The less she knew the better.

"For the record, I don't condone what you're doing," she called out. "We should ask around first." Her first remark came off a little harsh. She must have realized it because the second request sounded sweeter. The mix of nice and sassy suited her.

"You do that. I'm going to check out his place." Fortunately, she turned around and honored his request instead of trying to drag his ass down the steps—not that she would have succeeded.

While he didn't open any drawers, he did search for car keys or a printout of an itinerary, anything to indicate what might have happened or where the Senator might have gone. When nothing looked disturbed, he allowed himself to relax. Once he completed his search, Kane climbed down the steps.

He was almost surprised to see her waiting for him since he thought she'd be checking with the neighbors. She squinted since the sun was right in her face. "I found something," she said.

"What would that be?"

"I need to show you." He followed her to the back of the trailer. "See those shoe marks?" She dropped to her haunches and pointed to the impression.

He shrugged. "I'm sure lots of people walk around here, and with the lack of rain, there's no telling when the footprints were made."

She stood. "True, but this one," she said, pointing with her toe at one of the indents, "is a drag mark."

"You think someone took the Senator?"

"Maybe, but that's not all." A small smile turned up her lips as she produced a business card from her pocket that she'd wrapped in a tissue. "I found this a few feet from the first footprint. It's from a company in DC. Not saying it belongs to the Senator, but it could."

"You might be right, though the card alone doesn't indicate foul play. It might have fallen out of his pocket."

"Agreed."

They walked back to the front where he scanned the rest of the fifty or so vehicles parked there. "Do most live here full time, or is it more transient?"

"A little of both." She sounded friendlier now.

"If those heel marks did belong to the Senator, he might be in trouble. If they didn't come from him, perhaps he made the acquaintance of some locals and decided to go off for the day."

"Sounds reasonable."

The meeting could have fallen through or his contacts could have driven the Senator to the rendezvous point. "How about we start knocking on doors?"

"Didn't I just suggest that?" she asked.

He couldn't tell if she was angry or feigning outrage—probably a little of both. Hell, she could be flirting with him for all knew. He believed in giving credit where credit was due. "You did."

The first three neighbors didn't answer, possibly because Sky's uniform might have stopped them from coming to the door. The fourth person, who drove a small camper, did respond. The man had a barrel chest, a blond ponytail, and a beer dangling from his fingertips. He had pit bull written all over him and didn't seem the type to work at a research lab.

"Sure. I saw him drive in. He talked with Pat and Clay Wilson in the Coachman for a bit, but the Wilsons pulled out a few hours later and they haven't been back since. That's not unusual for them though. They often take off for weeks at a time."

Helpful bugger. Looks sure were deceiving. Maybe Pat and Clay were the Senator's contacts. He turned to Sky. "Do you have time to ask around about these two?"

She glanced at her watch. "I'm good for a little while."

As they were halfway to the next trailer, a man in a motorized wheelchair wearing an NRA cap came down the road with American flags attached to the sides, flapping in the wind. He waved. "Excuse me."

Kane closed the gap. "Yes?"

"Hi, I'm Pete. Betty told me you were asking about the Senator."

A quick shot of adrenaline coursed through him. "You know something?"

"Not exactly, but Pat was all excited the Senator had agreed to go cave hunting with them."

"What's cave hunting?" He glanced at Sky who had a twinkle in her eyes, and he decided this couldn't be good.

"I can see you're not from around here," the old man said.

"Phoenix."

"I'm guessing Sky hasn't told you about all the UFOs that have landed here?" She shrugged. In her defense, she had warned him. "Well, you see, the government is trying to cover up the fact that spacecrafts often land, or crash in the Arizona desert. They don't want us plain folks to know about the space people, so they hide the ships in the big caves until they can retrieve them at night."

Either this man was loco or he'd been brainwashed. "You know the location of these caves?" Not that he believed the wild story, but perhaps Overton decided to see something unique for himself.

"Sure. Everyone around here does. Sky can take you."

He bet his tour guide wouldn't volunteer for that job. While she'd been polite and even patient, from the way she frequently checked her phone, she wanted to return to town and do her thing—like find the identity of her mystery man. "Thanks for the heads up."

Before Kane had a chance to even ask her if she'd be willing to take him around, her cell rang. She turned her back and walked away, the conversation appearing to be personal.

"If I see the Senator, you want me to tell him you're looking for him?" the NRA man asked.

Kane handed him his card. "I'd appreciate it."

Sky returned. "We need to leave." The color in her face had receded, and her eyes had lost a little of their sparkle.

"What's wrong?"

"Someone else just went missing."

CHAPTER THREE

The fear in Pearl's voice when she'd called to report her daughter missing echoed in Sky's mind. Good thing Kane was driving, or she might have broken a few speeding laws on the way back. With him at the wheel, his strong profile allowed her to focus on something nice instead of on the possible crime.

Every woman in Savory would have called Kane Cornell hot. Some would claim it was the way he filled out his military camouflage pants, others how his biceps bulged every time he turned the wheel. The problem with someone like him was, the moment he delivered his urgent message to the Senator he'd high-tail it out of there, and she'd be back to breaking up bar fights, finding lost dogs, or looking for disappearing aliens all by herself. He appeared to be the type to do things *his* way, and win-win probably wasn't in his vocabulary, which meant she needed to keep her libido in check—seriously in check.

Until recently, Sky had a boyfriend. Right before Chris moved to New York, he'd suggested they see other people, but she wasn't sure if he said that because he didn't want to come right out and break up with her, or he didn't think it was fair for her to wait for him. Furthermore, she wasn't sure if his New York job was permanent or not, so Sky was kind of hanging in limbo, waiting on a definite answer from him on where things stood. God, her love life was a mess!

Cornell parked in front of the station, and before he cut the engine, she jumped out and raced up the steps in need of some space. Pearl Smith, who refused to acknowledge she even had birthdays anymore, was waiting on the front porch. The older woman's shoulders were bone thin but her hips were wide and full. She pushed up from the bench and wobbled for a moment. After giving Pearl a hug, Sky introduced Kane. From the body scan Pearl gave Kane, the sixty-two-year-old woman's eyesight was working a little too well.

"Hands off, Ms. Pearl." Sky didn't really mean it, but she thought making light of a terrible situation would alleviate some anxiety.

"Who me?" She dabbed her eyes, but Sky caught the twinkle. Her ploy worked.

Glad that Pearl had recovered some of her composure over Mary's disappearance, Sky wrapped an arm around the woman's shoulder. "Come on in and tell me what happened." Inside the station, the warm air still held a hint of the morning's chocolate chip cookies.

She thought Kane would excuse himself once they stepped inside, but instead, he dragged three chairs from the empty desks and placed them in a small circle. She shot him a look, but he didn't seem to take notice, so she strode over to him and stood face to chest, and then raised her chin. "This is a matter for the sheriff's department. I don't think you should stay." It looked as if he was working hard not to smile.

"I was an MP in the service and understand how the law works." He looked around the office, empty except for Harriet. "Looks like you could use some muscle in case the kidnapper calls or makes a demand."

Pearl never said Mary had been kidnapped, though it was a sound conclusion. Pearl did seem calmer being around him, and getting someone to relax under these sad circumstances was a plus. Sky wouldn't lie. Having him near certainly made her a little less edgy after the shooting. This one time she'd allow her instincts to win over logic and permit him to stay.

"Okay, but I have the right to ask you to leave at any time."

He nodded. "It's your show." He followed his comment with a smile.

Once Sky poured coffee for Ms. Pearl and Kane, she asked for details of Mary's disappearance.

Pearl turned first to Kane. "Mary's my only child. If anything happened to her..." Pearl broke down again.

Sky grabbed Pearl's hands. "We'll find her."

She dabbed her eyes and sniffled then looked at Kane. "Mary works at the bank until four then likes to ride her bike for a few miles before coming home. Only yesterday, she never arrived home."

Sky jotted notes on her iPad, a gift Chris had given her. It made taking notes much easier and more legible than writing them down. "Why didn't you call us right away?" She tried not to use a reprimanding tone but failed.

Pearl blushed. "Well, you know Mary. She's a little head-strong. I figured she met some fellow and hooked up with him. It was her birthday and all."

Mary had gone missing three times this year already and returned after a few days. "That is one possibility, but would she have stayed out all night without calling?" They lived together in Pearl's house.

"No, and that's what worries me. She usually calls me when she isn't coming home." Pearl knit her fingers together. "Only yesterday, I forgot to charge my phone, so she might have called." She looked down and seemed to examine every floor-board one by one. Pearl glanced up. "Actually, I was with Dan Joe, and I didn't get back to my place until almost ten this morning. That's when I realized Mary hadn't come home last night. There weren't any dishes in the sink or clothes tossed about or anything. I tried to get a hold of her on her cell but got no answer."

"Did you call the bank to see if she showed up for work this morning?"

"I did, but they said she hadn't. That's when I decided to head out to the park to see if I could find her. Mary sometimes skips work, you know. I found her bike in the bushes, and all I could think of was that poor woman last year, who was raped and killed there."

"Terrible tragedy." Sharon Filmers' death had sent the town into a tizzy for months. Sky leaned over and grabbed Pearl's hands again. "I'll do everything I can to find her. Don't you worry."

"I know she'll show up soon."

"When she does, be sure to let me know."

"I promise." Pearl stood and glanced over at Kane. "Sorry to take up your time with Sky. You looking for a runaway too?"

"Something like that."

After Pearl left, Sky wanted to work on her headless man's case since this was her first shot at a homicide. Too bad, all she could think about was finding out more about the enigmatic man sitting next to her, as he'd stimulated her curiosity something fierce. Kane was on the right side of the law, and while he'd tossed her a few smiles, he didn't appear interested, which fit into her plan just fine. She had a job to do.

However, if Chris had been serious about seeing other people, maybe she should too.

On the drive back to the station, Kane had asked about exploring the caves, but she'd told him she'd never found anything in any of them. Now that she thought about it, they might have fun dipping into the darkness and squeezing through small holes. The only problem was that while getting lost with Kane might be fun, it wouldn't help her find a murderer.

Kane rose to his feet and pulled his shoulders back so much

that she half-expected him to salute. "Thanks for your time and help."

"No problem." No man deserved to be that fit and so in control.

The moment the door closed behind him, Harriet swiveled around. "Woohee. That is one amazing man. You going to try to land him?"

"What?"

"You heard me. I know you've been in a long dry spell."

"Harriet, please. Our one-day relationship was strictly professional. And mind your own business." Sky added a smile to soften the response. Sarcasm wasn't an attractive trait.

"His eyes say he likes you. In case you didn't know, our boss left right after you took off with Mr. Kane."

"That's because he has a regional meeting in Flagstaff to attend."

"Which means he won't be back until Monday. Maybe when you come to work tomorrow, you should wear that revealing red top you wore last Christmas in case Mr. Sexy returns."

She glanced to the ceiling and exhaled. "There's nothing between us. Kane is solely focused on finding the Senator." At least one of them had their priorities straight.

Harriet rolled her eyes. "Then admit that Chris never got your motor running like this man does."

He used to. "I'm not discussing it. My shift is over. Tomorrow morning, I'm going to Page to see the Medical Examiner about the body Earl discovered on his back forty."

Harriet held up the plate of cookies. "Have another one before you go."

Sky's pants were tight enough. "A girl's gotta watch her figure."

"I don't think that Mr. Cornell thought your figure needed improving. I saw the way he watched you strut your stuff this morning."

"If you're implying I was attempting to be sexy, you're wrong." *Get me out of here before I say something I'll regret.* "Bye."

***

Given how tired she was, Sky thought she'd sleep well, but she was wrong. Visions of Kane Cornell kept floating in her head, and while she tried to ignore those fluttery feelings, they wouldn't go away. Even thinking about Chris didn't dampen the growing lust. She really needed to have her head examined. If she ever wanted to make detective, she had to focus on her job.

With a lot of effort on her part, she managed to fall asleep, and Kane had the starring role in every one of her dreams.

Once she rose and had her coffee, she called Dr. Williams, Page's medical examiner, to let him know she was on her way to learn about his findings regarding the decapitated man.

Williams' receptionist told her the doc was tied up with an important autopsy and wouldn't be able to see her until eleven. It was only nine now, but she wasn't in the mood to go into the office and be subjected to Harriet's teasing. She'd experienced enough guilt dreaming about Mr. Military Man and didn't need Harriet to pull the truth out of her.

With a bit of time to kill, she headed to Willows Park to search for potential evidence of foul play regarding Mary's disappearance. For Pearl and Mary's sake, she hoped there was a big misunderstanding, and Mary would show up soon with a smile on her face.

Twelve minutes later, Sky pulled into the near empty parking lot. Pearl had given her the exact location of Mary's abandoned bike, and while finding the Acacia tree took some work, once she found it, she took photos and made notes of the scene. The ground underneath the limbs was slightly disturbed, but there were no broken branches, no torn clothes, or anything else to imply Mary had been abducted or kidnapped, which was a huge relief.

To make sure she did a thorough job, Sky walked around the hard-packed dirt jogging path, hoping to find someone who'd noticed Mary. Unfortunately, on a Friday morning, there weren't as many people exercising as she would have liked to see. The few folks she did manage to stop either didn't know Mary or didn't remember the last time they'd seen her. In all, Sky wasn't any closer to finding her than she was to identifying the slain man.

Climbing back into her bright orange VW, she stopped at the only fast food place in Savory for some very bad-for-your-figure food, before heading up north to Page. Once on the desolate highway, she turned on her radio to her favorite news station. "This just in. Arizona's Senator Paul Overton has disappeared." Sky's pulse sped up, and she turned up the volume. "The spokesperson for the Senator won't release any details but asks anyone with information to call the FBI at 602-555-7672."

Since when had the Senator officially become missing? Kane implied Overton was only out of phone reach. Given Kane's intensity level, false clues would have him running all over the place, probably resulting in him asking for her help. If this had been the result of a leak, Kane would be royally pissed that this information was made public.

Something about Kane Cornell kept her off balance, and she didn't like it one bit. If he'd asked, though, she would have taken him around, despite having a murder to solve and a missing woman to find.

As she entered downtown Page, she forced her thoughts away from him. While the neighboring town might have only eight thousand residents, they enjoyed the benefit of more than three million visitors a year because of the Glen Canyon Dam and the local caves.

A horn beeped behind her, bringing her attention back to the road. A few minutes later, she turned down the side street where the ME's building was located. Sky parked and entered, flashing her badge at Darleen, the receptionist, before introducing herself.

"Why, Sky Nash. I know who you are. It's only been what, three years?"

It seemed longer. "I guess."

Darleen smiled. "Follow me. The doctor's in autopsy, but he's expecting you."

As soon as Sky stepped inside, she covered her nose. Even the bleach and disinfectant couldn't mask the stench of death.

She knocked and the medical examiner pulled open the key-coded door. "Hiya, Doc."

He smiled through his face shield. "Sky, you're looking good."

"Thanks." He'd aged. The addition of a toupee made him look older, or perhaps it was the extra twenty pounds.

Dr. Williams pulled off his mask and ripped off his latex gloves.

She stepped closer to the smelly corpse. "Is there anything you can tell me about John Doe here?"

"Whoever took the head was medically skilled, as there are very few nicks on the bones. Cutting off a head isn't easy."

"I've never had the privilege." She tried not to inhale deeply. At least the doc had drained the blood so the body didn't look too bad. "Can you tell the type of knife used?"

"A big one with a very sharp blade."

"Funny. Anything that will help me identify the man?"

He sobered. "A tattoo on his shoulder. I took a photo for you and enlarged it." He nodded to the manila folder on the counter.

She slid out the picture. An eagle grabbing a banner with the words *US Air Force* blazoned with three gold stars covered his bicep. "A military man."

"That would be my guess." He opened a drawer and pulled out the prints. "This is a copy of his fingerprints for you. I've sent the originals to the lab to be processed. They'll email you the results. If he's in the service, he'll be in the database."

Worked for her. "Did you do a tox screen?" The white

powder she'd spotted on the man's fingertips looked like it might be cocaine.

"Sure did. As soon as I get the results, I'll let you know."

"Great."

He nodded. "Good luck finding the murderer."

She thanked him again and left. Well that was a bust, although speaking with the medical examiner in person was always best, in case she had more questions. The day had been clear and sunny, and the break helped her sort through a few things.

Close to Savory, her cell rang, but she didn't recognize the number. "Hello?"

"It's Kane. I'm glad I got a hold of you. Harriet and Harvey have been trying to reach you for an hour."

Her stomach tumbled. "I turned off my cell when I was inside the morgue. What happened?"

"Someone ransacked your house, and from what I can tell, you might be in danger too."

CHAPTER FOUR

Sky's pulse shot up. "Tell me."

"The intruders smashed the back window in your house and left two sets of motorcycle tire tracks in the lawn," Kane said.

Her hands nearly slipped off the wheel as her mind raced to think of the names of possible suspects. To be safe—and have a moment to think—she pulled off onto the shoulder of the road. "Did anyone see them?"

"Your next-door neighbor heard the loud engines and raced over but not in time to get a close look or give a description. Good thing she noticed the glass on the ground under the window and called the station."

"Harriet must have freaked when the call came in. Why did she call you? You're a civilian."

"She was worried the intruders might come back and asked if I'd stand watch."

Sky's stomach nearly erupted at the violation. She had no doubt that Harriet would use any excuse to get the two of them together. Christ, Sky's hands were still trembling, and she had to grip the steering wheel tight with one hand. "I don't know why anyone would target me. I know everyone in town, except maybe the few tourists who pass through. No one has a beef against me that I know of. Hell, I'm a cop for cripe's sake."

She debated calling her adoptive dad, but since he was on the City Council, he might cause more trouble than it was worth.

"Just drive carefully. I'll make sure the place stays safe."

She appreciated that he sounded so calm and in control. "Thank you."

Sky pulled back onto the road to head back to Savory. Up ahead, a lone convenience store came into view. Needing a cold drink and to settle down before she drove home, she pulled into the parking lot. Her throat was dry, and her heart pounded way too fast. Inside, she bought a drink then stopped in the bathroom to comb her hair and dab on some scented hand lotion. Chris had always insisted she keep up with her appearance because *no one took a Plain Jane seriously*. She believed he was looking out for her well-being and wanted to see her succeed.

Wait a minute. What was she doing worrying about her looks? Someone had violated her home.

I'm scared, that's all.

Believing she hadn't lost her mind after all, Sky finished her drink then tossed the empty soda can in the recycle bin and slipped back into the car. One thing she knew for sure was that the criminals weren't local. For one, she never locked the back door, much to her dad's frustration. Everyone in Savory knew her house was open for company any time of day or night. These idiots had to be out-of-towners or they would have walked in instead of breaking the window.

Less than twenty-five minutes later, she arrived at her house. As promised, Mr. Security Guard was outside leaning against his Jeep, wearing shades and looking calm. His demeanor brought her some comfort. At least he'd have a level head. Kane pushed off from the Jeep and kept his focus on her, almost as if he expected her to have some kind of hysterics.

She wouldn't. Or so she hoped. *Now focus.* On the outside, the house looked quaint and safe, and the neighborhood appeared deserted. She took a deep breath and grabbed the door handle, but Kane managed to open her car door before she had the chance. Even though he leaned an arm against the roof, he towered over her as she stood. His midsection caught her attention first, and then her gaze traveled over his chest to those intense brown eyes.

Sky blinked. "Thanks for giving me the heads up about the home invasion. If I'd come home and found out someone had broken in, I'd have been too pissed off to investigate."

"I thought you might need some time to process what happened." He nodded toward the house. "Harvey's inside."

Harvey. Inside. Right. His cruiser must be in the back. "There won't be any fingerprints you know."

He cocked a brow. "You psychic?"

Her jaw loosened. "I have no idea why I said that, but I'm thinking they might be the same men who took a shot at me before. They'd be smart enough to wear gloves."

"Could be," Kane admitted.

She shot her gaze to the ground before looking at his too handsome face. "We probably should see what Harvey's found."

The front door clicked open and her coworker came out, easing down the steps. "You might not want to go inside just yet." He peeled off his latex gloves. "They emptied drawers, broke glassware, and even smashed the picture of your mom and dad."

She took a step and faltered, but Kane was there to hold her up. His touch was firm, but strong. Once her legs regained their strength, she straightened. "Sorry."

"Hey, it happens." From his quirked brow, she could tell Kane wanted to ask what had caused her to misstep.

She might as well air out her issues. "My parents were murdered when I was eight, and all I have to remember them by is a three by five photo."

"Jeez, that's tough. My father died three years ago. It's not the same thing, but I'm not sure I'll ever get over his death." His gaze followed the horizon as if he were reliving the tragedy one more time.

Kane's outer shell appeared hard, but she suspected he needed the tough persona to hide the inner pain. A thin thread of connection formed.

"I was lucky," Sky said. "I found a good substitute for a dad, until my adoptive mom died. I don't think I mentioned it, but Dad's a member of the City Council."

"Ah."

He searched her face for a moment, and the intense scrutiny caused her to swing her gaze to Harvey, forcing her to address the damaged picture and not the man beside her. "What did they take?" They better not have stolen the necklace her mom was wearing when she died.

"You'll have to let me know." Harvey shuffled his feet.

"What aren't you telling me?"

He held up his hands and twisted his mouth. "They left you a message written in lipstick on your bathroom mirror."

Her heart sunk. "What did it say?"

He pulled out his pad and handed her what he'd copied. *GIVE IT BACK BEFORE YOU LOSE YOUR HEAD TOO.*

Her throat nearly closed up. "Give it back? I have no idea what they're talking about."

Kane leaned closer. "The recent death of the man you were studying might have something to do with what they want. Could they mean they want the body back?"

"I can't see why since they left him there, although they seemed to have been in the process of burying him when Earl took a shot at them." She stepped aside knowing she must smell. Besides, his closeness jumbled her thoughts. "What else could they mean?"

"Do you know the man's identity yet?" Kane asked.

"No, but he had an Air Force tattoo. The men who shot at me could have been military too." She told him the shooters had been five hundred yards away and hit their mark.

"I see you have your work cut out for you."

She straightened. "I'm not going to let them win. I'll figure out what they're after."

Kane's brows rose and fell. "I'm sure you will."

Too bad she had no idea where to start. "I'll need help, though."

Harvey stepped forward. "Just name it." She'd been facing Kane, but she wasn't one to turn down an offer. Harvey seemed suddenly alert, more focused.

"Thanks. Have you finished processing the scene?" She didn't want to deal with anything other than cleaning her house. She found repetitive acts often freed her mind to sort through the small details.

"I did. I'll write up the report as soon as I return to the station. I called Brady to bring over a new back window, and he said he could install it tomorrow. In the meantime, Kane and I located some wood and tacked it over the window."

She blew out a breath. "Bless you." Where had this kindness come from? Maybe she'd misinterpreted his usual sullenness for dislike when, in fact, Harvey was still depressed over his son's death.

The familiar knocking of an engine coming down the street behind her sent the tension in her shoulders packing. It was Harriet. The friendly dispatcher stopped, cut the engine, and eased out. Harriet waved then moved to the trunk where she dragged out a large bucket and mop.

Kane rushed over to her side. "Let me help you."

"Thanks, sweetie. I sure could use a strong man to help carry all these cleaning supplies inside." The moment Kane moved to the passenger side door, Harriet winked at Sky. Oh, boy.

Harvey stepped next to Sky. "Harriet took the call from your neighbor. Knowing her, she's probably put out a call to a dozen women by now. If those two passed through Savory, I bet someone will have noticed them and come forward with information."

"I hope so."

Harvey tapped the folder in his hands. "Best be getting back and log this in."

As Harvey headed around back where he'd parked his car, Kane carried the cleaning supplies inside then came back out. "I'll leave you and Harriet to do the cleaning. It's not really my bag."

"I don't blame you. Where are you off to?" She wanted to take her mind off the violation and focus on something positive.

"I'm going to head over to Wildacres RV Park again, in hopes that the Senator has returned."

"Betty would have called if he had. I'm not sure if you heard, but on my trip over to Page, I heard a news report stating the senator was missing."

"What?"

She held up her hands. "I thought maybe you had made the call, but then I remembered you had said you wanted to keep this quiet."

"It wasn't me. Dammit."

She wanted to rub his arm, but Kane seemed lost in thought. "Someone might spot the senator. The broadcast could help."

He looked down at her and nodded. "You might be right. If you need anything, let me know."

"Thanks," she said.

The moment Kane's vehicle disappeared around the corner, unease settled over her. She doubted the thieves would be back, but she'd keep an extra clip by her side just in case.

***

For the next two hours, Sky and Harriet swept and cleaned. Feeling violated and angry, it took all of Sky's control not to break down. Her own body was weary, and she imagined Harriet was beat too.

"I think it looks great, Harriet. I can't thank you enough. Why don't you head home?"

"Do you want to stay at my place tonight? No telling if these men will return."

Sky smiled, loving how Harriet was always looking out for her. "I'm good. I'll lock my door and keep my weapon on the nightstand."

"Okay, hon, but call if you change your mind."

Sky helped carry the supplies back out to Harriet's car then hugged her goodbye. Once her friend left, Sky stepped inside and dropped onto the sofa. All during the cleanup, she tried to imagine what she had that someone would want but kept coming up empty. When her stomach grumbled, she realized she hadn't eaten much all day.

Not in the mood to cook, she locked all of the doors and headed into town. Wanting nothing more than a quiet hour to eat her meal in peace, Sky headed to her favorite haunt. Other than the ever-present checker players in the corner and one table with a couple sitting at it, EBE's café was empty, which was perfect since she wasn't in the mood to socialize tonight.

As if on autopilot, Sky headed to the back of the restaurant to her usual table and sat facing the front entrance. The flashing pink lights sent a warm, comforting glow through the restaurant, and the soft banging of pots and pans in the kitchen created a comforting white noise, allowing her to think.

Cathy, Sky's favorite waitress, rushed over. "I heard about the break-in. I'm so sorry." The antennae on her silver tiara bounced wildly.

Good ole Harriet. "I'm just glad I wasn't there when they broke in."

"Did they take anything? I mean I'm sure they did, but did they take anything that can't be replaced?"

"Nothing as far as I can tell. Can I get a decaf, black?" Sky readjusted her sunglasses on top of her head. Discussing the details of the break-in wouldn't help her melancholia.

"You look like you could use the Comet's Tail special."

The Comet's Tail came with whipped cream and a drizzle of chocolate. She patted her stomach. "Old fashioned black will do fine."

"One Martian Minimal coming up. You want the usual Alpha Centauri salad?"

"Sure, but without the tomatoes. My stomach is acting up." It was nice to have the decision taken out of her hands.

The coffee arrived moments later and Sky nearly melted from the wonderful, rich aroma. She'd taken one sip, when the bell above the café door rang and Dan Joe staggered in, unshaven with bloodshot eyes and his shirt untucked. He made a beeline to her table, and she nearly groaned out loud. All she'd wanted was peace but *that* didn't seem to be in the cards today. He was a constituent who clearly needed her help.

Without asking permission, he pulled out the chair across from her. "Am I glad to find you."

"What can I do for you, Dan?" Her attempt to keep her tone upbeat failed.

"I need to report a crime."

She set her cup down. That caught her interest. "What happened?"

"I was abducted."

F-in' awesome!

CHAPTER FIVE

The sound of a plate crashed near the counter, and the restaurant quieted for a moment, but then the two-person table near the entrance applauded. Oh, boy. Someone must have overheard Dan's alien comment. He'd practically shouted they'd come for him.

One thing was clear: Dan was drunk. Normally, she would have dismissed his comment in a heartbeat, but something was different. He'd always made fun of the alien expert, Earl Chee, so why would Dan claim he'd been taken, if he didn't believe they existed? She sipped more of her coffee, hoping Dan hadn't taken any drugs. "How much have you had to drink?"

He swiped a hand across his mouth. "A lot, but that was only after the aliens nabbed me." He swung a gaze around the room as if he expected little gray men to jump out from behind the counter and nab him once more. She almost couldn't blame his paranoia. The walls were rimmed with alien artifacts, from *E.T.* posters, to drawings made by the children at the elementary school that depicted spacecraft and little gray men.

Cathy came over with Sky's salad, her hands shaking. She must have been the one to drop the plate. "I brought over some bread in case you wanted to share." She sent a furtive glance at

Dan and set a glass of water with lemon in front of him. "Hi, Mr. Joe."

He looked up and jerked back. Cathy's uniform had the face of an alien on it, embroidered in silver foil. Maybe he thought she was from outer space, or else he was just plain wasted. Dan blinked a few times. "Oh, it's you."

Cathy shot a look at Sky before hightailing it back to the counter, her rubber shoes squeaking against the tile floor.

He wiped his damp brow. "It was the damnedest thing. I lost track of time for two days."

Sky picked up the Roswell coaster and twirled it, needing something to do with her hands. "You passed out again, didn't you?" Two days was a really long time to be out of it though.

He straightened and crossed his heart. "I swear I gave up the drink a month ago, after I ran over my dog with the tractor."

Poor Rufus. She'd attended the dog's funeral. It had been very sad. "Start from the beginning." She was starved and dug into her meal. Damn. Tomatoes. She picked them out and set them to the side.

"Well, it was around noon, two days ago, when I was out back working on my truck. I know it sounds corny, but I swear the sun got brighter, so I looked up for a split second, and the next thing I knew, I'm in my bedroom, face down with a mean mother of a headache." His breathing increased as though he were still in pain.

"Go on." She could have pulled out her iPad from her purse and taken notes, but this story wasn't one she was likely to forget.

"With my head pounding, I took a couple of aspirin and had a bite to eat. Then I turned on the television, and that's when I saw two days had gone by, just like that." He snapped his fingers. "Scared the crap out of me."

"I'd be scared too. Did you see anyone hanging around outside? Or a spacecraft flying overhead?" Not that she believed there would be, but she had to ask.

He guzzled down half the glass of water. "No. There wasn't anyone. I was outside one minute, and in the house the next— only two days had passed."

"Maybe you passed out and someone carried you inside." There had to be a logical explanation. He tapped his foot and leaned closer, but the stench of alcohol made her sit back.

"No, I tell you." He looked right then left before pulling down his collar to expose the side of his neck. "Look here. They stuck me."

She relaxed at seeing the half-inch diameter red ring. "I think that's some kind of insect sting. You probably went into some kind of anaphylactic shock. Are you allergic to any stings or bites?"

"No, never have been. Besides, there ain't any bees or wasps this time of year."

He had a point. "Maybe when you came to, you were so disoriented you dragged yourself inside and don't remember."

"If I'd a passed out, I would a woken up next to my truck— which didn't happen. It's almost November, and I would have frozen to death, if I'd slept outside for two days." He pressed his lips together. "I knew you wouldn't believe me."

The temperature hadn't dropped below freezing since last winter but she didn't think she needed to comment on that. "I'm sorry, but you need to give me some tangible proof if you want me to do something." Not that she'd be able to do anything about it even if she had proof.

He fisted his hands and held them out. His knuckles were raw and cut. "I did not have this bruising until I woke up."

She leaned closer. "Looks like you punched a wall."

"I thought the same thing, but there's no damage in the house or on my truck."

"Are you sure there isn't some guy with a broken nose?"

"He hasn't come around if there is, but I have a hankering to beat the shit out of someone or something right about now."

She crossed her arms over her chest. "You need to stop drinking. It makes you ornery."

He shoved back his chair and stood. "I can't make any promises."

"How about letting Doc Roberts check you out? Maybe he can tell what the neck injury is."

"I know what it was. I had a dream about it, only I wasn't sleeping."

"You mean like a flashback?"

His shoulders relaxed. "Yeah, like a flashback." He grasped the top of the chair as if to steady himself. "All I remember is a sting in my neck, and then being in a big room with a lot of people. I swear I was in some kind of ring, only I wasn't wearing boxing gloves."

Now he got her curious. "Can you describe the room?"

"Everything is fuzzy, but there were mirrors with flashing lights bouncing off them."

Okay. This was way out of her league. "What about Earl Chee? He's an expert on aliens. Maybe he knows what happened."

"That old coot? You've got to be kidding. What happened to me was *real*. Someone is out to get me."

She'd play along. "Who?"

"If I knew, I'd find him and show him not to mess with Dan Joe." He straightened his shoulders and strode out, knocking into one of the tables on his way.

Guilt descended. Sky wanted to help him, but alien abductions weren't in her job description. All the time she'd worked at the station, she'd never come across a manual for investigating anything alien. As much as she wanted to believe him, he most likely got drunk and stumbled around in his own house. Just in case someone had drugged and beaten him, she'd make sure that she or another officer would take a look into what Dan had said.

For years very little ever happened in Savory that she would consider out of the ordinary. Now, a man had been decapitated,

Mary was missing, an incredibly hot security agent came into town looking for a missing Senator, and one of their very own claimed to have made contact with aliens. If that wasn't enough to spin her head, some guys ransacked her house but stole nothing. It was worse than trying to stop a major jailbreak without a gun.

Cathy refilled her coffee. "Do you think Mr. Joe was abducted?" She tilted her head to one side and smirked. "He's back on the bottle again, I see."

"It's possible."

Dan had started drinking again after Pearl had broken up with him, and that was how he'd ended up running over his dog. Supposedly, they were back together now, so she'd have to ask Pearl what was up with Dan.

Exhaustion touched every muscle, but Dan's story had temporarily rejuvenated her. She pulled out her iPad and her fingers flew over the screen. Pearl had knitting club for another hour, so tomorrow would be soon enough to question her. Dan might not see the need to find support with his old flame until he'd exhausted his regular channels.

Just as she waved for the check, the bell rang over the door. Instead of taking note of the new arrival, she faced away from the door. The last thing she needed was someone else approaching her, claiming to have witnessed an exorcism or something.

Hell, maybe EBE's café, which stood for Extraterrestrial Biological Entities, had damned the town to weird events.

"This seat taken?"

She didn't need to look up to know *he* had walked in. Her luck, she hadn't showered after cleaning her house or put on makeup. Sky glanced up and her smile disappeared before it reformed. "No."

From the tension rippling across Kane's face, something had happened, and she bet his tale wouldn't be about aliens.

He dragged his chair next to her. "I like to watch the

entrance." Their shoulders touched, and her traitorous body reacted. He smelled freshly washed, and his slight scruff made him look particularly rugged.

"Me too." She scooted to her left to give him more room and to keep her thoughts where they should be. "Did you find the Senator?"

"Negative. I asked around and between all the busybodies, I'm convinced he hasn't been back."

"What about Pat and Clay?"

"Betty made contact with them. They told her that after they spoke with Overton, they took off for a vacation up north and haven't been in contact with him."

"Are you worried?" Dumb question, but she didn't want to presume.

"Hell, yes. He's been missing for far too long."

She waited for him to tell her more, but Cathy rushed over with her chest stuck out so far she practically fell over. "Can I get you anything, Kane? I bet a big guy like you would like our Area 51 special. It's made with hazelnuts and has dripped caramel on top."

Kane? Usually Cathy called her customers by their last name.

"Got any plain coffee?"

"Oh, sure. How silly of me. A man who looks like you wouldn't want to put sugar in his perfect bod."

Dear God in heaven help me. Sky held up a finger to Cathy and then faced Kane. "How about we go for a walk instead? There are a lot of ears here."

Cathy's chin dropped. Not that Kane belonged to Sky, but they were working together.

He shrugged and gave Cathy a weak smile. "Next time." If her lips frowned any more, they'd touch her jawline.

Sky gathered her leather jacket and backpack then dropped money on the table before following him outside. The couple waved goodbye, and Sky bet the fact Kane and she left together would be news within the hour.

They passed Rosalie's B & B and the used bookstore before reaching the town square. On the far side of the block was Thomas Park.

He nodded to the small park bench. "Is here good?"

From the seriousness of his tone, something was wrong. "Sure. What's happened?"

"I've been lying to you."

Her legs gave way and her butt hit the seat hard. "About what?"

She hoped it wasn't that he had a girlfriend, or that he was leaving tonight. Her stomach churned at both scenarios.

"The Senator is the ranking member of the Armed Services Committee."

She leaned back against the seat, relieved he hadn't stated her worst fears. "I know." His brow cocked. "I Googled him, but what does that have to do with why he's here?"

"The Senator and his committee appropriate funds for a lot of black operation projects—secret stuff if you will—that the government won't give details about to the committee. It's why I was asked to guard him. I used to be with Special Forces."

So he was more than a private investigator. That made sense. She buttoned up her jacket. The sun had set and the cool air had taken hold of the town rather quickly. "Can they do that?"

He chuckled, but the tone held no joy. "They can and they do. Apparently, Senator Overton was fed up with all the secrecy and said his committee wouldn't fund this one particular project unless he was given more details."

"Good for him. I'll shake his hand when I meet him."

"Me too."

"Do you know what this secret project is?" she asked.

"No and neither does my source, other than this building or factory is near Page and requires this special funding."

She smiled. "You're making this up, right?"

He held up three fingers. "Scout's honor."

Sky twisted to the side to watch his face. "Why not tell me

before? Didn't you think this information was important?" And here she'd thought he was so honest; so much for being her fantasy man.

Somehow, Kane Cornell managed to look uncomfortable without moving. "It was a need to know basis. I thought I'd find the Senator right away and not have to involve you."

Aha. She could see where this was heading. "So now Mr. Solo *needs* help?"

"I work with others when needed, but yes, I could use some assistance." He held up a hand. "I won't have you do anything that would be dangerous."

"I'm not afraid of a little danger, but why me? I'm just a beat cop."

"Perhaps, but you've been spot on since we've met."

She had? "I appreciate that." Especially since her boss never gave her compliments.

"I do need a favor *from you*."

Here it comes. She hoped he wouldn't ask her to do something illegal. If so, he was in for a rude surprise. "What?"

"I want to check out the caves that Pete, the NRA hat guy, told us about. Since the Senator showed an interest in visiting them, he might have gone out on his own." He held up his hand. "I know you said there isn't anything in any of the caves, but the Senator didn't know that."

All he needed was her tracking skills. "I will admit the rock twists and turns can fool a person. The Senator wouldn't be the first person to get lost and die in the caves."

"Jesus. Why didn't you say so when we were at the RV Park? I would have headed out there immediately."

Because Pearl had called and told her Mary had gone missing. "Just waiting for you to ask." She smiled sweetly.

"It's too late now to head out, but how about if I pick you up first thing tomorrow morning?"

Now that he'd asked nicely, she couldn't turn him down, and from the way he twisted his hands together, this was important.

"Fine, however the Senator could have gone up to Page to look at the caves. Nothing is prettier than when the sunlight streams in from the top of Antelope Canyon. The Navajos run tours there."

"The Senator wasn't here to sightsee, so our trip needs to be a private tour. No one can know. Just you and me." He dipped his head, and her stomach dropped.

***

Kane and Sky had spent all afternoon searching for the Senator, most of which entailed him watching Sky's butt wiggle in front of him as she wove her way through the caves. Even though the view was no hardship, and he was enjoying it more than he would admit, Kane needed to focus on his job and not on the imp of a brunette. The shifting sand made maneuvering difficult, yet the woman walked without ever losing her balance.

After an hour of cave hunting, she'd braided her hair and managed to tie the damn thing into a knot to keep it from flying all over the place, even without a rubber band or anything. Amazing.

She spun around. "The Senator was never here."

Kane stopped short to keep from running into her. "How do you know?" After four different caves, he was hoping to find some evidence the man had been there.

"The sand would have been disturbed. Other than some animal prints, no human has been in here in a while."

He studied the evenly ridged curves of the sand. "That's not what that old Navajo man said. He claimed nightly winds were enough to blow away footprints, and that he'd seen someone who looked like the Senator go toward the caves."

"Jimmy is half blind and will lie to get a dollar." She leaned against the wall and closed her eyes for a second. "I'm starving and beat."

Now she'd think he was a jerk. "I'm sorry. I should have been more considerate. Your house was broken into yesterday, and I'm asking you to give me a tour when you probably didn't sleep a wink." He stepped toward her. "Now that I know where these caves are located, I can search on my own."

Without any distraction.

She smiled and never looked prettier. "You'll have to pay Jimmy double if you come by yourself."

He laughed. "I'll keep that in mind and hit the bank before I return. Let's go. Dinner's on me." He shouldn't have blurted that out. She'd probably think this was a date. Dumbass. He motioned her to lead.

She took two steps and stopped. "Wait a sec." She dropped to her knees.

"What is it?"

She hovered her hand above the ground. "The sand is a different color and is flatter than the rippled area around it."

"Meaning?"

"Give me a sec. It might be nothing, or it could be something." She dug through the soft sand about three or four inches down, grabbed something, and then lifted out a metal sculpture. She sucked in a big breath. "Oh my God."

CHAPTER SIX

The air around her seemed to evaporate as Kane dropped to his knees and wiggled his fingers for the mystery object. Sky wasn't sure he'd treat this prize with the needed respect. "Be careful."

His mouth opened slightly as if he were in awe and then twisted the nine-inch tall metal object in his fingers. "The artwork sure is something else."

She puffed out her chest a little. "Those engravings look like petroglyphs. It's possible they're from a spacecraft, and I don't mean one that flew for NASA."

She glanced at Kane to gauge his reaction to her suggestion that the object could have come from outer space, but his face remained unreadable. Damn. She shouldn't have said anything, but she'd wanted to see where he stood on the concept of the existence of life outside of their planet. This pineapple shaped object resembled something Earl had in his house.

"You really think it's alien?" Kane rotated the cone-shaped figure in his hand.

"Possibly."

"Looks like it came off a post or the top of a metal Christmas tree. I doubt it's from outer space." He dropped his chin and looked up with a twinkle in his eye.

She slipped the object from his fingers. "It's lighter than I would have expected," she said.

He sat back, resting his butt on his heels. "It's probably made from aluminum. That's a metal mined in America."

She lightly punched his arm as she chuckled. "Funny." Sparring with Kane would get her nowhere. Those who didn't believe could never be convinced. "I have a friend who's an expert in everything alien. Maybe he can tell us where it came from."

"Suit yourself." He stood. "Let me take a picture of you with your treasure so you can show your grandkids."

"Cool." No need to tell him she didn't even have a husband yet. She passed him her phone, posed with her newfound treasure, and grinned like a fool. Kane lifted the cell at arm's length and tapped the camera icon.

He handed her the phone back. "Ready to head home?"

"You're kidding, right? I've searched these caves for years and never found any treasure. This could be the proof the world needs to show aliens have visited us. We have to continue digging to see if there's something else down there." A gust of wind swept through the tunnel and lifted the hair from the base of her neck almost as if some spirit had flown by.

He laughed. "I thought you were starving and exhausted."

"I am, but what if I find more proof of alien life here, in Savory?" The words tumbled out before she had a chance to censor them.

"Seriously?" He lifted the piece out of her hands and turned it over.

He was close-minded. Dammit. "What are you looking for?"

"A Made-in-China stamp."

"Pu-lease." Just because Kane Cornell believed there wasn't anything down there, didn't mean something didn't exist. She began digging. Sure, they were here to look for the Senator, but a few extra minutes wouldn't hurt. "I'll always wonder if I don't search a bit." Three scoops later, her nail broke. "Crap."

"What?" He sounded concerned.

She lifted her hand out of the sand and examined the damage. "I broke a nail."

"That's all?" He frowned and squinted at the same time, and the look came off more comical that serious. "Are you going to write up a report?"

"You're a real comedian."

Kane's gaze shot to the side, and he eased a gun out from inside his jacket.

She froze. "Kane, what are you doing?" Before she could move, he fired, the sound reverberating in the small chamber. Sky fell to the side and curled into a ball, as dust filled the air. "Dear Lord in Heaven."

He hadn't aimed at her, but the bullet could have ricocheted off the wall. When no pain registered, she had to work to breathe. The loud echo still reverberated in her ears and the stirred up sand settled on her face.

He was on her in a second, cradling her in his arms. "It's okay." He whispered into her hair. "You're safe. I killed the snake."

"You killed a snake? I hate those things." She hadn't even heard the thing rattle, assuming it was a rattler.

His warm lips touched her forehead, miraculously drawing out the negative energy coursing through her, but she refused to do anything about the light kiss that elicited a strong reaction. It wouldn't be right to fall for Mr. Special Forces, only for the life of her, she couldn't remember why.

Sky cleared her throat and let Kane help her sit up, daring to look behind her. "Yikes. That was a poisonous snake."

Kane rocked back on his heels and stood. "I know. That's why I killed it."

"Let's hope the Senator never encounters one of these guys." Without Kane's reflexes, she might have been bitten.

"Amen."

Sky stood and dusted herself off. "I'm good. Let's get digging." If only her heart would calm down.

"You sure you want to continue?" He stepped behind her and piled sand on top of the snake, giving it a fitting burial. Flies would be attracted to the creature if he hadn't encased it.

"Yes. The near death experience only heightens my desires."

He could take her comment any way he wanted. Right now, she wasn't sure what she was experiencing, other than adrenaline flooding through her veins, raising every sense from the confinement of the cave walls, the sand in her mouth and hair, the burnt smell of the gunpowder, and the wobble in her knees. Add in the excitement of her find and she'd never felt so alive.

"You're all right, Officer Nash. Let me get the shovel from my car."

Her laugh came out a little forced but held a lot of relief. "You carry a shovel around? You are the Boy Scout."

"You have no idea." He winked and trotted out.

Did his wink mean he was flirting with her? Wasn't he the one who claimed he preferred to work alone? *Stop analyzing.* He probably figured in the few days he would be here, that it was better to enjoy himself with a little companionship, than act professional and standoffish all the time.

He returned minutes later with a portable shovel in hand and a larger flashlight. She held out her palm and wiggled her fingers. "I'll dig first." She didn't believe males had to be the dominant ones.

"What? And have you break another nail? I won't be responsible." He planted a hand on his chest.

She laughed. If he wanted to play macho man, she'd let him. After all, watching his muscles ripple across his back would be a real treat.

Sky slid down to the sand and kept her back to the wall. She alternated between watching Kane work and keeping an eye out for other creatures of the cave. Once the light faded, even with the flashlight bouncing off the ceiling, the cave turned creepy, possibly because animals liked to seek shelter at night.

"I think you've done enough work today. It's getting dark," she finally said, sad that this adventure was about to end. She enjoyed the fact he'd put so much effort into her find. "I'll ask a few people to come back tomorrow and continue digging."

"You still think there's some big alien spacecraft buried here?" He wiped the sweat from his brow with the back of his sleeve and grinned.

"Go ahead and mock me. Someday, you'll see." She waved a hand. "As for there being a craft below the sand, I don't think so."

He stabbed the shovel into the earth. His jaw loosened. "Then why did you have me dig?"

To see if you would, and to watch your body sweat and writhe under the effort. "To make sure."

"You're something else, lady." He cocked a brow before brushing off the sand. "I'll need to clean up if we're still going out."

She slapped a hand to her forehead. "Crap. Can I take a rain check? I forgot it's Saturday, and I promised my dad I'd cook tonight. He laid a major guilt trip on me for not spending any quality time with him last week."

"Sure. Whatever you say." From the slight slump to his shoulders, he might be as disappointed as she was.

***

No sooner had Kane dropped her off at the station so she could drive to her dad's, than her cell rang. For a second, Sky hoped it was Kane calling to ask if he could see her after her meal. Instead, it was Dad. "Hey."

"I'm sorry, hon, I have to take care of some official business, and I won't make it home for our father-daughter get together after all."

"Da-ad. You begged me to make time after last week's fiasco." Something always seemed to come between them.

"It couldn't be helped. I'm sorry."

She'd given up a date with Kane for him. "Maybe we can do it
tomorrow?"

"Sure, tomorrow sounds good."

That's what he always said. There were sacrifices to having a
father who served the community. With that obligation gone,
she debated whether to turn around and stop at Rosalie's to see
if Kane still wanted to go out, but then she nixed the idea. She
wouldn't feel comfortable being on a date when covered in sand.
She'd have to shower and change, and by the time she primped,
he'd have already eaten.

As she rounded a curve, the metal object pinged as it rolled
on the floor and hit the metal undercarriage of the passenger
seat.

Well, if she couldn't get any enjoyment from seeing Kane,
she'd visit Earl. He wouldn't care if she were a dirty mess. The
old guy spent his days outside, but nights were lonely for him,
and she liked to keep him company. In the past when she visited,
he would spend hours talking about his experiences on the other
side of the galaxy. As a thank you for his potential help in identifying her object, she stopped at a liquor store and picked up a
bottle of wine.

A few minutes later, she pulled into Earl's drive and cut the
lights. Well, well, lookie who was here—Pearl. She was probably
there to discuss Dan's abduction with someone knowledgeable,
since he wouldn't come within a mile of this house.

Not wanting Ms. Pearl to see what Sky had unearthed, she
left the silver object on the floor of her VW and stashed the
wine in the back. Music sounded from inside—a slow, sensual
beat. Definitely not the type of music the former space explorer
would play. She tapped on the door, but no one answered. Curious, she knocked louder. "Hello. It's Sky."

She debated heading back home but thought she could add

something to Dan's abduction tale. Besides, she really needed Earl's opinion on her prized find.

Voices sounded followed by a moan. Her cop instinct kicking into gear, Sky pushed open the door, stepped inside, and stilled. Oh, my God.

CHAPTER SEVEN

The room flickered with candlelight, and incense perfumed the air. Pearl and Earl were together, which was cool, but Pearl's outfit was anything but. Wearing a red, satin thong and a matching bra, the wrinkly skin clumped over the waistband. Pearl was facing Earl and had wrapped a pink boa around his neck. He wore plaid boxers and had his hands on Pearl's hips, his upper body swaying to the music, and his smile beamed brighter than Venus on a dark night. Sky wanted to look away, but like a bad accident, she couldn't help but stare.

As soon as Earl noticed her, he tore the boa out of Pearl's hands. "Sky. Whatcha doing here?" Thank goodness, he didn't sound angry.

Pearl twisted around and slapped her hands on her abundant hips. "Not a good time, dear."

Sky backed up not sure how to respond. "Sorry."

She was halfway out the door when Earl called out. "Don't go. Give us a sec. Pearl and I have all night to do our thing. Right, honey?" He looked up and winked at the nearly naked woman.

"Sure." Sky ducked outside and pressed her back against the wall. Happy he'd found someone to be with after his wife died,

Pearl and he would make the perfect pair, in part because both believed in the possibility of interstellar space travel.

A few minutes later, Pearl opened the door, her blouse buttoned wrong. "You can come in now." She smiled. "I'm sorry you had to see that. I came over to celebrate, and one thing led to another."

"Celebrate?" Here she thought she'd come over to ask about Dan Joe.

"Yes. Mary came home."

Sky hadn't expected to hear good news, though a phone call would have been appreciated. "That's fantastic. Where was she?"

"With a man. She said she wanted to get away, claiming she called my cell a few times, but I swear I never heard it ring."

Good old Pearl. "Well, that's wonderful. Better keep a good eye on her."

"You aren't kidding. Thanks for all you've done."

Sky smiled, happy for a good resolution.

Earl had a blanket over his lap and now had on a sweater with holes in the right shoulder. She wasn't sure if she could be more embarrassed. "I'm sorry I didn't call first. I never thought—"

Pearl waved a hand. "Never you mind. Not only was I happy about Mary coming home, I needed some release after what happened with Dan earlier tonight. I was looking for some advice from my old friend."

Earl wheeled forward. "Pearl, you mind fixin' us some hot tea?"

She shot a glance between the two of them. "Sure, no problem."

Sky searched Earl's shelves for the object that reminded her of the silver pineapple, but all she saw was the gray fuel cell he claimed someone had recovered in a cave west of where she'd explored. Both were silver in color, and while hers was cone-shaped, his had a pyramid top and an inverted pyramid bottom. Not the same at all. Darn.

"You find out who killed that man?" he asked.

"Not yet." She stepped closer and kept her voice to a whisper. "I found something in a cave that might be alien though. It's in the car, and I'd like your opinion, but not while Pearl is around."

"Good thinking. Pearl likes to gossip something fierce."

The sexed up woman waltzed in with a tray in hand, the faint aroma of lemon and mint filling the air, which competed with the jasmine sticks. "Here ya go."

Sky took the cup. "Pearl, what happened with Dan?"

She placed the tray on the side table, handed a cup to Earl and another to Sky, and then sat down on the sofa. "He's a changed man. He told me he let you know about the abduction, but that you didn't believe him."

"It's not that I didn't believe him, it's that I need more information before I can help."

"I hear ya. I'm not so sure aliens were involved either, but something happened to him. He used to be sweet and always after me to... you know. Today, he was mean and unresponsive. It's almost as if he's looking for a fight." She glanced at Earl's lap.

"What are you saying? The aliens did this to him?"

Earl spoke up. "I don't know who did this, but according to Pearl, here, Dan doesn't care to have sex anymore."

Note to self: don't ask Pearl anything unless I want the whole truth and nothing but the truth. "Did any more of his memory return?"

She looked down and rebuttoned her shirt. "He remembers his lungs burning and not being able to breathe very well. His vision was mostly blurry during the whole ordeal."

"Dan claimed he hadn't remembered much other than waking in his bed and being in some kind of ring with bright lights. Did he tell you if anyone asked him questions?"

"No."

So much for hard facts. "Again, I apologize for interrupting. I just stopped by to see how Earl was doing after finding the dead body. Trauma has a way of creeping up on you when you least expect it." Though Earl seemed to have found a way to lessen his problems—better living through sex.

"'Preciate your concern, but I'm fine."

Sky smiled and hightailed it out of there, wishing he'd been alone so she could have shown him the artifact. Man, she'd never walked in on a couple about to go to it before. Sky grimaced at the visual.

The sun had set a while ago, and her stomach wouldn't stop making noises, so she decided to stop at EBE's for dinner. The engine took a try or two before it turned over, but once on the road, she reached downtown in good time. The café was mostly empty except for the ever-present Phil, Doug, Matt, and old Mr. Jameson. The foursome was at their usual table playing checkers—a game that never seemed to end. When one left, she swore another took his place.

Sky glanced around but didn't spot Kane. While disappointed, she could use the quiet time. Jimmy was on the evening shift instead of Cathy, which meant the cook changed shifts too. Getting her meal would take time.

"Howdy, Ms. Nash." Jimmy Torres had a large bandage on his arm and held his neck stiffly.

"You okay?" She hoped he hadn't been bitten the same way Dan Joe had.

He grinned real big. "Just a little football injury. I got head butted at last Saturday's game, and a guy in cleats stepped on my arm."

"I'm sorry."

"I'll be fine. What can I get you? Your usual?"

After the day she'd had, she wanted to splurge. "I think I'll have the Crash Site trout. Baked, and bring me lots of coffee. No, make it a carafe. I have some research to do."

"Can I interest you in a Galaxy coffee? Looks like you could use an extra dose of hazelnut."

"Just black."

"Coming right up."

While she waited for Jimmy to deliver the requested carafe, Sky dragged her iPad from her backpack and did a Google search on alien artifacts, hoping to find some object similar to hers. The diner filled up all at once, and her food arrived half an hour later. She forgot it was movie night, which often brought in half the town. She shut down the iPad with the intention of searching later.

She ate in peace and was about to pay when Harriet waltzed in, a surprise given the late hour. The chatter swelled as the department's receptionist stopped to talk with everyone. Finally, she swung over to Sky's table. "I've been looking everywhere for you. I tried calling but only got your voicemail."

"Whoops." She checked her phone and turned it back on. "Kane and I went cave hunting looking for the Senator, and I shut it off. You know how it is when the cell can't find a signal. It roams and roams and wears down the battery." Actually, she'd turned it off after her dad called.

"That happened to me once. So how did that go? Get into any narrow passageways with Mr. Hunk?" She winked.

Once or twice. "Nothing happened. We were on assignment looking for the Senator, but he wasn't anywhere to be found."

"So no ass grabbing when you bent down to examine the sand for prints?" She looked like the damned Cheshire cat.

The grilling wouldn't end until she gave her something. "Fine. He kissed my forehead."

Her friend clapped and sat down in the chair opposite her. "Do tell."

Sky detailed what led up to the snake shooting and the subsequent finding of the possible alien cone. "So you see, he was just protecting me. The kiss was an attempt to calm me."

"Sky and Kane sitting in a tree, K-I-S-S-I-N-G."

Sky laughed at her antics. "Remember, he'll be gone as soon as he finds Overton."

"You never know." Harriet opened her purse, pulled out a bag of brownies, and placed them on the table. "I made these for you, but you never came back to the station."

Sky glanced at the counter. "You can't bring food into the café."

Harriet waved a hand. "Don't be silly. Dixie doesn't mind."

Dixie was Harriet's twin sister and part owner of the café. "Okay, but shouldn't you be home? It's close to your bedtime."

"I'm not that old. Elmer called and asked if I'd find you. He received an urgent message for you at the station."

From the half-smile on her face, tragedy hadn't struck. "Did Kane call?"

"Don't you wish?" She pulled a piece of paper from her purse. "No, Chris is flying in tomorrow night for his mom's birthday. He wants you to pick him up at the Page airport at five." She leaned forward. "Tell him no. He needs to get his own damned ride to Savory. You're not his taxi."

The surge of excitement she'd expected didn't materialize. Yes, she was happy she was finally going to see him, but the fact that Chris was coming because it was his mom's birthday, and just wanted her for a ride from the airport, didn't sit well. It was clear they weren't dating anymore, so why call her? When Sky had celebrated her own birthday six weeks ago, he'd called two days late, implying he wanted to break it off, but then he'd sent her an amazing red cashmere sweater. She couldn't help but wonder if the gift was merely to keep her on the hook so she'd be available when he came to town. "I can't let him take a cab from Page. It would cost a fortune."

"He can afford it. Besides, he's no good for you. He should be coming to town to see you too, not just his mom."

Harriet was right. "Maybe."

"Remember, he only had time for you once a week when he lived here. Think about it. Gifts. Jewelry. Always wanting you to be made up like a fancy doll. He was training you to be his trophy wife. If you ever married him, you'd be together only when he needed to show you off or to give him some business advantage."

Sky shook her head. "So not true."

"Suit yourself." She leaned on her elbows. "Tell me this, what are you looking for in a husband?"

She never remembered Harriet being so serious. "Security, I guess. A steady paycheck and a man who's kind to me."

"Oh, honey, what about passion? Someone to see you through thick and thin? After your mom passed, you didn't have a role model." She shook her head. "Those qualities you listed are all well and good, but let me tell you what's important. The man of your dreams has to see deep inside you and connect with you as a person. Love you for who you are on the inside. He needs to excite you, make you want to be a better person, and push you to be all you can be."

That made her laugh. "You sound like the ads for the Army."

"It's a good slogan to live by." She tapped a finger on the table. "My gut tells me Kane's that guy. You're beautiful, but Chris doesn't see the real you. If he did, he'd make you his top priority and stop trying to make you into someone you're not. He also wouldn't suggest you both date other people."

That part was true. Chris always seemed to want her in fancy clothes and make-up before he took her out anywhere. She always thought it was because he cared, but now she wondered if he was thinking more about himself and the type of person he wanted to be seen with. "It's a moot point since Kane won't be around long enough to get to know me."

Harriet opened the bag of brownies and the rich, chocolaty aroma made Sky's nearly full stomach yearn for more. Harriet handed her one. Sky took her time chewing, not ready to concede her points. "These are really good." She finished the first treat and grabbed a second. "Besides, I get the sense that Kane's married to his job, so I wouldn't be any better off."

"If he is, I bet you could change his mind."

Something seemed off. "How do you know so much about Kane? You've only seen him a time or two."

She leaned back in her seat and got that I'm-smarter-than-you-think look. "While you were out and about, I had a long talk with Mr. Cornell."

"Really?" Sky wasn't sure she liked them talking about her.

"Yes, and so you know, he appreciates who you really are."

It was worse than she thought, especially if Harriet spilled Sky's secrets to Kane. She groaned. "He doesn't know what I want or want I need."

"You'd be surprised how sharp he is."

"Did you mention Chris?"

Harriet glanced away for a second. "Yes, I did."

Shit. "That's personal."

Harriet shrugged. "Do me a favor."

"What?" Sky wasn't in the mood.

"When you're with Chris tomorrow, think how different it could be with Kane."

Sky opened then closed her mouth not knowing what to say. The memory of Kane's warm lips on her forehead made her pulse speed. When was the last time Chris had spontaneously showed her affection?

Don't go there.

Fortunately, Jimmy interrupted them. "Hi, Ms. Harriet. Can I get you something to go with those brownies?"

Harriet held up the bag. "I'm just leaving since I failed to talk sense into our officer here. Take these and share them with the others." She pushed back her chair and raised her brows at Sky. "I'll see you in the morning."

Before Jimmy left with the goodies, Sky grabbed a few more. She still had the wine in the car. Tonight might be a good time to get drunk.

CHAPTER EIGHT

Sky's head pounded. The light coming through her bedroom window pierced her lids and shot straight to the back of her skull. She never should have had that fourth glass of wine, but after she Googled Kane's name and found he'd attended Columbia University and graduated at the top of his class before he entered the service, she realized he was clearly out of her league. Disappointed, she'd fallen into bed but then couldn't sleep. She tried to convince herself she wanted to see Chris again, but doubt kept intruding. Her new feelings for Kane seemed to be overshadowing those for Chris. Damn.

Someone knocked on her front door, and she slammed the pillow over her head. "I'm not answering."

Whoever it was knocked harder, clearly not going away anytime soon.

"Fine. I'm coming."

She patted the nightstand for her sunglasses and slapped them on top of her head. She knew she might look stupid, but the glasses helped tame her bed-mussed hair. With a blanket wrapped around her shoulders, she dragged herself to the door, her bare feet freezing on the cold floor. *Slippers*. She should have put on slippers.

Given all the weird stuff going on in town, she'd locked her doors. Sky peered through the security hole before opening up. Uh-oh. It was Kane. "Just a minute." She spun around and slammed her back against the door, her pulse racing. What was he doing here?

"Sky?"

She couldn't let him see her like this. On the other hand, she couldn't let him stand outside while she showered and changed.

After unlocking the door and opening it an inch, she leaned close to the edge, not letting him see her face. "Can you give me a minute before coming in, so I can make it back to my bedroom to change? Go ahead and make some coffee if you want."

Shit. Shit. Shit. Not only was she in her pooh bear pajamas, her mascara had probably streaked down her face. If she hadn't been so tired after all that wine she would have at least washed up. If Kane saw her now, he'd run for sure. Hell, she didn't even want to look in the mirror.

"Okay." Damn him for chuckling.

Not that it mattered, but she wasn't even sure there was coffee in the cabinet. She raced back to the bedroom, and a second later, the front door opened. She grabbed her sexiest underwear, tightest pants, and that low-cut red top Harriet wanted her to wear, and ducked into the bathroom. Once the water warmed, she jumped into the shower and was full of soap when she thought she heard a soft knock followed by a squeak of the hinges.

"Sorry to barge in, Sky, but I found out that someone saw the Senator yesterday at some perfume factory west of 89. The caller has to be someplace at ten this morning, and it's a little past nine now. We need to hurry."

Even though the shower door was opaque glass, she wrapped her arms around her chest. "You go ahead."

"I want you to come with me." Her heart skipped a beat. "I might need to request a surveillance video, and your authority will come in handy."

So much for him liking her company. Sky wasn't about to tell him she had no jurisdiction outside the Reservation. "I'll be right out." She rinsed her hair then turned off the water.

The door clicked close. Oh my God. Had he been waiting there the whole time? For an insane moment, she wished he wanted to catch a peek, but her rational side dismissed the thought.

In record time, she towel dried, and threw on her clothes, not taking the time to put on makeup. Dear God, she looked thirteen. Sky opened the door, took one step, and halted.

"Oh, my," she blurted. Kane was dressed in black slacks, a crisp white shirt open at the throat, and polished loafers. *Whoa.* "You fix up good."

His pupils dilated. "So do you. You ready?"

"Absolutely."

On the way out, she grabbed her leather jacket, hoping it didn't still smell from the morgue. A cool breeze and bright sunshine greeted her. "How did this person know to call you?"

Kane opened the passenger side Jeep door and she slid in. "I stopped by the station to find the location of all the local factories within a thirty-mile radius of Page."

That's when Harriet, the traitor, must have interrogated him. "And?"

He jammed the key in the ignition and started the engine. "I called everyone on the list and asked them to let me know if any of their employees spotted Overton. This morning, I received a call from someone."

That was highly resourceful of him. "Did you show this person a photo to make sure he identified the right guy?"

"Yup. My contact, General Stentfield, emailed one to my phone."

He backed out of her drive, and when he sent her a knowing smile, heat rushed up her face. Her body was one big traitor.

After a fifteen-minute drive, the air inside his Jeep overheated, and she rolled down the window. The sweet smell of something burning blew in, forcing her to glance to the horizon where a dark plume puffed off in the distance.

She faced Kane. "What would the Senator be doing at a perfume factory? Does he collect perfume bottles or did he need to shop for his wife?"

"I'm not sure. The manager merely spotted him. I'm thinking he might have taken one of the tours."

"I thought you said Overton came to Arizona on official business."

Kane turned into the factory's parking lot and pulled to a stop. "That's true, but from the looks of this place, there's nothing top secret about it, so maybe he decided to take a break."

Sky waited for Kane to do his gentlemanly thing again and open her door. "Thanks." She'd never been treated so well.

The Fleur de Paris perfume factory was a large square building with five huge air conditioners on the side. Off to the left stood four greenhouses. She'd lived in Savory for over twenty years, yet had never been inside this place. In fact, she hadn't realized the factory was even open on the weekends. Then again, if they catered to tourists, it made sense.

Kane escorted her into the building where the aroma of sweet orange and sugar filled the air, and everything looked expensive. One whole wall contained a display cabinet filled with perfume bottles, all of which were beautiful and exotic.

"May I help you?" A tall thin brunette, dressed in an Armani suit and Jimmy Choo shoes approached them. Wow.

Kane glanced at Sky, forcing her back to the moment. She pulled out her badge and hoped the woman wasn't up on her area of jurisdiction. "Mr. LeFloch called about Senator Overton."

"Oh, yes." Her gaze shot to the side before looking Sky in the face. "Please follow me."

To Sky's surprise, Kane didn't give the woman a once over despite the fact that she was gorgeous. They followed her down a long corridor, her tall heels clicking on the tile floor. As they rounded the corner, a group of tourists huddled inside a room, the chitchat echoing off the walls.

"They're on one of our tours," Ms. Jimmy Choo shoes said. "You two should definitely take one. The history of perfume making is so interesting."

"We aren't here to sightsee," Sky said in her most professional tone.

The brunette's brow rose for a fraction of a second. "Here we are." Her nose high in the air, she knocked on Mr. LeFloch's door before pushing it open.

A short, reed thin man seated behind a large mahogany desk stood. "Come in. I trust you're Mr. Cornell." He turned to her. "And you are?"

"Sky Nash." She flashed her badge. "Savory PD."

His lips thinned for a second, and she could have sworn his pupils dilated, a sure sign he was uncomfortable. He straightened his perfectly neat tie and adjusted his too large black glasses. When he tilted his head, the light from the window showed a slight bead of perspiration on his brow. "Please sit."

Kane did so and then leaned forward. "Can you give me any details about the Senator?"

"I was checking the greenhouses when I saw Alan, our horticulturist, with the Senator." Mr. LeFloch pressed his lips together.

"That drew your attention for a reason. Was that a problem?" Kane asked.

"Alan isn't supposed to take visitors in there. In fact, we've installed fingerprint biometric sensors to prevent unauthorized access. Besides me, Alan is the only other person authorized to be in there, and only during regular business hours."

Sky found it odd that someone would need to put such hi-tech scanners on a greenhouse. "Are the flowers that rare that someone might steal them?" Sky asked.

His stare looked a million miles away. He blinked before turning back toward her. "Yes. What we do here is secret. The recipe for making our perfume came from my family in France. We're from Eze." He said it with such reverence that she almost laughed.

She'd never heard of the place. "I guess you wouldn't want your competitors to find out how you mix the fragrances."

He smiled like a priest beaming down at a new parishioner. "I see you understand."

Kane tapped his foot. "If no one is allowed in the greenhouse, why was the Senator inside?"

"I asked Alan about that. He said he didn't see any harm letting the Senator inside since he's a government official." From the way Mr. LeFloch's lips pursed, he disagreed.

"Do you have any surveillance videos of the area? I want to make sure the Senator didn't go inside under duress."

Mr. LeFloch's mouth opened, and he slapped a hand to his chest. "Heavens no. Someone might get a hold of the tapes and learn how we work."

So his outrage wasn't over concern the Senator might have been taken against his will, but rather that company secrets might be revealed. She'd have to see what Kane thought about Mr. LeFloch dodging the duress angle.

"Thanks for your time, Mr. LeFloch." They both rose, and Kane shook the manager's hand. Interesting how LeFloch wouldn't even make eye contact with her.

She wanted to see if he would acknowledge her, so she remained still. When she made no effort to leave, Kane slid a hand around her waist and escorted her out. It was no love hold by any means since his fingers were pressed firmly around her waist. Guess he could tell she wanted to make LeFloch uncomfortable enough to slip up and say something.

Once in the hall, he lowered his arm, and the lack of contact unsettled her. She had never been attracted to the aggressive, must-be-in-control type, yet when he broke contact, she missed it.

Focus. "What do you think?" She failed once again to get a read on Kane's thoughts.

"About?"

"The fact that he's lying."

Kane said nothing as he walked outside and headed straight to his Jeep. "Are you thinking he didn't spot the Senator?" He held open the door.

She slid into the passenger seat. "No, I believe he saw him, but from the way he didn't maintain eye contact, he was hiding something."

"I thought that too. You're the law. Perhaps you can help me find out more." Once inside his vehicle, he sped out of the lot.

She twisted in her seat. "This property isn't on the Reservation, which means I have no authority here."

"You never told me."

"I guess I forgot."

His brows rose, clearly not buying her story. "I think LeFloch thought you did."

"From the way he dodged your question about Overton being in the greenhouse by force, I agree with you. On a slightly different note, didn't you find it strange that a building that couldn't be more than thirty thousand square feet would have such a massive air conditioning system? I know orchids and other flowers need a specific temperature, but why all the exhaust fans?"

"You tell me."

"I wish I knew." She faced front. "And why would someone build a perfume factory in a desert?"

He shrugged. "The land's cheap. The labor's probably cheap too. Besides, greenhouses are self-contained and prevent the outside air from getting in. Add in Arizona's abundant sunshine, and it makes sense."

She wasn't convinced. "Perhaps Mr. LeFloch grew up here."

"He said his family comes from Eh-ze." He drew out the

name of the little French town. Kane glanced over at her with a small lift to his lips.

She chuckled. "His accent was very slight, implying he could have come here as a child."

"Good point again. Since I roused you out of bed so early and never thanked you for taking me around the caves, can I at least buy you lunch?"

Her heart nearly stopped. "You have time? I thought you had to track down the Senator?" Or was he a polite man needing to pay his debts?

"For you, I'll make time."

CHAPTER NINE

Sky had an amazing lunch with Kane. They discussed possible explanations for Mr. LeFloch's nervousness but were unable to come up with any definitive conclusion. Then not only did they talk about some of his cases, he asked about her work too. It was refreshing to have someone understand what she went through on a daily basis.

On the drive back to her house, they discussed, or rather disagreed, whether aliens existed. They even stayed in the car for close to an hour talking about all the possible government conspiracies, and she had to admit it had been a while since someone had valued her opinion so much.

Their time together seemed to fly, and when Sky finally said goodbye, she was so invigorated by the exchange that she cleaned the house from top to bottom and then called her dad to tell him she couldn't make it to dinner because she had to make an airport run. He said he understood.

By four, she was ready to pick Chris up at the airport. She put on makeup and even curled her hair the way Chris liked it. To be honest, she thought she looked good without the changes, but old habits die hard.

Sky took one final look in the mirror. She bet Kane would

scowl at her heavy-handed attempt, whereas Chris always said makeup enhanced her face and made her look pretty. Damn. The two men were like night and day. Kane was reckless and rugged, whereas Chris was...safe, probably because they'd known each other for so long.

Stop comparing them.

Time to go. She threw on her jacket and headed out, wishing she could have picked Chris up in the new cruiser instead of her beat up VW. It took her fifty minutes to get to the Page airport, and by the time she parked and rushed inside, Chris was at baggage claim waiting for her. When he saw her, his face broke into a smile.

"Sky!" He hugged her hard and swung her around. "Let me see you." He set her down and held her out. "You look fabulous. I love what you've done with your hair."

Heat rushed up her face. "Thanks." She hadn't cut it since he left, anticipating he'd like it longer. She gave him a quick kiss and checked him out. His silk tie went well with his fitted navy blue suit and his starched beige shirt. "I see you have a new haircut too."

"Styles are shorter in New York. You like?"

"I like."

Chris lifted his carry-on over his shoulder then faced her. "I'm starving. How about dinner at Bonkers?"

"I'd love that." It was only the most romantic place in Page. He must have decided he couldn't live without her. When the anticipated rush failed to materialize, she pushed it aside. She nodded to his one bag. "You don't have any other luggage?"

"Nope. Just this." He tapped the side of his bag.

They maneuvered their way to the parking lot. "How long are you staying?" Perhaps they could spend a day or two at the lodge overlooking the South rim of the Grand Canyon, though the overnight bag implied he wouldn't be here for long.

"I have a flight out at six tomorrow night."

Even though he said he was here for his mother's birthday,

she thought he might have come to rekindle their relationship. Guess she'd been wrong. "Why such a short trip?"

"I wanted to take a week off, but to keep my job I have to make sure my clients stay happy."

"I understand." *Liar*.

"I appreciate you giving me some slack."

Did he think of her as a friend now or still as his girlfriend? When they reached her car, she popped the trunk.

"You drove that?" he asked.

"The cruiser's in the shop."

He tossed her an irresistible smile. "I didn't mean to make fun of the old heap. It doesn't matter what you drive."

She waited for him to open the car door after he placed his carry-on in the trunk, but instead, he climbed in the passenger side. Oh, well. His mind was probably on all those rich clients. She slid in and was thankful when old reliable started on the first try.

Ten minutes later, Sky pulled into the restaurant parking lot. Chris leaned over. "Stay here. I want to give you something that I have in my case." A moment later, he returned and handed her a box wrapped in gold paper. "Just a thank you for putting up with me. I know I should call more often."

Why? They weren't dating.

Excited at the gift, she tore off the paper, opened the lid, and gasped. Inside was a bright blue Donna Karan silk wrap blouse. "I'm speechless."

"I'll be the one without words when I see you in it tomorrow at Mom's birthday party." He smiled. "Let's go in."

Suggesting she wear this particular blouse was a bit controlling, but she would have chosen it anyway. Inside, about eight couples were in the waiting area of the full restaurant. Damn. She'd starve before they were served.

The maître d' motioned them to a table. "Right this way, Mr. Renford."

She leaned over to him. "You made reservations?"

"I didn't want my pet to wait. I know how hard you work."

Pet? She bristled at the demeaning name. His mixed signals were throwing her off, but discussing their *relationship* in a restaurant wasn't cool. As soon as they were alone, she'd ask him.

During the meal, Chris regaled her with wonderful stories of New York City and the high profile people he'd entertained. He reached across the table and took her hand. "I have something to tell you."

"Yes?" Too many conflicting emotions prevented her from becoming too excited.

"I received a promotion that will earn me an extra twenty grand a year."

It was not what she'd expected him to say, but she knew how much success meant to him. "That's fantastic."

"Oh, Sky. You should come to New York. We'd have so much fun. We could see Broadway plays, go to museums, and eat like this." He waved a hand around. "And I could really use your help decorating my bachelor pad. It's a sad little place without a woman's touch." He turned his lips into a frown.

Did he want her to fly out to New York so he could show off the city and just lend a hand decorating? "I'm sure women are beating down your door to help."

Chris was acting strange. She had a brain, but he didn't seem to care about that—only Kane did.

"That's not—" His cell rang, and he held up a finger. "Just a minute."

For the next ten minutes he talked to the caller about interest rates, PE ratios, earnings, and other financial gobbledy-gook to someone who she guessed was a client.

He mouthed, "I'm sorry."

She nodded, placed her napkin on the table, and headed to the bathroom, figuring he wanted privacy. When she returned, he'd finished his conversation.

"Babe, I'm so sorry. We have so little time together, and I

don't want to spend it on work. So tell me how you've been doing?"

The old Chris had returned. "Good. I'm working on a case that might be related to my house break-in."

He leaned forward. "Jesus. Why didn't you tell me you were burglarized? Did they take anything?"

She had called to tell him, but when he didn't answer, she didn't want to leave a message. "No."

"Good." Chris checked his watch. "Damn, babe, we gotta go. I want to get to Mom's before she heads to bed."

Sky slumped in her chair. Wasn't he curious as to why someone would break into her house and not take anything? "I thought maybe we could have some quiet time at my house before you saw her." She needed to ask him if he even wanted to be together. Right now, Sky wasn't sure she did.

He tilted his head and pulled her hand into his. "I would like nothing more than to spend all night with you, massaging your feet, adoring your supple body, but I came here for Mom's birthday."

And not for her. If that wasn't clear enough, she didn't know what was. "She's taking your dad's death hard. She'll be so happy to see you."

"I know." He motioned for the check. Chris signed the bill and walked her out, the cool air biting into her skin. She shivered, and he wrapped an arm around her lightly.

The drive back to his mom's was strained because Chris talked the whole way and never gave her a chance to voice an opinion, but she understood he was excited to share his adventures with someone.

When she drew to a stop in front of his mother's house, Chris rubbed her shoulder. "You want to come in?"

Not really. His mom usually ignored her, and she'd have to listen to Chris tell his mom how successful he was. "I'll let you two have your reunion in private."

"Don't forget. The party is at one tomorrow. Wear the blue blouse."

He was out in a flash. Once he grabbed his overnight case, he was at the front door before she'd even pulled out of the drive. Sky shook her head. She'd been such a fool in believing he'd wanted to get back with her. Chris only cared about himself.

She wasn't halfway home when her cell rang. The caller I.D. read Cornell, and a blast of unwanted lust raced through her. She couldn't imagine why he'd call at 8:00 at night, but there was only one way to find out.

"Hello?"

"You'll never guess where I am."

"Where?"

"I found the Senator and he's safe."

She sagged against the seat. "Thank goodness."

"Listen, I really need your expertise. Can you come to the RV Park now? I want to tell you everything."

She loved that he wanted to include her, though how she could help, she had no idea. "Sure."

More than anything, Sky wanted to rid her mind of what had occurred with Chris. She debated stopping home and changing into something more practical, but there wasn't time.

As quickly and safely as possible, she headed to Wildacres RV Park. Perhaps because she was in a hurry, it seemed like it took forever to get there. It was close to eight thirty by the time she slipped through the gates. The lights in the office blazed brightly, but given the late hour, she figured it was okay to go on ahead without checking in with Betty.

Finding the Senator's RV was easy since his remained the only RV on the east side of the park. She knocked on the door, and a smiling Kane answered. His even, white teeth, surrounded by those full lips, made her heart race and appealed to her on so many levels.

Stop it. He'll be leaving soon.

"Be right back, Senator." Kane wrapped an arm around her

shoulder, and when he led her down the three steps to the ground, his touch altered something inside her.

"Hey, I appreciate you coming on such short notice. I hope I didn't interrupt anything."

"No, I just dropped Chris off at his mom's."

"Chris?"

She didn't know why he asked since Harriet had already filled him in. Perhaps Kane didn't want to give away his little conversation with the traitorous dispatcher. "A friend who is visiting from New York."

"Everything go okay?"

No. Chris was an ass, just like Harriet said he'd be, which pissed me off for not noticing it before. Kane seemed to doubt her, but she wasn't about to discuss her issues with him.

"It went fine. So tell me what you need." She dug her hands in her pockets to keep from accidentally touching him.

"I'll let the Senator fill you in. I told him to wait until you arrived before going into detail, but do me a favor and do not react to what he has to say."

"What do you mean?"

"He remembers almost *nothing* after he got to the RV Park."

Her heart plummeted. Shades of Dan Joe's conversation filtered through her brain again. "You're kidding me, right?"

"I wish. I know the basics, but when he tells you about it please stay cool and be logical. I know what conclusion you'll want to draw, but let's see if you can refrain from suggesting aliens took him, at least right now?"

"But what if they did? According to Betty and Barney Hill, abductions create lost time." For some reason, she was now willing to believe the Senator over Dan Joe.

"Who?"

Clearly, the man had never studied any of the documentation. "Two abductees."

The door opened, and the Senator looked out. "Everything all right?" the Senator asked.

Kane grabbed her hand and led her inside. "Just fine."

She loved the strength of his fingers. Kane let go and made the introductions, seemingly unaware of the charge of electricity that arced between them.

The Senator looked like his picture except he wasn't clean-shaven, and his hair was mussed. The bloodshot eyes didn't help with the sophisticated image the media presented. "Nice to meet you."

As if Kane lived there, he motioned she sit next to him on the sofa. The inside air was warm and smelled of vanilla air freshener. "Senator, will you bring Sky up to speed?"

CHAPTER TEN

Overton paced in front of them. "I remember driving into the park and expecting someone from the research facility to contact me. At first, I thought maybe Pat and Clay were going to take me on the tour, but they left without a word, and I wasn't about to bring it up to any of the other locals."

"Do you know the name of the facility?" Sky asked. Maybe she'd visited it.

Overton swiped a hand over his head. "I'm afraid not. That's one of the reasons for the trip. The government actually expected the Armed Services Committee to fund this secret project without any information. That's bullshit. I made such a stink over full disclosure that the government set up this clandestine meeting." He faced Kane. "I'm not even sure how your general friend found out about it."

"He has his contacts. Are you saying you know nothing about the nature of the project?" Kane asked.

"All I know is it involves national security. Quite top secret."

Sky had to interject. "You sure this facility is in Savory?"

Overton shrugged. "All I know is that it's near here." He staggered and practically fell onto the chair facing them. "Wow. I just had this image rush."

Kane shot a glance at her. "Image rush?"

Overton waved a hand. "A memory where I was driving my RV, and there were six beautiful women in a van stranded on the side of the road. I pulled over to help them."

Kane leaned his elbows on his knees in a very masculine pose. The man oozed sex. "What did these women say when you stopped?"

"I can't remember. Only bits and pieces appear. Nothing solid."

She had to ask. "Do you think you were abducted?"

"Abducted? That's ridiculous." This came out close to a shout.

The man was clearly in denial. "So how would you explain this time loss?"

He rubbed his head. "At first, I thought I'd been in an accident and had amnesia, but nothing hurts. I've checked out my body. I have no bruises and don't have a headache, which means I don't have a concussion."

This was different from Dan Joe's case. He'd had a severe headache.

Kane leaned forward. "You do realize your RV hasn't left this lot since you arrived?" He held up a finger. "The manager keeps track of everything."

"That's impossible." While his voice was loud, the anger had disappeared.

"Senator, you keep rubbing your leg. You sure you weren't hurt? Kane asked.

"No. I'm fine." The Senator dropped his head in his hands. "I'm sorry to have dragged you both out here for nothing."

Her curiosity won. "Senator, would you mind pulling down your collar?" He lowered his chin, acting affronted, though it wasn't as if she'd asked him to strip. "I'd like to see if there's a mark on your neck."

He lowered the material, and sure as hell, there it was. She shot a satisfied look at Kane.

Kane moved closer and checked out the raised welt. "Looks like a bee sting to me."

That had been her logic with Dan Joe. "I'm betting it's an injection site."

"From?" Kane asked.

She was no doctor. "Whatever they give people to knock them out, and *drag* them to *their* vehicle." That would be consistent with the marks behind the RV.

Kane laid a hand on the Senator's shoulder. "Given what's happened, I'm going to stay here with you until we figure out what's going on."

He shook his head. "That won't be necessary." Overton scratched his neck. "Damn. I don't remember the bite."

Sky held up a hand. "Is it possible you were abducted by—?"

Kane swiveled toward her, his dark eyes indicating trouble. "May I speak with you for a moment *outside?*"

"Sure." She was tired and not in the mood for a yell fest, but she followed him down the steps. The wind had picked up, and the air was downright cold. "I'm sorry if I stepped out of bounds, but even you have to admit—"

"No. Your conclusions have merit—albeit out there." He ran a hand down her arm, spreading warmth. "Would you consider working the case with me, as in a full commitment?"

That was totally not what she expected him to say on several levels. "I can't."

She jammed her hands in her pockets again. Yes, she wanted to work on a big case, but Kane was dangerous for her.

"Why? This case is big, and the citizens of Savory could be in danger. It needs the highest level of professional expertise, and while I can provide the security and safety, we need your help."

That sounded like a line of bull to her. "I'm already keeping the citizens of Savory safe. If I work with you full time, who's going to stop the bar fights, catch the teenage kids doing stupid stunts, or break up the domestic violence?" *Look for other alien abductions or monitor the hog races?* "Remember, I have to find out who murdered our Air Force man."

"You can still do that. I'm not asking you to quit your job altogether."

"I would like to help, but Carl, our detective, is still in the hospital, Elmer hasn't been feeling well, and Harvey, well, if he had his way, he'd stay at the station doing nothing all day."

"I need to find out what happened to Overton."

"I can't help you."

"You're already involved. You're the one who found the drag marks and the business card behind the RV."

She shook her head. "Picking up a piece of trash hardly counts as helping with this crime. I was in the right place at the right time."

He lifted her chin, and her heart tripled in speed. *Stop reacting. He'll leave as soon as this case is solved.* "Do you really want to let down the Senator and the US government?"

What could she say that would not make her come off as a traitor to her country? "I'd like to help, but I can't."

Kane stepped back and blew into his cupped hands. "The case needs you."

The case? Not you? "I can't let down the family of that decapitated man." Even to her, it sounded lame.

He moved closer and dropped his gaze. "What are you afraid of? I won't let anything happen to you."

She withdrew her hands from her pockets and stuffed them under her arms. "Nothing." She looked up at the stars.

He couldn't guess how her history affected her behavior. First, her parents died then her adoptive dad emotionally left after her adoptive mother passed away. Next, the man she thought was the love of her life headed off to New York. She knew working closely with Kane would cause her emotions to grow stronger and she wasn't ready to put herself out there only to be left again.

Kane leaned back and gently placed his hands on her shoulders. "We won't tell anyone that you're helping, if that's what is worrying you." His voice came low and warm, like a rich cognac.

She stepped out of his grasp. "I'm sorry."

Before she let him convince her to help, she trotted off toward her car. She half expected him to run after her, but instead his boots sounded on the metal steps leading back inside the RV. Damn. Now she'd messed up everything, but it couldn't be helped. Everyone would be safer if she stayed away from him.

***

Sky's red taillights flashed, sending a shaft of colored lights across the lot, reflecting off the eyes of a raccoon. Rocks scattered as the forager disappeared behind a trailer.

Kane hated to ask for anyone's help, especially a woman's, but he needed Sky's cooperation if he was going to figure out what happened to the Senator. It wasn't as if he would ever put her in danger. God help him if that happened.

He wished he understood why Sky had been so reluctant to be part of the team, especially if she thought this case had something to do with aliens. There'd been bags under her eyes, so perhaps with a good night's sleep, he could convince her to sign on. If not, he'd go to her boss. Surely, he'd want to see one of his officers succeed and get some experience under her belt. Hell, her boss might be willing to do some legwork to find out who the dead man was, especially if it meant Sky might learn something.

Oh, crap. Perhaps Sky was mad at him because he'd interrupted her time with that no good boyfriend. He wasn't usually one to judge, but Harriet told him Chris didn't give one hoot about Sky as a person, and that gnawed at his gut something fierce.

For the first time since his wife died, he was attracted to someone—not just physically, but for the woman he knew she could be. It was a shame he lived so far from Savory. With his investigation company in Phoenix to run, a relationship wouldn't work. He should be happy she liked someone else, but not if that someone was a dick—Harriet's name for the boyfriend, not his.

"Kane?"

Shit. He'd been daydreaming, something he could ill afford. "Sorry, Senator." Kane stepped inside.

The Senator faced him. "You don't have to stay. I'm going to be fine."

"We've been over this before. The General told me you might be in trouble. I don't know what kind of mess he was referring to, since he couldn't know that someone would kidnap and then return you, but I'm here to make sure your trip doesn't have any more hiccups."

His eyes sparkled as if he was glad Kane wouldn't take no for an answer. "If you're going to insist, you might as well call me Paul. I'm having a beer. Care to join me?"

"Sure, but I stop at one." With Sky gone, he could relax somewhat. Thinking of her, he pulled out his phone and texted her to call him once she arrived home. That might be over-the-top, but that was who he was.

The Senator retrieved two beers from the fridge and handed him one. "I didn't want to mention this in front of the young lady, but I remembered something else."

Kane swigged his beer, and the cool liquid soothed his throat. "Tell me."

"I had sex with four of the six women I met. It's like I was on some kind of super Viagra pill."

The beer nearly flew out of Kane's mouth. "You do realize this was probably a dream?"

Overton chugged over half his drink. "I'm not so sure. If what you say is true, I might not have been in my RV, but the euphoria I experienced couldn't have been my imagination. Having several pairs of large boobs pressed into my face for hours is something I'm not likely to forget. I can still feel their soft, wonderful pressure on my lips and cheeks."

He'd be happy with one particular set. "Must be nice."

"I'll swear in court they were real."

"Let's hope your wife doesn't find out." Sore subject, he imagined, but he wanted to understand Paul's level of faithfulness.

If the Senator could have turned any whiter, he'd be a snow cone. "You can't tell her. I was out of my mind."

"So you were drugged?"

"I must have been. My moral compass didn't even engage. All I could think of was sex. I swear if a group of terrorists had been shooting at me, I wouldn't have moved away from those women."

"Not that I believe in it, but maybe the government is conducting experiments in mind control." Sky and he had talked about that topic. She claimed the government engaged in such practices, and it looked like she might be right—again. Damn it. Why did she have to change her mind about helping now when he needed her the most? She'd been so cooperative, and then bam. He must have done something to make her skittish.

"You'd be surprised what the public doesn't know," the Senator said, bringing Kane back to the present. "However, I'm not at liberty to discuss any of it." Paul waved the bottle. "So are you and Sky a couple?"

Kane spotted the question as an evasive tactic, mostly because he doubted the Senator cared about the answer. However, Kane didn't want to piss him off by ignoring him. "No."

"Why not? She's a real peach."

"I lost my wife two years ago, and I'm not ready to move on." *And because Sky doesn't seem interested.*

Paul laughed. "Son, I've never waited two years between my women."

Too much information. "My wife was my soul mate, and you only find one of those in a lifetime." *Unless that was a myth.*

"That's total bullshit. I was married twice before I found my Julie. Each of my wives was wonderful in her own way. Unfortunately, my job forced me to be away too much of the time, so they left me. I'll run for re-election once more then quit. I want to make sure I don't lose wife number three. She's the best."

"I appreciate the advice."

"Do more than appreciate it. Go after Sky. From the way she looks at you, she likes you."

"She has a boyfriend."

Paul chuckled. "She's not married yet."

"True, and the guy lives in New York, not in Savory. When I'm ready, I'll find out from her where she stands." Or maybe not. He didn't need the distraction right now.

The Senator shook his head and finished his beer. He stood, winced, and then rubbed his thigh. "I'll bring you some pillows and blankets. You can bunk out here." He set the bottle on the counter.

"You sure you're okay?"

"Yes." He walked down the hall with a slight limp and returned with the bedding. "See you in the morning, assuming I don't get taken again," he said with a laugh.

For a moment, a wistful glimmer filled Paul's eyes, almost as if he wanted to have sex with those women every day for the rest of his life.

"I'll make sure nothing happens to you." Kane turned on the tube and watched the news before shutting off the lights. He glanced at his cell, but there was no return text from Sky. He thought about calling her to make sure she'd gotten home safely, but at this late hour, he didn't want to wake her. He had no real reason to believe something bad had happened.

Unfortunately, sleep eluded him. He kept thinking of Sky and how she'd actually looked afraid to work with him, but he couldn't figure out why. Sure, she had to find the name of the dead man, but she had little to go on. No. There was definitely something else going on, and he was damned if he knew.

He draped an arm over his eyes and sighed, giving up on trying to figure out the answers tonight.

***

At the sound of a loud motorcycle, Kane jerked awake. Sunlight streamed in the RV and his cell told him it was 7:00 a.m. He'd overslept for the first time in a long time, probably because he'd only fallen asleep a few hours ago. After checking that Paul was still in bed, Kane decided to go for a short run before breakfast. Not only would he have the chance to exercise, he could check out the other trailers for anything suspicious.

After a thirty minute hard run, he slipped back into the motor home just as the Senator stepped from his room.

"You're back. Good. I think something's wrong with my leg." He rolled up his pajama leg enough to expose the bottom half of his thigh. "I was getting dressed when I noticed this lump."

It was about half an inch in diameter. "Looks more like scar tissue." Kane wiped the sweat from his brow with the back of his sleeve.

"I never had a scar on my leg before. I'd remember."

"The mark looks old. Perhaps you forgot."

"It's new and rather tender. Put your finger here." Kane did so. "See? It feels like there's metal under there."

"It is hard." A sense of unease crept up his body. "What do you think it is?"

"What I'm about to tell you is classified."

"My lips are sealed, sir."

The Senator nodded. "Back in 2009, there was a lawsuit against the CIA claiming they had implanted devices into the noses of unsuspecting people in order to control their behavior." He dragged a hand through his hair. "Jesus. Maybe my behavior was affected by this... this thing."

Even though the Senator was parroting Sky's fears, Kane wasn't buying it. "Your leg is a little far from your nose."

"To fool us, the government might have put it elsewhere. I want to get this out." The Senator paced. "Now, and you're going to help me."

CHAPTER ELEVEN

"You said what?" Harriet followed Sky to her desk, pulled up a chair, and placed a plate of blond brownies in front of her.

Sky didn't need any sugar today to mess with her mind or add to her mood swings. "I told him no."

"Why?"

"For several reasons. First off, Kane needs to bring in the FBI to solve this case, not some lowly officer from small town USA."

Harriet reached across the desk and nabbed a brownie. "Don't be silly. This is a chance of a lifetime. If you work with him, you'll be one step closer to being a detective."

"Second, you know me; I can't abandon this town. I also need to find out who murdered that headless man. You heard the Chief. If I mess up this case, it's sayonara to achieving any advancement here."

Harriet's shoulders fell. "It's so unfair."

"You mean it's unfair that the Chief doesn't like Caucasian women in law enforcement? Ever since he took over, he's been busting my chops."

"True, but if you help Kane solve this high profile case, it might put you in a better light." She raised her brows.

Sky had been wondering if that might be true. "Even if I'm

not working on my big case, who would watch out for the speeders or make sure no one steals from the diner again." She crossed her arms. "Carl should be here."

"But he's not." Harriet shook her head. "Don't use him as your excuse. You know what you are? A chicken. Harvey can take care of the town."

"Since when has he ever cared enough to help out?"

"Talk to the Chief and see what he says. He'll ride Harvey's backside to get the job done. Hell, maybe the Chief will volunteer to look for the murderers." Harriet chewed on her brownie while she held up a hand. "You want to know what I think?"

Not really. "What?"

"You're afraid to work day in and day out with Mr. Sexy."

Sky chuckled. "Oh, really, and why is that?"

"Any woman who spends even two days with that man would decide he's Mr. Right."

Sky shook a finger at Harriet. "I think someone in this office has a crush on Kane Cornell."

Harriet fluffed her gray curls. "I admit I find him attractive, but I think I'm a little old for him, don't you think? You, on the other hand, are perfect."

"You forget he doesn't live here."

She smiled. "My point exactly. You're afraid that if you work together, you'll fall in love with him, and then the pain would be greater when he leaves for Phoenix."

"That so? Have you forgotten Chris?" That was a cop out. Last night, she'd decided to break up with him.

"Chicken, chicken, chicken. And no I haven't."

Sky laughed and scooted back her chair. "I have to go. I need to find a murderer. In the process, I'll see if I can find out anything about the Senator's abduction."

"Are you going to tell Kane you're helping, on the side, of course?"

Sky blew out a breath. She should speak with the Chief about hiring more people, but perhaps she could work both cases at once. "I'm not helping Kane as much as I'm looking out for my advancement."

"Sure, sweetie."

As Sky moved toward the front, the door to the station opened. Harriet came up behind her and whispered. "Well, well, lookie who the cat dragged in. Why it's Mr. Kane and our very own Senator Overton." Harriet snatched the dessert plate from Sky's desk and hurried to the front. "Welcome, boys. Have a brownie."

Kane shook his head, but Overton stepped forward. "Don't mind if I do."

"How can I help you two handsome men?"

"I need to speak with Sky." Kane lifted his gaze to her—intense, powerful, and demanding.

Even though she'd planned to work on her case today, he drew her in like a small fish on a ten-pound line. Kane closed the gap between them.

"Hey," she said, trying not to sound excited. Damn. He'd reduced her to a gawky teenage girl.

"Is there some place we can speak in private?" He hadn't shaved and there wasn't a hint of a smile on his face. It didn't matter. He still turned her insides to mush.

"If you've come to ask me to help again, the answer hasn't changed." Harriet's words had made her realize how vulnerable she was in Kane's presence.

"I know you have your own work to do, and I'm not here about that. I promise I won't take up much of your *valuable* time."

She didn't miss the hint of sarcasm. "The conference room is free." Harriet frowned probably not happy that she wouldn't be privy to their discussion, though Sky wouldn't be surprised if she stood with her back to the door, listening to Kane's every word.

She didn't know if the Senator was invited to the tête-à-tête, but she held her head high as she made her way inside the empty but cramped room. Kane closed the door without the Senator. It was just the two of them, and her heart raced.

"Look. I know you're afraid you'll lose your job or something if we team up, but I'd really appreciate it if you could help the Senator with a little situation."

"The Senator?" That didn't sound bad. "What kind of situation?"

Kane scrubbed a hand down his chin. "He thinks he has an implant in his leg to track his whereabouts, put there by the *government*."

She smiled for the first time since yesterday. "I knew it."

That brought out a matching smile. "Okay, okay. You were right. Can you help?" He stepped closer, almost as if he understood his invisible power over her.

"I can try. I know a few good surgeons at the Page Hospital."

He shook his head. "The Senator doesn't want anyone to know. He thinks if word leaked out the government did this, the press would come swarming and crucify him, calling him a kook, or worse, a traitor."

She leaned back against the table. "Do you know the government is responsible?"

"No." He smiled. "Nor am I claiming little men from outer space did this to him. While I did feel something hard inside his leg, I doubt it's an implant. Right now, all he can focus on is getting it out, so my plan is to help him. Can you find someone who'll *remove* what's theoretically in his leg but won't document the operation? The Senator is willing to pay."

Giving a name wouldn't hurt. "I know just the man." Sky pulled out her cell and called Dr. Williams, Page's medical examiner. After a short conversation, he said he could operate, but that he had no drugs to numb the Senator's leg when removing the implant. He was, after all, a coroner. But because national security was involved, a physician friend of his from the nearby hospital might be willing to perform the procedure at the morgue, and properly numb the area.

Sky didn't consider her story a lie exactly, but telling the good doctor how important the removal was stretched the truth a bit. She hated to admit it, but this cloak and dagger stuff excited her.

"Well?" Kane looked excited, his eyes wide.

"He'll call me back with the name of someone. I'm guessing it'll take a good hour. I'll let you know as soon as I hear." She headed toward the door. Being in the small room alone with Kane didn't help her composure.

"Thank you." His warm brown eyes turned dark.

Don't do this to me.

"Don't forget to call me," he said as he motioned her out.

"I won't." As if she could ever forget anything related to Kane Cornell.

As soon as Kane and the Senator left, she returned to her desk to do more research on the headless man, but her mind wasn't on her job. Forty-five minutes later, she heard from the doctor with good news, and she immediately called Kane.

"That's great," he said. "I'd like you to come with us."

Oh, no. Being in a car with him for more hours would only cause problems. "I can't."

"Please? I don't know how to get there," he said a bit too quickly.

She smiled. Talk about excuses. "That's what your GPS is for." She shifted the phone to her other ear.

He chuckled, and it was good to hear the cheer in his voice again. "Guilty. I asked because I want you to come, to keep me company."

She nearly melted in her seat. Sky was helpless against his genuine charm, but she held fast. "You're a big boy. I doubt you need me to hold your hand at the morgue."

"If we have to do follow-up work, I'll need your help. Come on, I don't bite. It won't take more than a couple of hours. Surely, Savory can stay safe that long."

He did have a point, but with Kane, one thing always led to another. As much as she wanted to learn if there was a probe, she probably should go to Chris's mom's birthday party, as it would be more polite to break up with him in person. "I have another obligation."

He huffed out a breath. "Look, I won't ask you to do anything else for me. Please, just this once?"

Harvey was reading the paper at his desk, which meant he could handle any minor crisis. Harriet was right. Sky was a chicken. She could just call Chris. Hell, that's how he would do it. "Okay, but no more after this." She shouldn't have given in, but being with Kane was exciting.

"Meet you out front in a few."

She disconnected and pressed the phone to her chest for a moment, wondering what it would be like to have someone like Kane to talk to any time of day. *Stop dreaming.* Sometimes she hated that stupid voice in her head that believed in white picket fences and a family.

Now for the hard part—calling Chris. She didn't want to have this conversation, but she had to tell him not only was she not going to the party, the spark she'd thought existed between them no longer burned. Breaking up with someone over the phone sucked, but he'd practically done the same thing to her.

When he picked up, she was actually surprised. What followed was terribly uncomfortable, but he seemed to understand. In fact, she swore she detected a hint of relief.

After she hung up, she sagged back against her seat, and decided not to tell Harriet what had just occurred. There would be time later to tell her. It would also be best not to mention where she was going or with whom, as the ribbing would be endless.

Sky did let Harvey know she wouldn't be back before her shift ended. As usual, he grunted his response.

She waited at the curb for only a few minutes, and when Kane pulled up, she bent over to look inside his Jeep. Great. The Senator took up most of the back seat, which meant her only choice now was to join Kane in front. Being an adult, she could control her emotions or so she hoped.

As they headed north to Page, she wanted to ask Kane about his theory of what could be in the Senator's leg, but she didn't want to put him on the spot with the Senator in the back seat. Not that Kane would have had the chance to even respond since the Senator chatted the whole way there, regaling them with some of the projects his committee had funded—like the thousands of marines still in Okinawa, a carryover from a war that ended close to seven decades ago. It was amazing what the government thought was important to our security.

Once they made it to Page, Kane turned onto the morgue's street. She then gave him instructions where to park. "Dr. Williams said you two could enter through that gray door without the secretary seeing you. Let me check in first then I'll show you in."

"Perfect."

She crossed her fingers that everything would go smoothly. Once she entered, she chatted a bit with Darleen before heading back to Dr. Williams' lab where she knocked on the key-coded door.

"Come on in," Dr. Williams said after opening up.

The odor of death still lingered, despite the fact the room looked sterile. Inside stood a tall, thin African American woman garbed in a green surgeon's outfit, seemingly ready to begin the procedure. The ME introduced Sky to Dr. Patty Deland, who was on loan from another hospital for a year.

"Where's the Senator?" Deland asked in a crisp British accent.

"He and his security guard are around back." Kane was so much more than a guard, but it was what he preferred to be called. He would put his life on the line for the Senator; it was his job, his calling. "I'll bring them in. I wanted to check with you first to make sure you were ready for them."

The doctor nodded. The ME unhooked his swipe card from

his belt. "You'll need this to get back in."

Sky stepped out the back entrance, escorted them inside, and made the introductions.

Once Dr. Williams helped the Senator onto the table, he faced her. "I think it best if you and Mr. Cornell waited in the reception area. I'll let you know when we're done."

Sky peeked around the ME at the Senator to see if he wanted them there or not. Sweat beaded his forehead, but he tossed her a weak smile then shooed her out. "Go. I'll be fine."

She wanted to be there when the doctor removed the metal object, but if Dr. Williams thought it best to let Dr. Deland operate in peace, so be it. "I trust them," she told Kane. She faced her friend. "You'll let us know as soon as it's out?" Whatever *it* was.

"Most definitely."

They returned to the front office where the air was warmer and sweeter, a nice relief from the autopsy room. While Darleen said nothing as they waltzed past her, her raised brows implied she wondered how Kane had entered the building.

The only place to sit was on hard wooden chairs crammed into the corner of the entryway, but anything was better than the chilly, smelly room. While she believed Dr. Williams would be discreet about the procedure, there were lab technicians and others who could leak the information if they found something.

Because the receptionist sat not ten feet from them, Sky leaned close to Kane, and kept her voice low. "If the Senator does have a probe in his leg, how long do you think we can keep this quiet?"

Kane stretched out his long legs. "I don't think we have to worry. I doubt his lump is anything more than inflammation under the scar tissue."

"Scar tissue?" she asked. He nodded. "Don't tell me that it's crescent shaped?"

He stared at her for a moment. "Yes. Did Overton tell you?"

She held up a finger before pulling out her iPad from her

purse. Once she booted up, Sky navigated to a bookmarked page. "Here's an article on alien implants. The incision is new, but the scar appears old because of a special cream the aliens have developed. And the scar's in the shape of a half moon." Darleen looked up, smiled, and then returned to her work.

Kane clasped the iPad tightly. "Okay, now I'm a little freaked out."

"Are you starting to believe?" It was her turn to wink.

Kane chuckled. "God help me if I do."

She did more searching until Dr. Williams appeared. "Come back with me." He nodded at Darleen who showed little interest in the two visitors. From the frown on Williams' face, things hadn't gone well. As soon as they stepped in the corridor, the doctor stopped and faced them. "We found something. I'm not sure what it is, but it's definitely metal and about half an inch in diameter. There appears to be a microchip in it."

Her breath caught. "Ohmigod."

"My thoughts exactly. Do you want me to send it to the lab to determine its origin?"

A small shiver raced up her spine, and she looked at Kane, not sure if he wanted the government to be exposed.

He stepped forward and handed Dr. Williams a business card. "Please tell them to let me know the results, and ask them not to discuss this with anyone."

"The lab I use is very discreet."

She wondered how the Senator was taking the news. "Is Mr. Overton okay?"

"He's angry."

"I don't blame him."

Dr. Williams addressed her. "I forgot to tell you that I received the lab result this morning for the tox screen of your headless man. He had no cocaine or trace of any illegal drug in his system. Besides the military tattoo, he had about four percent body fat that was covered by a lot of muscle, convincing me he was military and not some drug user."

"Good to know." Sky shivered, not from the cold, but at the fact someone who was trained to fight, had died quickly. "Any results from his fingerprints?"

"Not yet."

The doctor led them back to the lab where the Senator was sitting on the table, looking uncomfortable. He slid off the table and winced. "Get me out of here. I have some phone calls to make."

Dr. Williams nodded. "Use the back exit. I don't need a leak coming from Darlene."

They all left. After they stopped for lunch, Kane drove them back to Savory. During the whole trip, the Senator was quiet, not that she blamed him. Not knowing when or how someone had implanted a foreign object in his body would scare the bejesus out of anyone.

Halfway back to town, her cell rang. "Hey, Earl. Everything okay?" Last night's heavy cloud cover would have prevented him from another sighting, so she couldn't guess what he was calling about.

"I found something you need to see."

"What is it?"

"Well, I was out on my golf cart when I seen this piece of plastic sticking up right near where the man was killed. I took out my grabber and lo and behold it was an ID badge."

"Was there a name on the badge?"

"Sure was. Crandall Thompson."

"Never heard of him. Is there a photo on it?"

"Nope. It's plain white plastic with a black strip on the back, like one of those credit cards."

Adrenaline kicked up her heart. "Does it look like the kind one might use to get into a protected area?"

"Could be."

She glanced over at Kane, whose eyes were riveted on the road, but from the way he gripped the wheel, he was listening to the one-sided conversation with attention. "I'll stop by when I return to town."

"You on some kind of fancy mission?" His question held way too much excitement.

"No. I'm visiting someone in Page. Later, Earl." She disconnected and turned to Kane. "I think I might know why someone broke into my house."

"I'm listening."

She told him about the found ID badge. "I'm thinking this guy could have worked at a secure facility, so if we can figure out where Crandall Thompson was employed, we might be closer to solving a few mysteries."

"We? I thought you had to take care of the Savory population and didn't have time?"

He'd caught her. Had Kane not delivered his comment with a smile, and if he hadn't been driving, she might have punched him in the arm. "My main goal is to figure out who killed Crandall Thompson. If that serves your purpose too, then all the better."

The Senator leaned forward in his seat. "I couldn't help but overhear. You think this secret facility might have a connection to the place I was supposed to look into?"

If she could answer that question, she'd already be a detective. "To be honest, I'm not sure what his card opens. My imagination might be working overtime. It's probably not something secret."

Kane pulled in front of the station but let the engine idle. "While you take care of your work, I need to find out who messed with Paul's leg."

She had no idea how he planned to accomplish that, and she wasn't about to ask. "Works for me. I need to meet Earl anyway."

Once she said goodbye to both of them, she hightailed it over to Earl's farm, without stopping inside the office to check in. The news of the implant would surely be written all over her face, and she didn't need Harriet grilling her.

When Sky arrived at the farm, thankfully Pearl wasn't there. From the backseat, Sky grabbed the silver cone-shaped object she and Kane had unearthed in the caves. If anyone could tell her what the item was, it would be Earl. Before she opened the car door, he was down the ramp to meet her. He must have a camera at the entrance since he always seemed to know when she was there. She pushed her sunglasses up onto her head and eased out.

He motored closer. "What do you got there? Oh, is that the thing you found in the cave?"

"Yes."

"Well, lemme have a look-see." She handed it to him. "It's light. That's good. Could be alien."

She leaned in closer. "You think?"

"It's hard to tell. Mind if I keep it for a few days? I want to do some research."

"Sure." If anyone would keep it safe, it would be Earl.

"Come inside. I left the ID tag on the counter."

She followed him in. "Are you burning candles? It smells like jasmine."

She swore he blushed. "Pearl brought a bunch over. Said my house needed romancing up."

That sounded like something Pearl would say. Sky spotted the white ID tag and picked it up. Light from the window reflected off the plastic to reveal a hologram—something Earl failed to mention. "Did you notice this image?"

He wheeled closer and wiggled his gnarled fingers. "No." He tilted the plastic. "Well, I'll be. What do you suppose it is?"

She studied the small reflective figure. "It looks like a perfume bottle. Kane and I just visited the Fleur de Paris. They have a white logo like this on the front door."

"Now why in the dickens would the dead guy work at a perfume factory? He was no sissy."

She'd leave that comment alone. She doubted she would have connected the dots if she hadn't made the visit. "Perhaps he worked as a landscaper at the perfume factory, or worked to maintain those massive air conditioning units. Something macho like that."

Earl nodded. "You might want to call Ray Strand or Cecelia Roberts. They both work at the Fleur de Paris." He pronounced it, Flour-de-Pear-ee.

"I forgot about that." Cecelia was basically a bottle washer, and Ray worked on the landscaping crew. She wouldn't have been surprised if Ray knew about the Senator's visit.

Sky pulled out her iPad and looked up the number for the factory. After three transfers, she finally got a hold of the manager, Mr. LeFloch.

"This is Dalton LeFloch," he said in his distinctive lilt.

Sky introduced herself, and he said he remembered her, though not fondly she was sure. "I found a badge that I believe belonged to one of your workers—a Crandall Thompson."

Paper rustled. Finally, Mr. LeFloch cleared his throat. "We don't have anyone by that name."

Right and she wasn't a cop. "You're familiar with all the workers? Even the names of those who work outside?"

"Yes, but I can have my assistant double check in case we hired someone recently who I wasn't told about."

Liar. "You do that." She gave him her number and disconnected.

Earl tapped his leg. "I'm bettin' he wouldn't admit the man worked there?"

"No. I'm thinking there's a definite connection between Crandall and the factory."

"I can't remember the last time you were wrong about anything."

"You are too sweet."

"Say, I hear you're working a case with Senator Overton's security man."

She opened her mouth and shut it just as quickly. "How did you hear that?" Earl never claimed to be a mind reader.

He lowered his chin and looked up. "A little birdie told me."

"Damned Harriet." Sky had said nothing about going to Page with Kane. She needed to remind Harriet not to make stuff up.

"Now don't go getting yourself in a tizzy. She's worried about you. Thinks you need to hook up with a good man."

Sky didn't need this conversation. Defending her decision not to openly work with Kane was her choice and no one else's. "I know she means well." Sky picked up the badge and stuck it in her purse. With Earl's fingerprints all over the plastic, there was no need to preserve the evidence. "Let me know if you learn anything about my find."

"Will do. Be careful now."

"Oh, before I go, I want to run something by you." She told him about the new theory of her break-in. "If they didn't find the badge at my place, they might think to come back here."

"Don't worry about me. I got more fire power than a small army."

"That's what scares me the most."

He laughed, and she hugged him goodbye. An energy she hadn't felt all day zoomed through her. She couldn't wait to run Crandall Thompson's name through the military database to see what else she could learn about the mystery man. His tattoo fit in with the fact most of the bases around here were Air Force. In fact, both Luke and Williams Air Force Bases were located near Phoenix, and the Davis–Monthan Air Force Base sat next to Tucson. However, this Thompson dude could just as easily have come from an Air Force base in Utah. Clearly, research was in order.

The drive home only seemed to take a few minutes since her mind raced from one topic to another. If the government had put the implant into the Senator's leg, why would they need to know his location? A simple GPS would have done the trick. When they'd taken him for the procedure, had they used sodium pentothal or some kind of GHB to erase his memory? Sheesh. She was just glad she didn't live in Washington where espionage happened day in and day out.

CHAPTER TWELVE

Sky rose early, ate a quick breakfast, and headed into work, eager to find out about Crandall Thompson. For safekeeping, she entered the ID tag as evidence and then logged the find into the murder book.

Next, she typed in Crandall Thompson's name into the database and tapped her foot while the computer ball spun on her screen. Sixty seconds later, it came up empty. Damn. He'd been in the service, so why wasn't his name showing?

As she pondered why his name didn't show, her email dinged with the results of the dead man's fingerprints. Ah, ha! That's why. His real name was Randall Tyler. He'd been commissioned at Hill Air Force base in Ogden, Utah, and was still listed on active duty at his death. So why did he have a swipe card with a different name on it? Was he working undercover?

After further investigation, his death brought up more questions than it solved. Sky found his home address and debated how to proceed. Even though Randall Tyler aka Crandall Thompson was no longer among the living, he might have confided in a neighbor or a girlfriend about what he was really doing.

Sky pushed back her chair, and then explained to Harriet where she was going. "I don't think I'll be gone long."

"You should take Kane with you."

"Why's that? I can handle myself."

Harriet shrugged. "Just saying. You start poking your nose in where it doesn't belong, and the next thing you know the killers will come after you, or worse, the U.S. Government."

"I'll be fine. Don't worry."

As soon as she stepped outside of Harriet's hearing, she forwarded the information to Kane, thinking this might help the senator. It was possible the senator knew this Randall Tyler and what kind of undercover work he was doing while working at the perfume factory.

Once Sky arrived at his address, she was a bit disappointed that he lived in a rundown area about fifteen miles from town. No one was on the street to talk to, so she'd have to go door-to-door.

One hour later, she left, having learned that Crandall Thompson was an honest and helpful guy. None of the neighbors had ever seen him with a woman and said that he kept to himself. Only one elderly gentleman had been aware Randall aka Crandall had been in the military at all.

After running into that dead end, she returned to the office.

"How did it go?" Harriet asked.

"No one knew anything."

"That's a shame."

All during the ride home, Sky couldn't help but wonder how the perfume factory was connected to some secret operation. Even the senator didn't know. While it was a farfetched idea, she wondered if the factory was a front for some kind of deep underground military base, or DUMB for short. Many of the locals claimed there were several in Arizona.

Time to do more research. She searched Google for anything related to these military bases. On the third link, she hit pay dirt. Someone listed as whistleblower2 authored one site. He said he'd worked at a place called Blackthorn Base, off 89, near Page. No address was listed, but as outrageous as it appeared, it was possible there could be an underground base below the perfume factory. The many air handlers outside the greenhouse made that seem possible.

She read on. When this person learned of the atrocities conducted there, he decided it was time to quit. While he was now in hiding—which was why he couldn't reveal his identity—he wanted the world to know what the military was really up to.

She read the introduction. "Oh my God." Blackthorn was five levels deep. Six, if she counted the underground parking level. That made sense since a secret operation wouldn't want a lot of cars parked right above it.

Not that everything she read on the Internet was correct, but this was detailed enough to give her pause.

Level 1 was plain creepy. Apparently, all of the workers first weighed in, were given a navy blue jumpsuit, and had their weight logged into the computer. If the worker gained or lost more than three pounds in a day, they were subjected to a physical exam, most likely because the base believed their workers were capable of stealing stuff.

Level 2: This was where the human research was conducted. Shivers crawled up her spine at that concept. Among the topics were mental telepathy, mind control, hypnosis, remote viewing, and out-of-body experiences. Okay, that last one was actually kind of cool. She'd like to learn more about that. Intergalactic space travel wasn't included in this list, but perhaps that happened at another military base. There was mention of a laser weapon that could cause some major discomfort to its target. Thank God the military men who shot at her and Earl weren't from this Base. Bullets seemed benign compared to a laser that burned holes in its victims. Also on this level was a section where the scientists could lower a person's heartbeat to put him into static shock. Sky wasn't sure exactly what that meant, but apparently, this condition enabled them to reprogram the brain. "Jesus." Had this happened to Dan Joe or the Senator?

Level 3 - Alien housing. Her fingers nearly slipped off the mouse. Was this for real? Sky leaned closer, not wanting to miss a word. This level was circular in order to house the electro-magnetic generator, which was nearly two hundred feet in diam-eter. There were five entrances, plus an escape door to the fourth floor, though she couldn't figure out why they'd build such a thing on the floor where the aliens were housed. The article went on to describe the intense security, probably like Kane was used to. Armed guards patrolled constantly. To move about, one had to use a handprint or a retinal scan station.

She leaned back in her seat, recalling that the greenhouse had some kind of scan. Oh, shit, maybe the entrance to the Base was through the greenhouse. She'd have to ask the Senator how he got in—assuming he remembered that part of his experience.

Level 4 – This was given the name, *Hell-hole Hall*. It held the genetics labs. Experiments were done on fish, otters, birds, and mice, which made them different from their original forms. Using otters, however, made little sense given this was Arizona.

She scrolled down. "Holy crap!" she whispered.

There were pictures, probably doctored in Photoshop, of multi-armed and multi-legged humans, as well as those of bat-like creatures up to seven-feet tall. She read out loud. "Aliens have taught the humans a lot about genetics, things both useful and dangerous." The article went on to say that people, usually drugged, were kept in cages, often crying for help. She had to admit this seemed too ridiculous. What was even more absurd was the reference to shifters—people who could change into an animal at will and then change back again.

Level 5 – Prison cells.

She couldn't finish reading. This was too gruesome. Kane would laugh at the article, stating whoever had created this had a vivid imagination with too much time on his hands. He might be right, but what if he wasn't? Sky decided it wouldn't hurt to

check out the perfume factory tonight and see for herself—
without Kane's skeptical help.

***

Right before her shift ended, she'd asked Harvey to drive her to
the garage to pick up the repaired cruiser. She wouldn't have
bothered, but in case she needed to investigate something at the
factory without them shooing her away, she needed to look
official.

Once she picked up the cruiser, she began having doubts
about going to the perfume factory alone at night—a factory
that could possibly be hiding Blackthorn Base underneath it.

Don't be a wuss. She was an officer of the law, duty bound to
find out who'd killed Randall Tyler. It wasn't as if she planned to
sneak around; she'd be in her cruiser.

Since she and her dad had planned dinner together, she'd eat
with him and then head over. As much as she wanted to ask him
if he knew anything about any military base nearby, she feared
he'd do something to stop her.

She called and asked if he wanted to come over to her place
assuming he didn't have something planned.

"How about we eat out? There's a new place that opened I've
wanted to try out."

"Sounds great."

It was a new steakhouse. A good meal would help settle her
stomach. A half hour later, they met and had a really nice meal.
"I broke up with Chris," she announced, wanting to keep the
conversation off her job.

"I'm glad. I never did like the guy."

Now he tells her? "A long distance relationship was never
going to work. So what have you been up to?"

For the next hour, he told her about what was going on with
the City Council. She always learned something. And knowledge
was power.

Just as they finished, his cell rang. Apparently, he was needed for some emergency. She didn't like that he put his job above family, but if she didn't have something to do, she might have complained.

Once they hugged goodbye, she headed toward Page. Gray clouds scudded overhead, covering the moon for most of her drive. The winds, with nothing to block their path, made her cruiser shake as she fought to stay in the lane.

Spotting the factory up ahead, she drove past the entrance and parked a short distance away. The cop in her said to call Kane, but her emotional side said she wasn't ready for his ridicule. Kane also wouldn't leave the Senator just to do a stake out for hours on end with probably nothing to show for it.

It wasn't as if she'd need his protection anyway. Sky had already decided that this was a reconnaissance mission only. A rookie might have charged into the parking lot and looked around but not her. She was fairly certain there were cameras trained on the lot. She merely planned to take notes on who came and who went. A dirt road turnoff on the far side of a hill provided the perfect location. The headlights from any vehicle coming from the factory wouldn't spot her. If they did see her and asked what she was doing there, she'd claim she was on official business. What that business was, she didn't know.

Her stealth position, however, was unwarranted. By eight, only three delivery trucks had driven by, and none of them had even slowed as they passed by the factory. If something secret were going on, it might happen later. It didn't matter. Sky was determined to stay here for as long as was needed.

When her cell rang, she nearly jumped, adrenaline jacking her heart. She checked the screen. It was the gossip queen herself. "Hi, Harriet."

"I am glad I caught you. After you left, Kane stopped by to say that some lab called with the results you wanted."

Sky sensed Harriet only called because she was dying to know which lab results. Sky could lie and say they were Randall

Tyler's tox screens, but dishonesty wasn't her thing. Her pulse raced and she sat up straighter. "Did he say what was in it?"

"I tried to pry the information out of him, but his lips were sealed tighter than a frog's ass."

"Har-ri-et." The woman didn't have a censored bone in her body.

"Sorry, but it's true. He told me he'd tell you and only you. Listen, I'm on my way out and just wanted to let you know."

"Thanks."

Sky pocketed the phone and leaned her head back to take a quick break when the rumble of large cars sounded up ahead. She sat up and lifted the binoculars to her eyes. Holy shit. Three camouflaged Hummers were pulling into the factory lot.

She waited a few minutes for something to happen but nothing did, though she wasn't sure what she expected—that they'd storm the perfume factory with their guns blazing?

She had to assume these men worked in the underground Base. They would probably sneak in through the greenhouses, take an elevator down a few levels, and replace the other guards on duty. If so, those guards might be exiting soon.

Her stomach tumbled at the thought there might actually be captives below ground. In cages. Drugged. Needing help.

She rolled down the window, hoping to hear either voices or perhaps a door opening and closing. In the cold, dry Arizona air, sound traveled far. She waited for anything to indicate the occupants had left their vehicles or a new shift had started. After another fifteen minutes of sitting in the dark, she figured it was time to get a closer look at the mystery vehicles and check out the greenhouses that might be used for more than just growing plants to make perfume.

She drove to the factory. Except for a few emergency lights in the entranceway, the place was shrouded in darkness. She hadn't noticed it when she and Kane had visited, but there were no street lamps illuminating the parking lot, nor did the sign stay lit to advertise its existence to passersby.

She headed up the driveway, but before she could put the car in park, three sets of bright lights flipped on and blinded her. Stunned, she sat there and blinked.

A man, dressed in a camouflage uniform, exited one of the trucks, the light from inside the cab illuminating the rifle slung over his shoulder. *Oh, shit.* He walked toward her, shoulders erect.

I got this. Sky eased out of her cruiser and stood tall.

"Can I help you?" he asked.

Think. "I received a call about a disturbance." Sky looked around.

"Everything's quiet here, officer."

She smiled, hoping he couldn't tell her lips were trembling. "I can see that. It must have been a false alarm. Probably some kids thinking it was a fun prank. Good night."

Sky spun on her heels, pulled open her door, and eased in. As if this had been a routine check, she turned the cruiser around and left, keeping an eye on the rear view mirror. Thankfully, they seemed to have bought her story and didn't follow her, but as soon as she turned left out of the lot, she floored it, trying to put as much distance between them as possible.

After two miles, she relaxed and slowed. Her mind spun, trying to figure out who those people were. A curve up ahead forced her to slow, and as she rounded the bend, the road narrowed, pinched by two cliffs of red rock. Suddenly, her car lurched, and her foot instinctively hit the brakes, her neck snapping forward. Sky managed to brace herself from hitting the wheel, but barely. What the hell was that?

Pulse jackhammering, she checked the side view mirror then the rear view mirror, but no one was behind her. She must have hit something. Once she caught her breath, she slowed, ready to pull over to check it out.

Without warning, a loud bang was followed by a clang. Someone had slammed into her. Shit. Then that someone, or something, hit her again, forcing her hands to slip off the wheel.

She pressed on the brakes, trying to stop, but the pressure from behind pushed the car off the road straight into the rocks.

As she crashed, the airbag exploded, smashing the material into her face. Her nose pressed in, and for a moment, she couldn't breathe. Her body continued its forward momentum, and stopped only when the seatbelt pinned her. A huge pain stabbed her chest and shoulders. Finally, the car halted, and her head slammed back against the seat.

Nothing registered at first. Then like an unexpected tsunami coming ashore, a huge ache rushed in. Sky didn't move a muscle, fearing something terrible had happened to her. Blood rushed to her head and hammered against her temple.

Her vision blurred and she blinked. What looked like a larger than life wolf darted back across the road. For a split second, she wondered if that had been a shifter like the article claimed existed.

No, it couldn't be.

Then feeling returned to her feet and hands, along with the belief the damage was not as severe as she'd first thought. Anger devoured her. Someone had run her off the road and it wasn't her having swerved to miss some animal. The rearview mirror was askew but the side view mirror showed no one was behind her. How the hell had they disappeared? It had to have been one of those Hummers with the black tinted windows with its lights off. Fuckers. If the airbag hadn't exploded when it did, she would have seen them speed on by.

Sky grabbed the door handle and pushed hard to get out, but that only caused her shoulder to scream in pain. Damn it. Nothing better be broken.

On second thought, she wouldn't be able to drive out of there, so she might as well stay warm inside the car. The first thing she needed was help. She wanted to call Kane, but her dad would be royally pissed if he weren't able to play big man on the scene, directing the tow truck and the paramedics. On the other hand, he might be upset if she interrupted him during his emergency meeting. But hell. She was injured and needed help.

Fortunately, her cell phone hadn't dislodged from her top pocket. When she dialed her father's number, his voicemail picked up after the first ring. Ugh.

"Dad, it's Sky. Someone ran me off the road, but don't worry, I'm fine." Blood dripped down her nose, and she wiped the mess away with the back of her hand. "I'll call after I get towed out of here. Bye."

She leaned her head back against the seat, and her neck muscles tightened. "Ouch." Rubbing her neck didn't even help. Perhaps her prognosis wasn't as good as she thought. Steam hissed from the radiator, and she couldn't imagine the cost of this repair.

She didn't want to call her boss and tell him the just-fixed cruiser was once again headed for the shop, but she was duty-bound to report the accident, so she called the office. Harvey answered on the third ring. Using energy to keep her voice from shaking, she briefly told him what had happened. It didn't surprise her that he asked only about the cruiser, and not if she had been injured.

"I'll call Morton's and then let the Chief know you messed up his car again," he said. "He won't be happy."

"I know." She didn't need him to tell her that.

"I'll send Elmer to write up the report and take your statement."

She was pleased Elmer was well enough to return to work, though by the time he made his way out there, she might bleed to death. "Thanks."

Once she disconnected, she dialed Kane's number, wanting his expertise and comfort. A wave of lightheadedness swamped her, and she inhaled deeply to make sure she sounded strong. She had the sense Kane would freak if he thought she was injured.

CHAPTER THIRTEEN

Kane was debating which tactic to take with the Senator in regards to the probe when his cell rang. Sky's caller ID blinked on, and his pulse notched up. Maybe she'd changed her mind about helping. "Hey, there."

"Kane." Her voice came out weak, forcing him to increase the volume on his phone.

"Sky? What happened?" He jumped up from the sofa and headed outside for better reception.

"I need your help. I was in an accident."

"Are you hurt?" From the way her voice trailed off on the last word, it appeared she had been. The silence that followed sliced through his gut. "Sky?"

"Maybe a little. Everything's stiff, but there's only a little bit of blood."

"Jesus Christ. Where are you?"

"I'm on 89, about two miles north of the perfume factory." She sucked in a breath, clearly in pain.

"Do you need an ambulance?"

"No." She nearly shouted that answer, which implied she was better than he'd first thought.

"Hold on. I'll be right there." He swiped the *off* button and raced back inside the RV to the Senator. "Sky's been in an accident. Lock the door and don't let anyone in but me." He grabbed his keys and sped out to his Jeep without waiting for a response or providing any more information.

The next thirty minutes was the longest half hour he'd ever experienced, having no idea if she was bleeding internally or if she had a concussion. Sky seemed the type to understate her condition. Dear God, what had she gotten herself into? Fortunately, he encountered few cars on the road. God Bless the small towns of Arizona. The glow from her headlights bounced off the rock wall ahead, making her easy to find. Since there were no other cars nearby, apparently, he was the first to arrive.

Kane killed the engine and was by her side in five seconds. The driver's side window was up, and he flashed his light inside. Sky's eyes were closed, and blood had caked her forehead and cheek. His muscles tensed as he rapped on the window. She jerked and immediately covered her eyes. Damn. He hadn't even identified himself. He lowered the light. "It's me, Kane."

He waited a second for her to react before tugging on the handle. It was locked. At least she'd had the sense to protect herself. As he pulled, she pushed, and the door opened. When she levered her legs out of the car and stood, she swayed, and he grabbed her shoulders to steady her. The flashlight in his hand lit the front of the cruiser. The damage would be a bitch to repair.

She winced. "Ouch. My shoulder."

"Sorry." He eased her down to the seat. "Tell me what else hurts?"

"I don't know."

"I'm going to put you in my Jeep. Did you call for a tow?"

"Harvey is taking care of it."

Kane slipped his arms under her legs before she had a chance to resist. "Wrap your arm around my neck." Not only did she hold on, she rested her head against his chest, and an overwhelming sense of need rushed through him. He tried not to think of her body next to his as he carried her the ten feet to his Jeep, but he couldn't help it.

Once at his car, he slid her onto the seat, careful not to let her head hit the roof. "Hold on. I have a blanket in the back."

"Are you always so prepared?" Her voice quivered.

"I was a member of FAST."

"What's that?"

"Fleet Antiterrorism Security Team. You have to be prepared for every eventuality."

"Hence the shovel, the flashlight, and the blanket."

He chuckled. "Yes. If you get hungry, let me know. I have some power bars too." He smiled. "I never know when I'll have to rescue a beautiful damsel in distress."

Before she shot back a retort, a tow truck rolled up behind them. A young man jumped out, waved at Kane and Sky, then surveyed the damage and whistled. "Ms. Sky, you sure are hard on your vehicles. It might take me more time to fix this than it did to repair all those bullet holes."

She held the blanket tight around her shoulders. "Please don't repeat that to the Chief."

The young man smiled. "You betcha. I'm getting rich off your bad luck."

"Ha. Ha. Not funny." Sky shivered.

Just then, a cruiser rolled up. An older officer eased out and walked toward them. Kane leaned in. "I thought Harvey was coming."

"No. He sent Elmer Peacemaker. He has the late shift."

She explained he'd been ill, which might be why Kane hadn't met him. He vaguely remembered Harriet mentioning that.

"You okay, Sky?" Elmer asked.

From the blood on her shirt, he had to see she'd been injured.

"I'm good."

"Care to tell me what happened?"

Kane stepped over to him, and kept his voice low enough for

Sky not to hear. "I need to take her to the hospital. Can the report wait?"

"Oh, sure. I'll make note of the damage, and Sky can tell me everything later."

Kane nodded then turned back to her. "Elmer will take care of everything. Let's go." For once, she didn't argue.

On the ride back, Sky kept her eyes shut, and he worried there was more to her injury than she was saying. As he reached the turn off at 89 to Savory, he headed north toward Page instead of returning back. While he assumed Savory had a local doctor, she might need an X-ray or need some other type of advanced exam and assessment that the small town couldn't provide. Good thing she kept her eyes closed, because if she knew where he was headed, she'd be upset.

In less than fifteen minutes, he entered Page proper and followed the signs to the hospital. After parking near the emergency room entrance, he cut the engine and came around to her side. When he opened the door, she was sitting up, her lips pressed together. He was happy there wasn't a lot of light to see the fire in her eyes.

"I am not going into any hospital. I'm fine."

"What are you worried about? That your boss or your dad will find out about this?"

She flinched. He must have hit a nerve. Harriet would have to fill him in on the father-daughter relationship. The boss relationship, as he understood it, was bad.

"No." She flicked off the blanket. "Oh, crap. My purse is in my cruiser."

"I'm sure the tow boy won't steal it."

"That's not the point. My insurance card is in there."

"Don't worry about it. I'll take care of your payment."

She cocked her head to the side and stared at him, acting as if no one had ever offered to do something nice for her. And here, he thought *he* had demons. Sky Nash was one complicated bundle, though in truth, it might be fun to unravel her, one issue at a time.

Inside, he made her sit wrapped in the wool blanket while he spoke to the admittance nurse. After Sky filled out the paper-work, they were told to wait until the next doctor was available.

"Tell me again what happened," he said. She opened her mouth then shut it. "Don't leave anything out," he commanded.

She started with learning the name of the beheaded man and his connection to the perfume factory.

"That's excellent work."

"Thanks."

"What happened once you arrived at the factory?"

She told him about the three Hummers and how she thought she'd left the lot alone. Their lights-out maneuver reminded him of his military days. Christ. This was worse than he thought.

A very tall male nurse approached them. "The doctor will see you now, Ms. Nash."

She stood and looked back at Kane. "You'll be here when I get out, right?" She clutched her hands by her side.

"I can't stay. I've got to get back to the Senator, so if you don't mind walking home, I'd appreciate it." All fifty miles of it. He then tossed her a smile and winked. When her chin dropped, he shot out of his seat and stepped close. "I'm kidding. I'd never leave you."

Her shoulders sagged, and then a bright smile captured her lips. "I knew that."

Sky Nash was something else. She turned and followed the nurse through a door. By the time she returned an hour later, he'd come up with a plan.

Her forehead was bandaged, but she wasn't sporting a cast or showing any sign of a serious injury. The relief took his breath away. Kane stood and met her halfway. "You're okay?"

"Just cold and hungry. No broken bones or internal injuries. Thanks for asking. The doctor said I'll be quite sore tomorrow, and I'm supposed to rest, but you know me. That ain't goin' to happen."

He laughed. "Let's put you to bed then." She stiffened for a split second. Oh, boy. That reaction implied someone had done a serious number on her, and he could only hope it wasn't that boyfriend of hers.

On the way home, they went back and forth about who might want her to stay away from the perfume factory and why. She told him about the article she'd read claiming aliens might be kept in a kind of underground detention camp, but he wasn't willing to entertain something that farfetched even though he couldn't come up with a better alternative.

"You just passed the turn off to my place."

Here came the argument. "I don't want you staying alone."

"Why? I'm a cop, and I own a gun." She turned in the seat to face him. "You think someone will try to harm me?"

"You mean, harm you again? I don't know, but I don't want to take any chances. My other concern is that you might have side effects from the accident. Unless you think Harriet will stay with you, I'm volunteering for the night."

"You're overreacting."

"You hope."

She tugged the blanket tighter around her shoulders, and he slid the car's heater to high. "You know Rosalie's is the other way, don't you?" she said.

"Did I forget to tell you that I've moved into the Senator's RV?"

"No, but I should have guessed. You do know that if we stay in his motor home, you'll have to be on your best behavior." For the first time, a smile claimed her lips.

Call the press. Sky Nash was flirting with him.

As they pulled into the Wildacres RV Park, she sucked in a breath. "I forgot to ask about the results from the Senator's probe. Harriet said you had information."

"Yes." He cut the engine and faced her. "I'll tell you, but please let's not discuss your opinion in front of the Senator."

"You keep saying that, and here I believed you valued what I thought."

He groaned. "I do. All right, here it is. The lab said that the probe wasn't made from any kind of material they were familiar with."

She pumped her fist and winced. "Shoulder. Bruised. Damn. Remind me not to get excited. You know what this means?"

He was afraid what she'd say. "Tell me."

"Lab equipment can diagnose every mineral and metal known to mankind."

"So that means you think the implant is alien."

"Yes. This is amazing."

"Sky, the government is developing all sorts of new materials, altering their physical properties to make them stronger and lighter. They don't want the terrorists to get a hold of this research, so they hide the information."

"You don't think the probe is alien then?" Her voice dipped low.

He didn't want to upset her any more. "All I'm saying is that we can't be sure."

She let out a breath. "What did the Senator have to say about this?"

"The Senator wants nothing to do with little green men. Can you imagine what would happen if the public got wind of the possibility the Senator was abducted or had alien technology implanted in his leg?"

She bit down on her lip. "He'd never get reelected."

"Right."

"So now what?"

"I'm going to find out who's responsible."

CHAPTER FOURTEEN

Sky was quite uncomfortable—not from the memory foam sofa she was laying on, but from Kane standing so close to her in a very intimate and warm RV. Leaving them alone, the Senator had retreated to the back bedroom. She could smell Kane's pine-scented cologne, and while she loved the woodsy, masculine aroma, the scent traveled to her heart, quickening her pulse, and that wasn't good.

He unfurled the blanket and let it float down on top of her. As the rush of air kissed her face, she inhaled and her muscles relaxed. When he leaned closer, she was forced to hold her breath or chance swooning, and she certainly didn't need him invading any more of her thoughts.

Kane then tucked in the blanket, an action she remembered her mother doing when she was alive.

He watched her for a moment. "You comfy?"

She swallowed. "Very."

"I have something else that might make you feel better." He tossed her a dimpled smile and disappeared into the kitchen. Cupboards banged and metal scraped metal, but she had no idea what he was doing. Less than ten minutes later, he came out with a hot cup of mint smelling tea and handed it to her. "My mom swears tea heals all aches."

Sky smiled. "Your mom is a very smart woman." She sat up and her body rebelled. "My neck will put her theory to the test." Sky sipped the drink and the strong, rich tea soothed her. "Delicious."

"You ready for some shut eye?" he said.

"More than you can know."

"Mind if I read for a bit?"

"Not at all."

He picked up a pile of magazines from the coffee table and leafed through them. She wished she could have seen the titles to know what topics drew his interest, but the idea of him reading while she fell asleep created a sense of security. She set the cup on the side table, lay down, and closed her eyes. A minute later, she propped herself up on her elbows. "Have you ever had s'mores?"

Yes, that had been a random thought, but his woodsy aroma had caused old memories to surface. She was dead tired, but the idea of learning a little more about him intrigued her.

"What?"

She studied him for as long as she dared. His eyes twinkled, and that sexy mouth of his was turned up just enough to form shallow dimples. Dear God, the man took her breath away.

A small smile caught her lips. "S'mores. Like kids make over an open fire."

"Not since I was young."

Her parents had loved to camp, and they often made their meals over an open fire. At times, it was all they could afford. "I love the smell of the wood burning in a campfire, the intense heat on my face while my back remains cold, and the gooey marshmallow melting the rich chocolate between the crunchy crackers."

"Sounds wonderful. Now get some sleep. The doctor told you to rest."

Her body said yes, but her mind was remembering those pleasant memories and sending healing endorphins through her. "The heat from the fire might help calm me."

He lowered his chin and gave her an evil eye. "Sky."

"Fine." She lay back down and tried to rest, but the flipping of pages kept her awake—at least for a while.

She jerked and let out a snort, like she had been sleeping. When she opened her eyes, Kane was in the same position. "I'm hungry," she said.

He turned around and popped up to his feet. "I'll see what the Senator has in the fridge."

"No. I'm in the mood to sit by a fire."

He chuckled. "You sure you want to sit outside at this time of night?"

The short nap had rejuvenated her. "Yes."

Kane huffed. "I spotted a general store near the entrance. I'm betting they carry everything we'd need."

She'd been to the store a few times but never this late. "It's closed, though I know where Betty hides the key." The manager was a trusting soul.

"Are you sure?"

She wasn't on the job, and after the day she'd had, a little recreation might be merited. Being near the too-hot Kane would be tough, but she was serious when she said the heat from the fire might do wonders for her muscles. That crazy person in her head told her to go for it. "Let's do it!"

He knelt in front of her, licked his thumb, and held it out. ""Secret mission time. It's a spit bond. If we're captured, nobody talks."

She'd never heard of anything like this, but hey, she was in. After licking her thumb, she touched her finger to his, and she swore a tiny electric shock jumped the gap. "We're good."

Never in a million years would she have suspected the rather focused, taciturn investigative bodyguard would be so fun and silly. Perhaps he was trying to take her mind off her near-death experience. For that, she'd be eternally grateful.

"Let me put on my boots." She reached next to her and carefully donned them. "Should you let the Senator know?"

"Let him rest. I'll keep an eye on the camper. We aren't going far."

She sucked in a breath and extended her arms. His large rough palms and strong fingers grasped her hands, and when he pulled her to her feet, she worked to ignore the slight pain rippling over her.

Their bodies stood within inches of each other, and her gaze locked onto his lips. Full. Perfect. Warm. *Stop it.* It was much too soon to be thinking about kissing the enticing man, so she stepped to the side and cast her gaze downward. Harriet's *chicken, chicken, chicken* rang in her ears.

"Hold on." He gently placed a hand on her arm. "Do you think we need face paint?"

She chuckled. "We don't need no stinking face paint."

"You're right, soldier. It's go time." He was out the door in a flash.

Good God, the man could move fast. The moment she stepped outside, cold air hit her, but she didn't mind, as the excitement of it all kept her warm. Sky wasn't sure she was ready for the adventure of snuggling up to Kane and sharing a marshmallow by a hot fire, but then again, it wasn't as if she was going to have sex with him or fall in love. They were two friends about to have a good time.

Do it.

She eased down the steps, holding in a grunt at the stiffness. When she didn't see him, she stopped and looked around. Surely, he wouldn't have left her behind. The sound of a rock tapping a tree caught her attention. That was too funny. Kane was crouched behind the trunk.

She jogged toward him, hoping the exercise would help loosen her muscles. As she neared, he motioned military style to go ahead and take up a position by the Buick parked in front of the next camper.

How fun was this?

Close to her destination, she tripped over a protruding rock, and before her hands hit the ground, he scooped her up by the waist.

"We FAST men never leave a man down." She laughed so hard at his antics that her sides hurt. He placed her on her feet and turned her toward him, his face within an inch of hers. "You okay, soldier?"

She held her stomach. "I'm good. Mission is still a go. I'll be more careful next time."

"From here on out, we don't talk unless we spot the enemy."

She gave him a high-five. This time, he walked next to her as they made their way to their destination.

The newly renovated convenience store, with two rocking chairs in front, sat behind a row of tall trees. She held up her hand for him to stop. "Did you bring the flashlight?" Not even the sign was lit nor had Betty left any lights on inside.

He chuckled. "I thought you knew where the key was, soldier."

She leaned closer. "I need light to see. She keeps it taped to the side wall behind one of the hedges."

He pulled out his car keys with a small penlight attached and dropped them into her hand. "See if this helps."

She loved the weight of his heavy keys. It was so manly—like Kane. She giggled at the comparison. What was wrong with her? Twenty-nine-year-old women didn't giggle when a man handed them a light. Boy, she was so out of practice being with someone new—especially when that someone was a self-confident man who had a great sense of adventure and who wasn't hard on the eyes.

They made it inside the store without a hitch. "Mission accomplished," she said with more joy in her heart than she'd had in a long time.

This was like when she was back in high school—before she had any idea she was going to be a cop. She and a group of her friends had climbed over the school fence to go skinny-dipping in the pool. They'd had tons of fun until the local patrolman caught them. That's when she decided it was better to be on the right side of the law.

Kane flicked on one panel of overhead lights and pointed down the second isle. "First stop, the food." He grabbed a large package of marshmallows, then a box of graham crackers, not seeming to care which brand he picked up, and rushed to the candy aisle to get the chocolate bars. After placing the goods on the counter, he jogged over to the rack containing the wine.

She caught up with him. "There is no prize for the person who shops the fastest, you know."

He laughed. "This gives me more time to decide on the perfect wine."

"If I get a vote, I prefer red over white." She should have mentioned that she rarely drank and that she got tipsy after one glass.

He lifted his chin, and the dark part of his eyes went extra wide, like he was drinking her in, trying to see what she really wanted. "You look like a red wine girl."

"What's that supposed to mean?" She laughed. God, it felt good to let go and have fun. As a cop, she always had to be a role model, but tonight, she was going to have the time of her life. Tomorrow, she'd reign herself in and go back to being Officer Nash.

He shrugged and picked up a Merlot and studied it then looked at two different Burgundy's, followed by a Pinot Noir, replacing all but the last.

She nudged his back. "Hurry up. You aren't buying wine for the Queen."

He turned around and lifted one side of his lip. "You'd be surprised."

She had no idea what that implied. He'd been quite the

professional with her, and now he seemed, well, interested. It would be easier if he held back since there would be less temptation on her part.

Once he seemed satisfied with his choice, he took the bottle to the counter and pulled out a twenty.

She didn't want to owe him more than she already did. "I'll pay you back when I get my purse."

"This is my treat."

A tingle charged up her spine at the thought he considered this a date. Once again, she wasn't sure whether she wanted it to be or not. "Okay."

She stepped toward the door, and he grabbed her hand before she'd taken two steps. "Wait, wait." His grasp had the solidness of steel but was gentle enough not to hurt. "I need to write Betty a note."

How considerate of him. She stepped next to him, shoulder to shoulder, ready to help if need be. He picked up the pen on the counter and wrote on the back of an old receipt, penning carefully chosen words, almost as if what he said held more meaning than just a list of items he bought. He then placed the pen back in the plastic cup.

"Are we ready now?" Not that she was impatient or anything, but the prospect of spending a night under the stars with Kane Cornell excited her—almost like enjoying her last birthday with her parents, before the accident.

"Very ready." God, what the smile did to her.

Once they doused the lights and returned the key, he gently, but firmly wrapped an arm around her waist. As he led her back to the RV, she relaxed against him, enjoying how his hipbone nestled snuggly against her waist.

At the door to the camper, he squeezed her side then let go. "Wait here while I pick up some blankets and wine glasses."

For one night, she wanted to put aside the car wreck and the abductions. "Bring a big flashlight too."

"You afraid of the dark?" His voice held a chuckle.

"No. It's so I don't knock anything over, funny man."

"Here, take the small light."

Kane's personal light. "I'll wait by the fire pit, which is behind those bushes, next to the picnic tables." With the quarter moon and the small Maglite to guide her, she set up while Kane retrieved the items from the RV. To her delight, someone had left a stack of logs, ready to use. When Kane arrived, he placed a blanket on a large rock, along with the rest of the gear.

"You want me to find a stick to roast the marshmallows?" she asked.

"Sure."

"Do you have a knife?"

"Always." He dug into his hip pocket, slipped out a small Swiss Army knife, and opened the blade. "Here, you whittle and I'll start the fire."

He really was a team type of guy, despite professing to be a loner. She stepped over to a tree. After she found the perfect stick, Sky whittled one end and then waited on the bench, marveling at his ability to light a fire on the first try while enjoying the view of his hot backside. "You're very good."

She was amazed by a lot more than his skill at making a campfire. She bet he was just as good at making love, going all night, keeping her happy with one escapade after another.

Stop it.

"Have to be. Sometimes lives depend on it."

The fire crackled, and the smell of the smoking wood brought back many good family memories. She needed to do things like this more often. Mother Nature had a way of drawing out the best in her.

Kane dragged a large log near the warm fire. "Let's sit down here. It will be easier to burn our marshmallows."

As she moved toward the seat, he looked not just at her face, but deep inside her, as if he was seeing all of her. For once, she didn't mind.

"Wait a minute. Did you just say you wanted to destroy a

perfectly good marshmallow? I like mine lightly brown, rotated just so, to give it an even glow."

He chuckled. "You're such a girl. Catching them on fire is the only way to go. Love that burnt taste."

She unpacked the groceries and handed him the package of marshmallows. "Let's see the master at work."

"Let me pour the wine first. It will keep my insides warm while I cook."

Using the plastic cups from the Senator's kitchen, he filled them to the brim then handed her the wine and smiled.

"Cheers!" The liquid cooled her throat and slid down so smoothly, she nearly polished off half a glass in one gulp.

He poked the fire to encourage it to flame then stabbed two marshmallows on the stick. Holding them high over the fire, he kept them there until they browned then burst into flame. Within seconds, Kane handed her two burnt marshmallows on the stick, as promised. "Make mine also."

She hadn't expected the rush of intimacy. *Get a grip. It's just s'mores.*

While she opened the package of graham crackers, he held up his cup in a toast. "To beheaded men, alien implants, and underground bases."

Sky did enjoy his humor. "Here, here."

She took out two wafers, one for her, and one for Kane. She placed four little squares of chocolate on top of each half then smashed the two marshmallows on top of the first one. Removing one marshmallow without the other proved difficult. "Can you hold this while I pull?" She handed him his half.

"Out of practice, huh?"

"I don't remember the last time I made these." She tugged on the stick and was rewarded with one remaining gooey marshmallow, which she then placed on her cracker and topped it with the second one. By the time she finished making her dessert, her fingers were all sticky. "I have goo all over me."

She wiped her fingers on the paper towel on her lap, but that only made things worse. She held up the paper and shook it. Kane laughed. She sent him her meanest glare, which probably made her look more like a mouse than a witch. "What's so funny?"

"You. Here, let me help." He set his glass on the ground and smiled as he pulled off the paper, which then stuck to his fingers.

Now it was her turn to laugh. "Let me." They looked like Curly and Moe from the old Three Stooges show, trying to get the damned thing unstuck. They laughed until her sides hurt.

She held up her hands, and her fingers were still smeared with marshmallow. She filled her mouth with more wine and stuck her fingers inside to wet them. Kane leaned closer, his focus on her. The fire crackled, and she froze. Whoops. She hadn't thought what that motion implied. As fast as possible, she lowered her hands to her lap.

She cleared her throat and shoved another bite of warm, gooey chocolate into her mouth so she wouldn't have to talk. He let out a soft groan, his lips slightly parted, and his eyes filled with a passion she'd never seen before.

In self-defense, she shut hers briefly. "Divine," she mumbled. It wasn't just the melted chocolate sending her libido into overdrive. As if to mock her, he jammed the entire s'more into his mouth until the corners of the crackers extended his cheeks into squares. She giggled. "You look funny."

"Look who's talking, Ms. Goo Fingers." The sentence came out garbled.

She polished off the glass and held up the empty, anything to keep her hands from touching him. He nodded and filled the glass again, but in the process, he leaned too near. This time she didn't care. Kane was funny, nice, considerate, and the list didn't stop there.

He picked up the package of marshmallows. "More?"

"Oh, yeah. I'm not stopping."

His brow rose, but he turned his head before she could see

his full reaction. After making another set, he waved the stick. "I'll do the honors this time. I'm neater."

The chocolate melted faster than the first round, probably because the marshmallows were hotter from the intense heat, and when he finished, chocolate streaked his cheek.

"You have something—" She swiped her own face to indicate where he needed to wipe his.

He turned his head and dragged a hand down his cheek. "Did I get it?"

"No." Their lips were less than an inch apart. She should have leaned back and moved away, but she couldn't. The flames danced on the logs, the colors turned brighter, and the air held more energy.

Between the too hot fire, the wine, and Kane being so close, her resolve broke. She leaned to the side and licked the melted chocolate off his face in one smooth stroke.

Oh my God. Sky couldn't believe she'd been that bold. She expected him to jerk away, but he held steady, probably waiting for her to make the next move. His chest heaved once, and he twisted his face toward her and held her gaze. His lips parted, and their warm, wine-filled breaths mingled. As if someone slammed into her back, she leaned forward and kissed him. Hard.

In a flash, his rough palms gently cupped her face and his urgent tongue explored her mouth. Her heart stopped right before the dam of resolve ruptured and her temperature rose— everywhere. Because she wanted to ravish him, she practically crawled out of her skin to get to him. His chest expanded as if he couldn't get enough air, and she placed her hands on his chest to explore his body through his shirt.

He moved one hand under her hair and rubbed her neck while he placed his other hand against her breast. Oh, my. She needed him now.

CHAPTER FIFTEEN

Kane broke the kiss, his eyes darker now, more intense. "We can't."

Wh-what? "Why?" She grasped at any reason other than he didn't want to kiss her anymore.

"Damn it, Sky, you're almost engaged." Kane stood.

Cold air poured over her. "I—" She was trying to think of a way to tell him that she'd broken up with Chris without sounding insensitive. He might believe he was just a rebound man, and he was anything but that.

"Let's get you back inside. I have a lot of legwork to do tomorrow." Distant and controlled, he appeared angry with himself, or so she wanted to believe.

Tell him.

Sky leaned forward to leverage herself up, but her legs wouldn't hold, and she dropped back down. "Whoops. I think I had too much to drink." She prayed her words hadn't slurred. The fire sent out a loud crackle, and embers floated to the beat of the music coming from down the road.

Before she was able to try again, Kane scooped her up in his arms as if she weighed less than a hundred pounds. "Nighty night, for you." His words held some humor, thank goodness.

Perhaps it was for the best they stopped, but dammit, couldn't he have waited until after a few more kisses before growing a conscience? She leaned her head against his chest, not caring if he wanted her to or not. Her fingers inched upward, enjoying the rough wool of his shirt.

His hand shot out and stopped her. "Sky, please." His voice held raw emotion, deep and cutting.

"Spoilsport," she grumbled low enough so he couldn't hear —hopefully.

Tell him. She would have if he hadn't broken the mood. Besides, it was safer this way. He'd keep his distance, which would make it easier for her when he left.

His boots clanked on the metal steps. He opened the door and then carried her across the room. She could have managed on her own but having his strong arms wrapped around her made her feel like a woman—wanted and desired. So what if he'd shot her down. Men were stupid sometimes.

Kane set her on the sofa with more care than he probably thought she deserved. It didn't matter if he blamed her or himself for the kiss, he was mad. "Time for sleep."

"I had a good time tonight. Thank you." She debated apologizing for putting the moves on him, but she wasn't sorry, so she didn't.

"Sleep." He sounded like her dad—impatient to the point of being gruff.

Kane stomped outside. She rose, needing to wash her sticky hands and face before he returned. Afterward, she sat on the sofa and stayed there for what she considered an eternity. She debated checking to see if he was okay, but she knew he could take care of himself, and that if she went out there, it would be to see if she could convince him to pick up where they'd left off.

When he finally returned, two empty glasses clanged against each other, and she fell asleep before he climbed into bed.

***

The faint light seeped in through the slats in the blinds and woke her up. Sky sat up and drew in deep, cleansing breaths until her muscles relaxed. The clock on the TV read 6:00 a.m.

She looked down at Kane's long form on the floor a few feet in front of the sofa, his snores soft and low. At least one of them appeared to have had a good night's sleep.

Before using the facilities, she listened for any movement coming from the Senator's bedroom. There was none. Sky's head throbbed from all the wine but not enough to ruin her mood. Moving slowly, she tiptoed past Kane and ducked into the bathroom down the hall. The mirror was wavy and warped, or at least she wanted to think it was the glass and not her face. She could only hope she hadn't looked this bad last night.

There was a large purple bruise under her left eye and a small cut on her chin. The doctor said she hadn't broken her nose, but it sure felt like something was amiss. She peeled off the bandage from her forehead and sucked in a breath. There was a dark red, ugly gash. For now, all she wanted to think about was a hot shower and breakfast. Once she returned home, she might padlock her doors and stay in bed for a week, thinking about Kane and what could have been.

Not wanting to use up the hot water, she washed quickly. Once dry, she put on the same clothes she'd arrived in, which now smelled of smoke, and slid past Kane to reach the kitchen. He hadn't changed into his pajamas before going to sleep, and she wondered when he was at home, and not in protective detail mode, if he slept in sweats, boxers, or in nothing at all.

She voted for commando, and envied the lucky woman who woke up next to him every morning. From Kane's response last night, however, it wouldn't be her. His rejection killed any chance of that.

Noise sounded down the hall near Overton's bedroom. *Move.* Time to pay him back for his hospitality. Once in the compact and functional kitchen, she located eggs, milk, cheese, bacon, bread, and jam in minutes. In less than fifteen minutes, she'd made omelets, fried the bacon, and had three slices of toast on a plate.

Kane rounded the corner. He looked like hell, which for Kane was almost impossible.

"You're up," he said with a gruff tone. He was in a pit bull mood this morning.

"No, I'm sleep walking, dreaming of a breakfast buffet on a resort island." She waved a hand and forced a smile.

"Got coffee?" he asked, without a hint of any joy. Great.

"It's over by the toaster. I never forget to make coffee in the morning." Here she'd thought last night started off uncomfortably, but this was twenty times worse.

Look busy. She dished up the meal, and as soon as she poured a cup of freshly made coffee for herself, the Senator rolled in.

"Good morning." He nodded to the food. "I'm liking the service around here." He stepped close. "How are you feeling? I'm betting the sofa wasn't all that comfortable."

"The sofa was wonderful. It's Kane you need to ask since he took the floor." Just as she handed him a plate, her cell rang, and she checked the ID. "That's my dad. I need to take this."

Glad for the interruption, she scooted into the living room. "Hi."

"Sky, your message said you had an accident. What happened?"

She told him someone ran her off the road, but that she was fine.

"Were you driving your VW?"

"No, the cruiser."

He whistled. "Lapahe is going to be pissed."

"Don't I know it? I bet he takes my keys away."

"Perhaps he should." He cleared his throat. "Sorry about not being available when you called."

He often wasn't around when she'd needed him—more so in the last few years. "No problem. I called Kane."

"Who's Kane?"

"I mentioned him when we were at dinner. He's Senator Overton's bodyguard."

"Oh, yes. I heard Harriet is gaga over him."

"Did she take out an ad I didn't know about?"

"You going into work today?" he asked without saying when he'd spoken to Harriet.

"Yes, but if I am going to make it on time, I need to get ready. Maybe we can do lunch."

"Oh, sweetie, I have a town hall meeting from ten till two. Perhaps tomorrow."

"Sure." Her dad worked too hard. Of late, it seemed as though he'd decided his sole responsibility in life was to take care of the town. Good thing he'd found time to eat dinner with her yesterday.

After saying goodbye, Sky edged back into the kitchen. Kane and the Senator sat opposite each other at the small table. She fixed her plate and stood at the counter, attempting to look everywhere but at Kane.

He pushed back his chair and rose. "I'm done. Take my seat." He didn't make eye contact as he strode past her. He scraped his dish and placed the plate in the sink. "I need to wash up."

Fine. Go. Sky sat and nodded at the large, orange bowl of candy on the counter, filled to the brim with Snickers, M&Ms, and Twix candy bars. "I forgot it's Halloween tonight, and I didn't have time to buy stuff for the kids."

"Betty dropped that bowl by yesterday, saying I should participate in the festivities. Like I don't have enough on my mind?" His lips thinned. The once handsome man suddenly appeared old and beaten.

"I always wrap packages of candy and take them over to the orphanage. Everyone lives so far apart, it's hard for the kids to go door-to-door," she said.

The Senator stared at her for a moment. "That's nice of you."

"I think I have more fun than the children." She wasn't about to tell him that she was one of the lucky ones. She'd never had to spend even one day in a place like that.

Kane returned all too soon, looking refreshed. "I'm taking Sky home."

The Senator ran his gaze between the two of them, his furrowed brow never relaxing. "Something happen I should know about?"

"No," they said in unison.

"Okey-dokee." He slapped the table then drank the rest of his coffee, probably happy not to have to deal with anything else.

"Keep your door locked." Kane gave the order like a man on a mission. "I won't be long."

The Senator saluted. "When you return, we need to discuss my little problem."

He must think Kane hadn't told her. For now, she wouldn't bring up anything about the probe being alien. Kane was pissed enough.

She thanked the Senator for letting her crash there last night and followed Kane outside. She rubbed her hands up and down her arms as the chill in the air was quite unpleasant.

"Slide on in, and I'll crank up the heat."

That was considerate. "If you don't mind, could you drop me off at the station? My car's there."

"Sure."

Kane said nothing for most of the ride, and from his rigid jaw he wasn't interested in any discussion.

"Do you plan to send the probe to another lab for confirmation? To see if they can identify the substance?" she asked.

"Yes."

O-kay. In what seemed like an hour instead of minutes, he arrived on Main Street.

"What are your plans for the rest of the day?" God, she sounded like a wife, but she didn't want to end their time together on a sour note.

"Keep the Senator safe. I need to speak with my supervisor,

General Stentfield, to see if he has any further information on the DUMB."

So he wasn't going to leave for Phoenix today then. Her pulse sped up. She wondered if he was interested in the factory because of the possible connection to the Senator or because someone from there had tried to kill her. "I'd like to ask him a few questions myself." Her tone had just the right amount of friendly concern.

Kane stopped in front of the station. "I'm afraid what we discuss is confidential."

Like water on a fire, any professional trust they'd built collapsed. Sky slid out and didn't look back.

***

Once Kane returned to the RV Park, the Senator and Kane spent much of the day trying to figure out who'd placed the probe in his leg. By six, Paul Overton needed some time to himself. "Kane, how about heading to town and bring back some dinner for us?"

Kane studied him, probably trying to understand his agenda.

"Sure. I need to pick up some clothes from the boarding house anyway. I shouldn't be gone long."

Once Kane left, Paul propped the computer on his lap, determined to catch up with emails and find his own answers. Unfortunately, he made little headway, partly because the pesky trick-or-treaters kept interrupting his work.

Another knock sounded on the camper door, and he set down his drink. "Shit." He didn't need the distraction, but it might raise more suspicion from the RV park residents if he didn't answer the door.

"Trick or treat!" the children said in unison.

He had to admit they were damn cute. He handed them candy and then went back to work. For what seemed like forever, he shuffled between the door and the sofa, passing out candy to the little buggers. He couldn't believe so many kids lived in the park. He was just thankful no suspicious adults came to the door.

He was given a short reprieve before another group knocked. During that time, he managed to make a few phone calls. Kids giggled outside, interrupting him again. "Damn." Where was Kane? He should have been back by now. Paul picked up the near empty bowl of candy and answered the door.

Five children, aged from about six to nine held out plastic buckets, eagerly awaiting their treats.

"You are all so cute." He wasn't sure why he felt the need to compliment them, but his nerves were shot, and he didn't have the energy to scowl.

"Thank you," they all said in unison.

Four of the kids drifted off to the next camper, but the littlest one held out a piece of paper. Paul was uncertain what it was, so he took it. "Thank you." The child ran off into the darkness.

He went inside, placed the empty bowl on the counter, grabbed a beer, and returned to his computer. After taking care of business, he decided to check what the kid had handed him. It was probably a flyer or a hand-drawn picture.

He opened the paper and froze.

CHAPTER SIXTEEN

Kane headed back to the Senator's with a sack of food and a bag of clean clothes. During the ride, he couldn't stop thinking about how he'd obviously upset Sky when he stopped kissing her, but he believed she'd regret her actions in the morning. Hurting someone pained him immeasurably, but it had to be done—for her sake.

Stentfield had called him when he was buying the food, and they'd talked for maybe two minutes when the General said he had to go. During that short conversation, Stentfield had relayed some pertinent information, or rather confirmed what Sky had found out. There was a secret base, Blackthorn, which operated under the perfume factory. The General heard rumors the Base performed experiments ranging from mind control to genetic engineering, just like the whistleblower had claimed. If the whistleblower was right about the Base and the mind control, was it possible there were aliens there too? He doubted it, but stranger things had happened.

Kane was within a mile of the RV Park when the Senator called. Kane hadn't been gone that long. "Yes, Senator?"

"You need to get back here now." The panic in his voice put Kane on high alert.

"What's wrong?"

"Just get here."

"My ETA is three minutes." Kane floored his vehicle and a few minutes later swerved into the park.

As he passed the fire pit, memories rushed in, and his cheek tingled where Sky had licked him.

Focus. He couldn't get sidelined until the mission was over. Dust billowed behind him as he slammed on his brakes, turned off the car, jumped out, and rushed up to the Senator's door where he knocked.

Paul opened up. "Kane, thank God you're here."

"Are you okay?" He scanned Paul's body, but found nothing wrong, other than he looked pale.

"Not really. One of the trick-or-treaters gave this to me. Look at it." He handed Kane a piece of paper.

Kane stepped over to the window for better lighting. "VOTE FOR THE MILITARY BASE APPROPRIATION OR YOUR FAMILY WILL DIE," Kane read. "Jesus. Did you get a good look at the kid who gave you the note?"

"No. Ironically, he wore a devil's costume."

At least they'd learned humans were behind all this mess, but using an innocent kid was sick. While he had no solid facts, he guessed the same people who ran Sky off the road had written the note to the Senator. They must be getting close to uncovering some dirty secret if someone was willing to kill to keep the information hidden.

"The message on Sky's bathroom mirror was also in all caps and had similar strokes." The cross line that makes the letter F wasn't touching the vertical stroke, just like in her note.

"I was hoping you'd say this was a hoax."

The Senator couldn't believe that, not with all that had happened. "Did you call home and warn your wife?"

"I did. I also called Tony, my assistant, and he's arranging for someone to keep watch over her."

"Good."

The Senator stood. "I need to go home."

Kane hadn't thought the Senator would return so soon. "You're not going to pursue the kidnapping or the note?"

"No. If I say the government implanted something in my leg that was made from an alien material, I'll look like a fool. I'm not sure what will happen next if I stay here."

"For your safety, it's probably a wise choice to leave." Kane paced the cramped room. "Is anyone bucking for your position on the Armed Services Committee?"

He shook his head. "Not that I know of, but who's to say there isn't some junior senator who's after my job?"

"True."

The Senator took in a big breath and exhaled. "And what about you? Are you staying to continue the investigation?"

No one would be picking up his tab if he remained, but he couldn't leave without making sure Sky was safe. "For the time being, I'll stay. If you head back, that will either take the focus off Sky or intensify it."

Paul polished off the rest of his beer. "Warn her that snooping could get her killed. Clearly, the government takes their secret projects seriously, and messing with them isn't worth it."

"Getting Sky Nash to back off is like asking the defending Super Bowl champs to throw the final game."

Paul tapped the paper. "Show her the note. Maybe she'll realize how serious they are." The Senator stood up. "I need another beer. You?"

"Hell, yeah." With the day he'd had, he deserved a few.

Kane served the meal, and by the time he and the Senator finished discussing who might be responsible for everything going on, it was past midnight.

Kane wanted to touch base with Sky, but it was late. He'd called her earlier, but her cell had gone to voicemail. Why wasn't she answering? Most likely, she was pissed at him. Perhaps it was for the best.

Kane had a hard time falling asleep, as part of him needed to stay alert in case the note writer intended to come after the Senator personally and partly because he worried about Sky.

Fortunately, his evening turned out uneventful, and by seven in the next morning, the Senator was ready to head back to Phoenix, promising to keep in touch. Both hoped the person who'd temporarily kidnapped the Senator would make himself known in Washington, allowing Sky to return to her safe little life, and Kane could go home.

He expected relief to loosen his muscles, knowing this case was nearing the end, but instead, a sense of melancholia descended. The spunky woman had gotten under his skin, though he couldn't decide when that had happened. It might have been the illicit kiss that sent him over the edge, or the way she seemed to come alive when thrown a challenge. Like a good soldier, she'd embraced their mission antics as much as he had.

Her sole purpose in life appeared to be helping others, like taking candy to the orphans or making sure her invalid friend, Earl, had whatever he needed. And the interplay between her and Harriet—like the love between a mother and daughter—warmed his heart. He envied her for the close connection. Since his wife died, he'd withdrawn and made work his focus in life. Now, he realized how much he'd been missing.

Even though Sky had shown interest in him by the fire, he obviously wasn't the right man for her. She loved Chris, and it hadn't helped that he'd acted like an idiot when he'd taken her straight inside after their s'mores date. Dammit, though, she never should have kissed him, and he never should have kissed her back, but when her tongue touched his face, all sense of propriety flew out the door. He had no one to blame but himself, since he'd seen how the first glass of wine made her giddy. He should have insisted she stop, but they were having more fun than he'd had in a long time.

If Kane had learned one thing in life, it was that starting a relationship with sex was risky. Until she told him she and Chris were no longer an item, he'd keep his hands off her.

It was still early when Kane stopped for breakfast. The closest food place was EBE's since Rosalie didn't serve breakfast until nine, claiming civilized people shouldn't rise until then.

At the restaurant, he ordered two double-sun omelets and a Martian Minimal coffee. Surprisingly, they called bagels and cream cheese just bagels and cream cheese, instead of something like the Double Rings of Saturn. Cathy waited on him, but he must have looked fiercer this morning than when they'd first met, because she didn't even flirt with him this time, not that he cared. Maybe it was because he hadn't shaved and had slept in his clothes.

After he ate, he walked to the police station where the inside smelled good. He walked up to Harriet and looked down at the cinnamon rolls. "What do you got there?"

She held up the plate. "I was hoping someone would appreciate my baking skills."

He picked one up and bit into it. "Mmm. My mom couldn't have made this better, and she's a great cook."

"I'm glad you like it."

"I'm looking for Sky."

She gave him an exaggerated frown. "And here I thought you wanted to court me."

He laughed. "Harriet Brown, you are a fine woman. If I were a little older, you'd be my first choice." He could have sworn she blushed. "Now about Sky."

"She hasn't come in yet. She usually doesn't roll in until ten-ish."

"I wanted to check the station first before heading out to her place."

"Want to take her a roll?" Harriet held out the plate. "I swear she never eats."

"I'll take two. One for her and one more for me." Harriet smiled.

In a better mood than when he'd woken up, Kane drove to Sky's, keeping an eye out for her VW. To his dismay, he never passed her on the road.

Her house was about seven miles away from town, east of Savory on 98. Once he arrived at Ransom Road, he took a right and drove for another two miles, passing about five streets, each of which contained no more than four or five homes on the block. He made a left on a small dirt road called Ivory Creek. He couldn't see any creek, but maybe years ago there'd been one. About six houses sat nestled together. While quaint, they weren't very well protected from intruders. What he didn't like about her place was its isolated location.

Her car wasn't in the drive, which he found odd. He would have noticed if he'd passed her driving into town. Bright orange VWs were hard to miss. Just in case she'd wrecked her car or had loaned the VW to someone, he knocked on her door. No lights were on, but then again, she could still be asleep. After a few tries to rouse her, he walked around to the back and peered in the window hoping to see some signs of her. Her bed was unmade and the door leading into the bathroom was open and dark, convincing him to conclude she wasn't home. He tested the back door but found it locked. At least she was being smart after the break in.

Back in the car, he ate both of the cinnamon rolls. Other than the s'mores he'd had with Sky, he couldn't remember anything tasting better. He pulled out his phone and called Sky again, but it went straight to voicemail. Damn. "Sky, it's Kane. Please call me. I have news from the General." That should intrigue her, even if she was pissed at the way things had ended between them.

Next, he called Dr. Williams. It was possible the doctor had asked her to consult with him up in Page, but the receptionist said neither Sky nor the doctor were in the office but promised to track down Williams and have him call Kane back. That call came less than five minutes later. Williams said he hadn't heard from her, but that he'd tell her Kane had called should she contact him.

Another dead end.

He snapped his fingers and dialed the office.

"Savory, PD, how can I help you?"

"Harriet, it's Kane. Sky's not home, but I'm thinking she might be with her friend, Earl."

"Why would she do that? She's supposed to be at work."

No way would he tell her there was an underground military base right outside of Savory and that Sky most likely wanted information on it from her alien expert friend. "You have that number?" His leg bounced up and down.

"Sure. It's 928-555-2948."

"Thanks." He disconnected before she could ask any more questions.

Earl answered on the second ring, and Kane introduced himself then asked about Sky.

"She was here last night, all right. I've been telling her all along about how the government don't like people to know what they're up to. That's a fact."

"Did she seem agitated?"

"Some. She hates people lying to her."

At least he hadn't lied. "Don't tell me she wanted to do more investigating of the base after she was run off the road."

Earl sucked in an audible breath. "I'm afraid so, and no matter what I said, I couldn't talk her out of it. Said she wanted to ask some questions but promised not to go inside."

Damn her. "I appreciate the intel. Let me know if she contacts you again. I need to speak with her."

"You betcha."

Damn Sky. The strong-willed woman would get herself killed for real this time. He'd expected her to have a bit more sense.

With the obvious options exhausted, Kane took off for the factory, hoping the three Hummers were nowhere in sight. While he carried a concealed weapon, he couldn't go against an

AK-47 and win. Less than twenty minutes later, he pulled into the nearly empty parking lot. When he spotted her orange VW parked on the far end of the lot, his heart hitched, not sure whether to be happy or royally pissed.

Inside, the same, tall brunette met him, and he asked about Sky.

"No, sir, I haven't seen that lady cop."

He didn't believe her. "Her car's in the lot."

"Maybe she's on a tour."

Not likely, but he'd check it out. "May I speak with Mr. LeFloch?"

She didn't blink. "He's not here."

Obviously, she wasn't going to provide him with any information. He'd have to investigate on his own and hoped no one would interfere with his snooping. He figured any kind of scandal in broad daylight would not be good for their secret project.

Before he left, he found the tour, but Sky wasn't part of it. Now he was pissed. Thinking cameras were watching his every move, Kane walked out, forcing his feet to keep a steady pace.

He pulled out of the drive and headed south, driving slightly under the speed limit so as not to attract attention. Yesterday, he'd parked at a desolate area that contained a few trees and hiked back to the factory, doing reconnaissance of the layout. He returned there now. About four hundred feet behind the factory was a ravine, half the width of the Grand Canyon and nearly as deep. The Colorado River had carved the canyon as it wove its way past the factory, emptying up north.

There was probably a tunnel from the river into the military base for the workers to get in and out of unnoticed, though from where he'd stood yesterday, atop the ridge, he hadn't seen anything to prove his theory.

If he had a small boat, he could have confirmed or denied his suspicion by traveling up the river. Without the craft, however, he'd have to rely on his trusty binoculars to figure out how the workers entered and exited.

He stuffed two power bars, a flashlight, emergency blanket, two water bottles, a hand line, and his phone into a backpack and strapped it on, all the while praying he could find Sky before anything happened to her.

From his vantage point, he spotted a small ledge about five feet wide and fifteen feet long, approximately four feet below ground level jutting out of the side of the ravine. Within two minutes, he reached it, hopefully without being detected.

He eased down to the ledge and then rested the binoculars at ground level. Either no one was aware he was there, or they didn't want to make a scene. He found it odd that he neither saw nor heard any movement from the hundreds of personnel that might be below him. At least Sky's car remained clearly visible, though he wished she'd leave. It would make him feel a lot better.

After three hours of surveillance, and two power bars later, he needed to take a leak. Stakeouts sucked from that standpoint. Since the area had no trees or any other natural barricades, he decided he'd be unseen if he peed over the ledge, watering the craggy red rocks below.

Once he finished, he popped his head up over the rim to return to his stakeout position, only to find a man in fatigues standing over him, rifle in hand, and aimed right at him. Oh, shit.

CHAPTER SEVENTEEN

Kane held up his hands in surrender. "Mind if I get up on level ground?" The army man wouldn't shoot him, at least not in broad daylight. Kane's only apparent offense had been to take a leak over the rim of a canyon.

The soldier motioned with his gun for Kane to proceed carefully. So as not to show he was a threat, Kane pulled himself halfway up, then let go, purposefully landing on his butt. A thin layer of dust rained down on him, and he moaned for effect. The sun slipped out from behind a cloud and speared him in the eye, and he squinted for effect.

The man stiffened, and Kane gave him a good-ole-boy laugh. "Not to worry." Kane rose slowly, dusted himself off, and tried again. This time he made it to the top, forcing air in and out of his lungs.

The soldier towered over him. "What the hell were you doing down there?"

Kane sat up with planned deliberation and placed a hand on his chest. He deserved a medal for his acting skills. "I wanted to get a little closer to the Colorado River, but I found out I couldn't get down there from here. Does this go to the Grand Canyon?" He waved a hand. Clearly, the guard wasn't buying his story. "Okay, I had to take a leak and was too lazy to go inside the factory."

A small smile crossed the soldier's face. "Done that before." The soldier's shoulders relaxed a bit. "You're crazy, you know. If you'd fallen, you'd be dead."

Or perhaps, if he'd gone down a little farther, he'd have found an entrance to the underground military base. "Yeah, I know that now." Kane eased to his feet and sneezed. "The dust around here will kill me faster than any fall." He cleared his throat. "Can I take a picture of you? My wife won't believe I was held at gunpoint by a real military man." He added a little southern twang to throw the guy off.

He could have sworn the man's chest stuck out another inch. "It's against regulations."

Clearly, the man was taking his orders from the military and not from some perfume factory owner.

"No problem. I best be going anyway. My wife's probably finished the tour by now." He attempted to sound like a tourist, though he wasn't sure if he'd pulled it off.

The man shouldered his rifle. "Next time, ask permission if you want to wander behind the factory."

"You can be sure of that." Kane tossed him a loose salute and grinned like a fool. This little trip showed him the level of security was piss poor and only above ground.

On his next mission, he wouldn't be here during the day and would use night vision goggles for a better feel for what went on after the perfume factory closed. The presence of the soldier implied there was something worth guarding nearby, but he wasn't ready to buy into Sky's spacecraft theory.

He headed to the road via the parking lot and scanned the area, double-checking the lot. Now Sky's car was gone, yet he hadn't heard that noisy engine fire up. Most likely, she left when he was down below taking a leak. If so, he could relax somewhat, knowing she was safe.

Kane looked back over his shoulder, noting the security

guard was nowhere in sight. Kane walked casually toward the road, but as soon as he was out of sight, he jogged the mile to his car, and then drove to Sky's house so he could give her a good talking to. She was crazy, approaching Mr. LeFloch by herself. The woman would get herself killed if she wasn't careful—cop or no cop.

Once on the road, he broke the speed limit by half again, thinking he could catch up with her. Only he didn't. All he could think of was that she wasn't headed home, but he still wanted to check.

When he arrived at her place, her car was there yet she didn't answer her door. Most likely, she was too angry to speak with him. He couldn't really blame her after the way he'd turned cold the last time they were together, but she shouldn't have expected him to let go of his emotional control when in the middle of a job. He took pride in his work.

Be honest.

He'd sworn off women for good after his wife passed, but then Sky had walked into his life and everything changed.

He banged on her door again. "Sky. Come on. I know you're in there."

Not one to give up easily, Kane walked around the house and looked inside each window. All of the lights were off, and Sky was nowhere to be seen. The bed was still unmade, and the skin on his arms prickled, the same way it usually did when a mission was about to go bad.

"I'm coming in, Sky. We need to talk." He figured he might be having a conversation with the walls, but he needed to warn her. Using a credit card, he breached the opening in less than ten seconds. As soon as spoke with her, he'd insist she get a set of good locks.

"Sky? Where are you?" The air smelled stale, as if there'd been no human activity in a while.

He checked everywhere, but she wasn't home, though she couldn't have gone far in a few minutes. Perhaps she went next door to visit the friend who'd witnessed the break in. After a quick check, he found the lady wasn't home either. Out of options, he visited the other houses in the neighborhood. The one person he did speak to didn't have a clue where Sky might be. Kane didn't know what kind of game she was playing, but she wouldn't win. He'd hurt her feelings, he knew that, but if someone threatened the Senator's family, they might come after Sky too, and he wouldn't let that happen. Not on his shift.

Four hours later, he was still sitting in his car in front of her house waiting for her to return, worry settling in his gut. He'd already called her father, Chief Lapahe, Harriet, Earl, and EBE's café, making each promise he'd be the first one called if they spotted Sky. Harriet swore Sky had never even checked in, and no one else had a clue about her whereabouts. Chief Lapahe said he'd sent Harvey out to all the local establishments but had no luck either.

Everyone, except Earl, appeared shaken by her disappearance. Her friend claimed the aliens had probably taken her, but that they wouldn't harm her. Kane wished he could be so sure about the military *aliens*.

His stomach complained about the lack of food, and his throat was dry, but he refused to leave Sky's house until she came home. The next-door neighbor drove in around 6:30 p.m., but she failed to provide anything useful either. As the sky darkened, his thoughts turned raw as ugly scenarios raced through his mind, but he wasn't going to leave without talking to her—not with things this unsettled.

After a full day of playing phone tag trying to find her, he was tired and frustrated. His cell rang, but he didn't recognize the number. "Yes?"

"Kane? This is Cathy at the café." She sounded out of breath.

His fingers gripped the wheel. "What is it?"

"You gotta come. Sky's here, but she's not okay."

Adrenaline flooded every muscle. The words, *she's not okay* rang in his ears, and he twisted the key and gunned the engine. "Tell me."

"She's in the bathroom, just sitting on the floor, staring ahead. She blinks but doesn't talk. I didn't know what to do."

"Is she bleeding? Does she need a doctor?" His mind latched onto the medical protocol he'd learned in the service. He tore out of there with the phone cradled under his chin.

"No. It's like she's hypnotized or something." Cathy sobbed.

Thankfully, she wasn't injured. "How did she get there?"

"I don't know. She must have walked in through the side door, because I'm positive she didn't enter through the front. I was working the tables for the last hour. I would have noticed."

"Who else knows?" His tires almost lifted off the road as he took the turn onto 98.

"No one, but I'm scared. I've never seen anyone look that way."

"Call Harriet. She'll know what to do. Tell her I'm on my way." He pressed the accelerator to the floor. "Stay with Sky." The command came out too abrupt, but dammit, he was scared.

He arrived at EBE's in good time, but every spot on the road was taken, so he double-parked. Anyone who drove down the road would have to go around him. Normally, he wasn't that inconsiderate, but Sky was in trouble, and he would do whatever he had to do to protect her.

Instead of entering through the front, he sprinted to the employee-only side entrance and let himself in. He wiped his hands on his pants, knocked softly on the Women's room door, and entered. "Cathy?"

The handicapped bathroom door opened. "She's in here."

In three steps, he was kneeling beside Sky. Harriet was holding her hand, and she shook her head. "Harriet, can you guard the door?" he asked. He handed her his phone. "Call her dad and the Chief to let them know we found her."

"Should I tell them anything else?"

"Say, she'll call when she can."

Harriet nodded. Cathy stood and her antennae banged together. "Can I do anything?"

"How about getting her some water?" He needed to be alone with Sky to check her for injuries.

As soon as Cathy and Harriet left, Kane lifted Sky off the cold floor and onto his lap. She fit snuggly against his chest, causing a wave of protection to blanket him. He tightened his hold and leaned over her. She smelled sweet, almost as if someone had sprayed her with perfume to disguise some other scent. Shit. The bastards at the factory must have done something to her. He whispered in her ear. "Sky, it's Kane. Can you hear me?"

When she didn't respond, he ran a hand down her soft cheek, waiting for her pupils to respond, or her respiration to change, but nothing happened. It was as if she was in a trance.

Anger bubbled inside him at the injustice, and the need to hurt someone surfaced, but he swallowed his rage. What kind of government would do this to someone so innocent? He could guess, but unless he had proof, he couldn't barge in and demand answers. Once he knew for sure who was responsible, he'd expose the fucking government's tactics to the world. Maybe the whistleblower Sky had discovered on the web had seen the human testing, which was what prompted him to run and hide.

Kane held her tighter, rocking her in his arms, praying she'd snap out of the drug induced state. The bathroom door squeaked open and Cathy brought in a cup of water.

"How is she?" Cathy gripped the plastic so tight, he thought she might crack it.

"The same." Her condition was beyond his scope of training. "Call the doctor, but when you do, emphasize the need for secrecy."

Cathy handed him the glass and rushed out, promising to keep out anyone except the good doctor.

If he hadn't rejected Sky, they could have approached LeFloch together, and she wouldn't be on the floor right now. If the military had been responsible for Sky's altered state, he couldn't see what their purpose would be for returning her. All he could think of, was that this was some kind of warning.

He dropped his chin, and when he kissed the top of her head, she wiggled in his arms, causing his pulse to spike. Leaning back, he looked into her eyes, trying to see how much she was aware of his presence. "Sky, honey, can you hear me?" She moaned. Yes! Then her body relaxed as if she gave up the fight. "Come on, Sky, stay with me." Too many bad thoughts raced through his mind, but he refused to go there.

He rubbed her arms and dragged a knuckle down her face to stimulate her senses. He lifted the cup of water to her lips, but she didn't take a sip, which wasn't a good sign.

Fifteen long minutes later, an elderly gentleman wearing jeans and a top that wasn't buttoned correctly pushed open the handicapped door. Since he was carrying a black case, Kane figured he must be the doctor.

His jaw dropped the moment he saw her. "I came as quickly as I could."

Kane relinquished his hold on Sky and moved out of the way. After closing the stall door to give them some privacy, he paced the small space in front of the sinks. The doctor's bag snapped open and closed. Paper ripped, and the man's knees scraped on the tile. After what seemed like an eternity, the doctor swung open the door.

Kane rushed up to him. "How is she?"

"From the welt on her neck, I'm guessing someone injected her with a sedative. I took blood, but it will be a while before I get the results back. We have to wait for the effects to wear off before I can tell how she's affected."

It appeared to be the same thing that happened to the Senator. He prayed whoever was doing this hadn't surgically implanted a device in her body. "I'm staying at Rosalie's B&B, so I'll take Sky there to make sure she remains safe. I'll contact you if she doesn't recover soon."

"And you are?'"

"Guess that would be helpful. Sorry. Kane Cornell. I'm a friend. We've been working on a case together." Kane pulled out his card showing his bodyguard status. "I can protect her."

"You might want to call her dad and the Chief."

"They've already been contacted." Once the doctor left, Kane knelt down beside her. "Sky, can you stand?" If she walked in here, she might be able to leave under her own power.

She turned her head and opened her mouth, but nothing came out, and a wave of fear stabbed his gut. If they'd harmed her, he'd break into the fucking DUMB and make them wish they'd never seen Sky Nash.

Kane moved his car to the side entrance for more stealth, returned, and then picked Sky up. Luckily, he was able to take her out of the building without notice.

* * *

Sky opened her eyes then immediately closed them, the sunlight streaming in the window acting like shards of glass poking her. Her mouth tasted like chalk, and her head pounded. She wasn't at home, that was for sure, but she no longer was in the back of a van either—a van that smelled of urine and vomit.

The brightness dimmed, and she eased open her lids. A large body blocked the window's glare, forcing her to blink. She must be hallucinating again. She fisted the blanket and scooted back to get away from the light, away from whoever was near, until her head hit a wall. She tried to swallow, but her mouth was too dry.

"Hello, Sunshine."

It was Kane. Her vision wouldn't stay focused, but she'd never mistake that voice. "Hey." She prayed he wasn't some illusion.

He moved toward her and eased down on the edge of the

bed, causing the mattress to sink lower on one side. "You okay?" His voice held a lot of concern.

Kane took her hand in his, his fingers warm and strong. The last time they were together, he'd dropped her off at work, and acted as if he never wanted to see her again. How did they get here, wherever here was?

"What's going on?" She blew out a breath. Her stomach was queasy, and she didn't have the energy to muster up enough anger toward him, even though the hurt from his rejection still coursed through her body. When she'd kissed him, he'd turned her away.

"It's a long story. You've had an incident. Tell me how you're feeling."

An incident? That didn't sound good. "Not doing so well." Once her vision cleared somewhat, she pulled her hands from his and sat up straighter. God, that took so much effort. "What's wrong with me?" She remembered the pain in her neck, the hard floor vibrating over a bumpy road, and then her mind weaving in and out consciousness.

"Someone drugged you."

That explained a lot. Her muscles tensed. "Why?"

"I wish I knew."

She rubbed her neck again, bringing some comfort. "It feels as if they injected poison in my veins." She squeezed her eyes shut and pressed the palms to her temples, trying to recreate the last few hours. All that came to mind was this recurring dream where she and Kane were making love under the stars, his magic hands creating new and wonderful sensations all through her body. He'd trail kisses from her lips to her belly, gently plucking her nipples with his teeth before diving into her with maddening energy.

Kane gently ran a hand down her arm. "Tell me what you remember."

Heat raced up her face. The last thing she'd tell him was her wonderful dream with him in the starring role. "Everything's a blur." She told him about the van and the bumpy ride. "Only bits and pieces float through my mind, but I remember watery blue walls that sounded like a rippling river."

"What was the first thing you remember?"

"I was driving home when I saw a car in a ditch." A hammer was cracking cement inside her head, making clear thoughts difficult.

"What kind of car?"

Though frustrating and painful, focusing on the facts helped calm her. "The vehicle was dark and big. Maybe an SUV." She rubbed her forehead. "I'm usually good with make and models, but I can't remember."

"It's okay," he soothed. "What else?"

She wet her lips. "I pulled up behind him, got out to help, and the next thing I remember I was bound in the back of a van."

"Christ. Did you get a look at the driver?"

"No."

"Did they harm you in any other way? Physically or sexually." He squeezed her hand.

Nothing burned between her legs, so she prayed the answer was no. She moved her toe, legs, hips, and shoulders. Nothing appeared broken. "I don't think so. Can I have some water?" His jaw relaxed as he handed her a cup. He must have anticipated she'd need a drink when she awoke. The cool liquid tasted wonderful. She studied him. "My God. When was the last time *you* slept or shaved?"

At least she had an excuse for looking bad.

"I'm fine. I've been worried about you, that's all."

Had he been searching for her? Her spine tingled. "Oh, no. I bet Harriet is frantic. And Dad will be upset." She didn't dare think about the Chief. He was probably celebrating.

"They're all worried. Harriet sat with you in the bathroom stall where we found you, and both your dad and the Chief have been notified. They want you to call them as soon as you're able."

All of this information was coming at her so fast. "Wait a minute. I sat on the floor of a bathroom stall? That's disgusting."

"I don't think you were worried about sanitation. I think instinctively you knew you'd be safe at EBE's." He leaned closer. "What else do you remember?"

Things weren't making sense. "What are you still doing in town? Last time I saw you, I thought you were on your way to Phoenix." No doubt Mr. Protector was probably doing his job like the good bodyguard he was trained to be.

"We'll talk about it later. I need to find out what happened to you."

She could deal with the delay. "I don't really remember much other than I woke up here." In between the van and *here*, apparently a lot had happened. She and Kane had gone camping, then snuggled together in two sleeping bags zipped together. He spent hours exploring her body under the bright stars and the roaring fire before they made love. It was amazing, sensual, and oh so romantic. But dreams were personal—ones she wouldn't share.

His eyes widened. "Do you even remember walking into EBE's, the doctor checking you out, or me sitting with you on the very cold tile floor?"

She sucked in her bottom lip. "No." That part was true. She took in a breath— horrified someone had ripped minutes, hours, or maybe days from her life. "How long have I been out?" She thought she'd only been asleep for a few hours after they took her—whoever *they* were.

"You mean how long has it been since anyone saw you?" She nodded. "A little more than a day."

Her jaw dropped. "Those bastards. They took me like they did the Senator—without my consent."

"If they'd asked nicely, would you have said, yes?"

"Smart ass. Ow. My head hurts." She rubbed her hands down

her thigh. "Nothing is tender so maybe they didn't implant me with a sensor." She wondered if Dan Joe had an implant when he'd been abducted. "I know I've asked you before, but who do you think did this?"

He shook his head. "Your guess is as good as mine, but you know me, I'm leaning toward the military."

"Me, too. Aliens wouldn't have been so rough." She was kidding, but it was amazing that he could keep such a straight face. She bet he could withstand torture quite well with his ability to shield his thoughts. "How's the Senator? Does he know about what happened to me?"

"He headed back home. And no, he doesn't know about you."

"Crap. I was hoping if I remembered something, we could have compared notes." She dropped back onto the pillow and blew out a long breath. "One thing is certain. I'm going to nail those bastards. You in?"

CHAPTER EIGHTEEN

Sky held her breath waiting to see if Kane would jump ship and hightail it back to his job in Phoenix, or stay around to see this crime solved. However, it wasn't the only reason she wasn't breathing. She *really* wanted to know whether he cared enough about her to stick by her. She understood he wouldn't be there for the long haul, but she wasn't ready to let him go just yet.

He ran a hand through his hair. "It's too dangerous for you to do anything."

So much for the brief sexual fantasy of him wanting to work with her because he couldn't leave her side. She gritted her teeth, mostly for effect. If he wanted to play protector, fine. She understood that, but it didn't mean she couldn't give him some grief over his comment.

"What's that supposed to mean? They could have killed me, but they didn't." His intense stare made her cast her gaze downward. So much for trying to add levity to the situation.

He scooted closer and took her hand in his, sending her right back to fantasyland. "The drugs are still in your system and clouding your mind." He leaned so near he was almost invading her space—not that she minded—but if he wanted to get this close, he should kiss her and put her out of her misery.

What did he say? Oh, yeah, the drugs. "I'm fine, really. Don't forget, I'm a cop with a job to do. This is my big chance to prove I'm worth something to the Chief."

He sat back. "Is that what this is about? Showing off to the boss?"

Was it? "No, it's more than that. I'm not going to let the government or the aliens take anyone else. They need to leave Savory alone. Wouldn't you do the same?"

Kane eased off the bed and stood at the window, keeping his back to her. His absence intensified her longing. "Sure, I'd fight back," he said, sounding far away, as if he'd been in the same situation before—or someone he knew had been.

She relaxed. "Are you willing to help me then?"

"Affirmative."

Her pulse slowed, and the ache behind her eyes lessened. Clearly, his actions weren't tied to how he felt about her. To him, this was a job. That was okay as long as they brought the perpetrators to justice.

Liar.

"So where do we start?" She tried to put some cheer into her voice. All this serious talk was not only depressing, it was downright scary.

"I told you before." He faced her. "There is no, *we* here. If the government is involved, next time they could make you disappear—permanently."

She flicked a hand in the air. "I'm willing to take that chance." She pulled the blanket up to her chin. If she didn't think she'd look stupid, she'd yank the dang thing over her face so he couldn't tell she wasn't being completely honest with him. Her chin wobbled, and a set of chills pricked her legs and arms.

"Let me handle it." He spread his legs wide, looking like a damned pirate or a gunslinger ready for a fight. "You don't know who you're up against."

"Neither do you. I'm not giving up until these bastards are behind bars." The bravado helped push the chills away.

"If they find out you're gunning for them, you'll be more dangerous to them. No telling what they'll do."

"I can say the same for you. Remember, I'm still the law."

His face contorted. "I won't let you die!" She'd never heard him shout before. His lips hardened, and then he stomped out of the room, the slamming door shaking the walls.

What the hell was that about? He went from concerned to irate in an irrational second. Kane never lost control, which caused her stomach to clench even more.

She tightened her grip on the soft blanket. Going after him in his state of mind wouldn't achieve anything, so she flopped back onto the pillow. He'd be back. After all, she was in his bed. Her muscles ached, and her lids became heavy.

Sky closed her eyes to think for only a second before something woke her up. It was a soft shake to the shoulder. Eyes open, her vision started out blurry then cleared.

Kane held out a steaming cup of cinnamon tea, his face looking more gaunt than when he'd run out. "I'm sorry."

"I'm sorry too." Her stomach was doing a tumbling act, and the headache had just returned in full force. "You do have a point about me not investigating."

Tomorrow she'd work the case—not today. She sipped the hot brew then set it on the nightstand next to her.

He raised a brow. "You aren't going to give up that easily, so what gives?"

Damn. He could see right through her. "I'm tired, that's all." *And I have a headache from hell.*

He sat on the bed and clasped her hands again. His callused palms set off tremors of heat between her legs, and she wished he'd put her out of her torture and have sex with her—rough passionate sex. She wanted him now—or at least as soon as her headache went away.

"How about if you rest then?" he said.

She'd have asked for some aspirin, but she wasn't sure that would be a good idea to mix it with whatever drug was in her system. "As soon as I'm feeling better, I want to speak with Dan Joe. Are you okay with that?"

The pressure from his fingers increased. "Who's he?"

"Didn't I tell you about him the other day? He claimed he was abducted and lost time for two days. I dismissed his claim because he used to be a falling down drunk. Now, I'm not so sure what happened to him wasn't real."

His jaw slackened. "How many other people do you know have had missing time?"

"Over the years? Maybe six or seven that I'm aware of. There could have been others who were too embarrassed to come forward."

His jaw hardened. "Did your department follow up on their claims?"

She shrugged. "I can ask the Chief, but he hasn't been here that long. The guy before him died, so he won't be telling us. I'm guessing we didn't do much about their claims, or I would have heard the stories about whether or not they'd captured the perpetrators. If you haven't figured it out by now, Savory has a lot of kooks."

"I've noticed." His gaze shot to the right as if he was doing mental math. "Go ahead and talk with this Dan Joe guy, as long as you trust him."

"I do. I've known him my whole life."

Kane dragged a hand down his jaw, and the hard plains of his face stretched taut. "Did that website you looked at tell you how long the base has been in existence?"

"No." She bet he was trying to calculate how many people were taken on average each year.

"I'm going to call my general friend again and tell him about the recent incident. Perhaps he can shed some light."

"Earl might be able to help too." Her stomach made noise.

Kane sat back on the bed. "When was the last time you ate?"

"Forever ago?"

"How about I take you to Page for something to eat? We can get away from all the prying eyes."

"For that, I'll dub you a saint."

And he would remain one unless he tried to interfere with *her* investigation.

***

Their meal turned out to be a bit of a challenge because Kane started off by insisting he move into her place. He claimed he could protect her better that way. At least her fierce headache had dulled, and she was better able to concentrate.

Needless to say, Sky argued at first, but in the end, she decided she would feel safer having him around. If by some chance she was able to seduce him, so much the better. Besides, with all that had happened, it might be better to have someone to discuss things with, and Kane seemed to be a good sounding board.

On the way back to Savory, she convinced him to drop her off at the office while he packed up his stuff next door. "I need to check in with Dad and speak with the Chief."

"Sure. You'll be safe there."

No longer could she keep what happened to her a secret and not raise suspicion when she asked her boss about the other abductees. She planned to fill him in on her drugging and the Senator's threatening note.

As soon as she stepped inside, Harriet hugged her and wanted to hear about her ordeal. "I'm fine. We'll talk as soon as I speak with the Chief."

Harriet waved a hand. "Sure." She picked up a plate of sweet rolls and handed her one.

Sky smiled and took one. "Thanks."

She knocked on the Chief's office door and stepped inside. After he asked questions about her health, the Chief studied her, but she couldn't tell what was going through his mind. To avoid his hard stare, she looked around his office. Papers were piled up on his desk, and three used coffee cups sat next to his computer. The man hated clutter of any kind, which implied he might have been upset over her disappearance or else was distraught over her crashing the cruiser.

He leaned forward in his chair. "Elmer told me about the cruiser. Tell me exactly what happened. You'll have to fill out a report."

So much for him being worried about her. Knowing this would take a while, she pulled up a chair. "First off, Richie swears he can fix it."

He blew out several heavy breaths through his nose. "You need to be more careful."

She fisted her hands and inhaled, trying not to explode. She took pride in her ability to handle a vehicle. "I was careful. A Hummer pushed me off the road. It had nothing to do with my steering ability."

He stared at her for what seemed like a minute. "At least you're safe." He fiddled with his coffee cup but didn't drink from it. "You know you scared the crap out of everyone at the office when you disappeared."

Perhaps he had been concerned. She always figured her boss would have been happier if he hadn't inherited her when he took over.

"About that." She told him what she remembered. "Please note it wasn't my choice to be abducted."

"I know."

Right now, she needed information more than she wanted sympathy. "Have you ever come across any record of other abductions?"

He went to the cabinet and pulled out a file. "Kidnappings?"

"Yes, either of the human kind or by something else, though I'm convinced the government was behind mine. I remember Robert Danvers and Margaret Hill were both abducted and then returned, but their abductors were never found. Danvers died over ten years ago, several years after his incident, and Margaret left town right after she was *taken* though I don't blame her for moving."

For the first time in a long time, sympathy filled his face. "Are you thinking of going away?"

She never thought she'd see the day her boss would show any affection toward her. "No, I'm fighting back."

"Good, but be careful. If, as you suspect, the government is involved, there's no telling what they'll do."

Lapahe sounded like Mr. Bodyguard. "Kane Cornell is helping, and trust me, he won't let me near the factory."

"Smart man." The boss leaned back in his seat. "What else do you know?"

She filled him in on what she'd learned, including what was written in the Senator's note.

"Interesting. So you didn't get a look at these people who nabbed you?"

"No." At least he seemed to believe everything she said, including the information about the Base. That might have been a first.

"Not even a glimpse?"

"I'm afraid not. All I felt was a needle in my neck. The drugs knocked me out right away." There were dreams, but she'd keep those erotic thoughts to herself. Sky then told him what she'd learned about the Base.

"I'll put out some feelers. Several folks in town work at the factory. There has to be someone who's suspicious about the goings on there. You can't have a five-level military base and hide it from everyone in town."

"That's what I was thinking." She held up a finger. "It would make sense for the Base to change shift only during the night."

He shrugged. "The workers have to live somewhere. They might not all be from Savory, but there aren't that many towns nearby for them to live."

She told him about Randall Tyler, thrilled the chief was

spending so much time discussing what happened to her, or even believing her.

"I read about him in the murder book, but I didn't put the pieces together. Good detective work."

This was a banner day. Her chest swelled with pride. Maybe she should go missing more often, though his sudden reversal seemed odd. "Thanks." She took a sip of her coffee. Cold and weak, yuck; "I'm going to call Earl to see if he can shed any light on what happened to me."

"What would he know?"

"Earl seems to hear things."

"Just don't let him convince you it was aliens."

"I won't."

She thanked her boss and when she stepped back to her desk, she called Earl. They only spoke for a few minutes before Kane arrived. "We'll talk later. Kane's here."

"I'll see what I can find out," Earl said.

"Thanks." She disconnected, not wanting to keep Kane waiting.

"Ready?" he asked.

"Yup." Once they stepped outside, she told him about the Chief's reaction. "He's going to ask around too."

"Great."

"I have to admit I'm in some shock." She told him how the Chief had suddenly been nice to her.

"Maybe he cared all along."

She doubted that. "He has a funny way of showing it."

Once they arrived at Sky's, she made a nice cup of Kona coffee, hoping that the caffeine would help jar loose some details about her capture. She had to admit that having Kane close by brought her comfort.

"You said you called Earl. What did he say?" Kane asked.

"He said he had some contacts that might be able to help find out who could have taken me."

"What kind of contacts?"

She laughed. "I didn't ask. He'd probably say they were aliens."

Kane pulled out the kitchen chair and sat at the table while she finished preparing her drink. "While you were at the station, I called the General and told him about your abduction. He thinks whoever took you is escalating, especially in light of the recent threat to Overton's family."

"Do you think the Senator will vote for the Base appropriations?"

"I can't say, but since his family's lives were threatened, I'm betting he will."

"That's got to be tough." She swung toward him. "Did the General say what kind of research the Base is conducting?"

He looked down for a second. "As a matter of fact, he did."

A slow smile crept up her face. "It's mind control, isn't it?" She stepped away from the stove and stood over him.

"That and genetic research."

She pumped her fist. "I told you. What about aliens? Did he know anything about them?"

"He's looking into it."

Well, hot damn.

CHAPTER NINETEEN

Without waking Sky to tell her what he was about to do, Kane left her house for his reconnaissance mission at the factory a few minutes before midnight. Between where he parked and his destination a mile away, he had to lie low for minutes on end in case motion sensors were strategically placed nearby. From his military experience, the intermittent stop and go often confused those machines. What he really wished for were a few trees along his path or a large rock to hide behind. The ground was dirt strewn with small rocks, which if accidentally kicked, would bounce and ping down the ravine to the river below. He might as well use a bullhorn to announce his arrival if that happened.

His goal for tonight was to find out how many men arrived and in what kind of transport. That was all. There'd be no heroics, as he did not intend to enter the Base to see what the military was keeping secret. Despite his credentials, they'd frown on his intrusion. In fact, they might imprison him underground for life if he snuck in.

Kane took close to an hour to reach his secret ledge, timing his entry to the sentry's movements around the building. Except for the wind occasionally slapping the side of the glass greenhouses and the even pounding of the sentry's boots on the pavement as he marched in a large circle around the perimeter, the place was as still as the ravine was deep. Up above, clouds swirled across the moon in a rhythmic fashion, gaining speed with each minute. One strong gust while he was standing on the narrow ledge, and he'd be free-falling the thousand feet to the river below, which was exactly why he'd snuck out while Sky was still asleep. This mission was too dangerous for anyone but a trained Special Forces operative.

Unfortunately, after four hours of surveillance, Kane still had no idea when the workers would arrive for their shift or if they had already arrived. He hoped their *day* didn't run from ten at night until six in the morning, as waiting until the sun rose would put his escape plan at risk.

He also worried Sky might wake and find him gone if he stayed away too long. She'd freak, but he needed answers about the military base in order to ensure her safety. If he'd written a note regarding his mission, it would either have calmed her, or prompted her to follow him. In the end, he opted for the safe route and said nothing.

All of a sudden, the drone of engines set him on alert, and with his night vision goggles, or NVG's, in place, he peered at eye level across the barren ground. All kinds of trucks, cars, and military vehicles came around the back of the building with their headlights off. The stealth implied a secret base existed after all. No one lived on the other side of the canyon to see their lights, but perhaps they worried a satellite view would show the stream of lights entering a normally dark region. These men were either paranoid or smart.

The vehicles stopped in front of a tool shed that was wide enough for one double garage door yet was rather tall. The door lifted up, and like robots, the convoy followed the first truck into the shed—a shed that couldn't house more than four cars end-to-end. After the fifth vehicle piled in, he figured there must be a ramp that led down to a parking garage as nothing else made sense. Sky and the General had both been right. There was a deep underground military base.

After about thirty vehicles had driven in, Kane lost track of their number. Then an equal number piled out, confirming a shift change. As much as he wanted to waylay one of the men, it was too dangerous.

A ton of questions bombarded him, but unfortunately, no answers followed. Had the military been responsible for the Senator's and Sky's kidnapping? If so, why take a public figure and an officer of the law? Sky had mentioned that a local man, Dan Joe, claimed he'd been taken too. Surely, he had nothing the military would want. Only the Senator's capture made sense.

Perhaps Sky had witnessed some event that alerted National Security, or they found out about the cone she'd discovered in the cave—a cone she claimed was alien in nature. He shook his head to clear out that kind of nonsense. This was military, no doubt about it.

The flow of vehicles exiting eventually stopped, and the large door squeaked closed. The temperature had dropped to around forty, and while he'd dressed well, the biting wind chilled his face, and the air smelled of rain. Maybe if they had a rare storm, the one security guard would be more interested in taking cover than in patrolling the area. From the way the man slumped as he walked, Kane doubted the guy had any Special Forces training.

With his intel complete, Kane was about to leave when he heard a group of men come around the corner laughing. They were on foot and dressed in jeans and camouflage jackets. They approached the side of the shed, swiped a card in a slot, and a side door opened.

The security sure seemed to be lax above ground, but he bet underneath, it was like Fort Knox. He wouldn't be surprised if the personnel had to pass a retinal or fingerprint scan to go deeper into the DUMB.

As soon as the men disappeared, Kane climbed up to ground level. Just then, another figure darted around the corner and pressed his back against the wall. Kane squatted and held still, ready to run should the person catch sight of him. The man had his face averted, but his hands glowed white in the moonlight.

The *creeper* edged along the wall in starts and stops almost as if he was debating his next move. Something wasn't right. If he was a worker, why wasn't he going inside?

From the gait, height, and small build, he'd swear he was a she. *She* turned her head, and the moonlight reflected off her face. Oh, shit. His NVG's allowed him to see her clearly. It was Sky. His pulse raced as he fisted his hands. She'd promised not to come here. What the hell was she thinking? If anyone else rounded the corner, she'd be a goner. Intruders were shot first and questioned later. The best case would be she'd lose her job, and the worst case, her life.

Kane stood and quietly darted to the east side of the building to check if anyone else was coming. All clear. He dashed along the back of the perfume factory while Sky closed in on the shed door that led to the *parking garage*.

Fearing she might cry out if he called to her, he snuck up behind her and clamped a hand over her mouth. No surprise, the feisty little woman elbowed him in the gut and stomped on the arch of his foot. He had to hand it to her. She was tough.

"Sky, it's me," he whispered in her ear.

She stilled, her chest heaving. He slowly lowered his hand and turned her around. Her lips were pressed together, and her eyes narrowed. Before he could question her or yell at her for being stupid for coming, another set of voices rang out from the side of the building, and escape routes raced through his mind. He needed to get them out of there.

Kane tugged on her arm to move her away from the perfume factory just as several people came around the side of the building. He did the only thing he could think of.

He kissed her, goggles and all.

He wasn't sure if she was grinding against him to get away or if she enjoyed the passionate kiss, but he wanted to believe it was the second option. The men closed in. Her cheeks were chilled and her nose frozen, so he softened his lips and drank in her lavender scent for one more second.

"Hey," one of the men yelled then followed it with a laugh. "Get a room." Sky pulled back and pressed her hands on Kane's chest, but he didn't lessen the pressure of his body against hers. He had no idea what she'd do if he let go.

Another companion chuckled. "That you, Starman?"

Starman? He wasn't sure how he could answer and not give himself away. Every muscle tensed. He then planted a hand next to Sky's face to block their view and placed the other on his weapon. He leaned close, and with their lips almost touching, he moaned loud enough to wake the dead. "Oh, baby, what you do to me." To his dismay, he didn't have to fake it.

"Yo, lover Boy. Better hurry before the Colonel catches you. He's on his way." The first one cackled, but they didn't harass him anymore, thank God. Instead, they continued to the door.

Shit. The parade of personnel seemed non-stop. Kane waited a few seconds to make sure his tormenters wouldn't return, and then he and Sky ran toward the far end of the building away from the parking lot. Thankfully, she didn't complain. As soon as they rounded the far corner, he stopped, and planted her back against the wall.

She opened her mouth and he placed a finger on her lips. "Shh." Now wasn't the time for their much-needed conversation or her excuses as to why she was there.

"Where did you park?" Dumb question, but he needed time to assess the situation since his head was swimming from that kiss, one that had been intense and exciting.

"Next to you."

How had she found his Jeep? The problem now was how to escape without being seen. If he'd been alone it wouldn't have been an issue. Perhaps if Sky had been closer to five-foot eight instead of five two, she might have passed for a military man.

"You packing?" he whispered.

"Yes."

At least they both had firepower, but he didn't want to have to resort to a shoot-out. They'd lose against the automatic rifles. The sound of rocks rolling down a hill put his senses on high alert. Someone was near, and he motioned with his hands for her to go north. Taking the south route would take them in front of the factory.

She nodded and took off at a trot. From the east, a flashlight hit Sky's face, the rays nearly blinding her. She stopped. Kane whipped off his goggles as the owner of the light raced toward them.

"Who are you?" the sentry asked.

He flashed the light directly in Sky's face and held up something. A click sounded that was too soft to be a gun. Sky squinted, but from the way her legs were spread and her shoulders squared, she was more pissed than afraid. *Please don't pull out your badge and act hostile.*

Kane stepped forward. "Yo, man. It's cool. I was showing my little lady here how I used to do it in the Special Forces. We have a few minutes before my shift starts." He knew he probably sounded like Sylvester Stallone, only not with as heavy an accent. Kane wrapped an arm around her shoulders. "That's right, doll?" This was worse than a bad B-movie.

The guard stood up taller. "Well, the game's over. You know the rules. No fraternizing. Now get inside. And check your watch. You're late."

That answered one question about shift times. Kane could probably take him down, but if Sky were hurt in the scuffle, he'd never be able to live with himself.

She then waved something small and white in front of her. "That's right, Tony. We need to get to work. We don't want to piss off the boss."

Tony? Either she knew the sentry or she was calling Kane by that name to throw off the guard. If that was the case, he had to admire her fast thinking.

She took off toward the shed and he followed, the light from the sentry's flashlight leading the way. He bet the guard was running names through his head to see if he could figure out just who the hell they were. Kane half expected the sentry to use some high tech equipment to check them out, but he didn't. Kane also wondered why he hadn't asked for ID. The General would have a heyday with this guy.

At the door, Sky swiped a card and miracles of miracles, the door opened, and his shoulders relaxed. Luck was on their side when the sentry didn't follow them inside. Kane checked out the small space. No one was standing guard, but he noted a ramp sloping downward that had to lead to a garage. The metal shed looked rickety from the outside, but the interior walls were reinforced with steel, and low wattage lights rimmed the ceiling. He wouldn't be surprised if they had mounted cameras around the inside. Kane turned his head away from the interior and leaned over her. "Is that the card Earl found?"

"Yes."

"How did you know the card would open *this* door?" He made sure his body blocked her face.

"I didn't, but I suspected it might be for the factory or this underground Base."

He wanted to question her logic further, but they needed to leave now. The only way out as far as he could see was the same way they came in. "Let me check to see if the coast is clear."

He pushed open the door and looked outside. The sentry wasn't there. Kane grabbed her hand and tugged her outside, and they headed south, this time toward the safety of the ledge. They were halfway there when the sound of more vehicles came toward them. Perhaps one contained the Colonel.

He dragged on his goggles and ran with Sky along the ridge. At the ledge's location, he stopped. "Climb down." Her hand tightened.

"No way."

"Don't worry, there's a ledge. Okay fine. I'll go first and then help you down." Kane dropped to his haunches and jumped the four feet to the flat surface below then held up his arms to help her, but Sky didn't move. The engine noise got louder. "Get on your butt. You have to jump."

"I can't."

Gravel crunched under tires as a vehicle approached. In a few seconds, she'd be found.

"Come on." He lifted the rope he'd left there, to ensure she wouldn't get tangled in it, since Sky probably couldn't see a damned thing.

The engine noises were getting louder—and closer. If she didn't trust him, she'd get caught and life as she knew it would be over.

She crouched on the edge of the ravine and as she leaned forward to take his stretched fingers, she must have tripped, because she tumbled outward as if an invisible hand pushed her —right over the edge.

CHAPTER TWENTY

Arms waving, Sky propelled into the darkness. *No. No. No.* The air rushed from her lungs, and all that escaped was a small eke. She belly-landed on top of Kane's face, and the momentum of her fall pushed him off his solid perch into the blackness below. Oh my God. Even though they were free falling, he managed to keep a hold of her. She wrapped her legs around his waist, and her hands clamped down hard on his head so they would stay as one.

"Whoa." The sound came out muffled since his face was buried under her.

So black. So cold. So deathly.

Fear paralyzed her. Rushing air sent her hair upward, and she was going to die without telling Kane she was falling in love with him.

They sped downward, his back to the ground into the nothingness below. Regrets and fear filled her veins. Then abruptly, their free fall ended with a hard jerk, and they bounced upward for a few feet.

Her heart raced so fast, she couldn't talk. All she could figure was that he'd landed on a branch jutting out from the rock wall, but the blood pounding in her ears prevented rational thought from breaking through.

Before she could comprehend why they'd stopped, the wind pushed them into the wall, and a sharp rock stabbed her arm, pain speeding throughout her body.

"You're safe," he whispered, as he cradled her back. "I'm here. Nothing's going to happen." His arm tightened around her waist.

"Safe?" She wanted to yell or rub her arm, but nothing was going to make her let go of Kane's rock hard body. She looked up and saw nothing but a big black sky dotted with gray swirling clouds. The river below roared, but she refused to check out that scene. Kane and she were upright but he was standing on air. "How did we stop?"

"As soon as I made it to the ledge, I attached a clip from my harness to a rope that I'd previously fastened to the rock face."

His preparation astounded her. She squeezed Kane tighter, as they swayed in the wind. "Thank you."

"We're not home free yet. Slip down a little so you have a better grip." He was talking with his cheek to her stomach.

With his help, she lowered her body a foot, feeling more in control even though her heart threatened to leap out of her chest. "Now what?"

"We have to climb up unless you want to live face-to-face with me for the rest of your life."

How could he joke at a time like this? "Up?"

Of course, they had to go up. Her brain had short-circuited. She'd never been into rock climbing like many of her friends and wasn't all that certain she could do this, especially in the dark, without losing her footing.

"I'll need my hands to haul us up, so hang on for dear life—literally. I'll do all the heavy lifting."

The second he let go of her, she sucked in a breath. Even though she couldn't see a damn thing and was dangling a thousand feet over a river, she wasn't as petrified as she thought she would be. After all, she was in Kane's arms, or rather Kane was in her arms.

Hand over hand he pulled them up the rope until they reached the bottom of the ledge. He then swung his leg over and hauled her up into his warm, safe embrace, and relief flooded her as he kissed her forehead then her lips.

"Are you hurt? Is anything broken?" he asked.

She was still spinning from fear. Sky moved her neck, hands, hips, and feet. "No. For nearly dying, I'm doing quite well, thanks to you," she whispered.

**

While Kane claimed she wasn't in any condition to drive her car home from the factory, she didn't want to leave any evidence of them having been there. She had to admit that driving after her near death experience had been hard.

Once home, Kane thankfully didn't lambast her for going to the Base. Tomorrow would be soon enough. Exhausted, Sky slid under the covers and fell into a deep sleep, but awoke a few hours later, because Kane was clomping around outside her door making a lot of noise. She hoped he wasn't planning another expedition. They'd both only had a few hours of sleep, and she was still weary from the adrenaline rush.

He was a guy who was probably used to keeping watch, standing for days on end. Clearly, he wanted her up, and it wouldn't be to praise her efforts.

Fine. She tossed on some jeans and a T-shirt and headed into the kitchen. Kane sat at the table scowling. *Wonderful.*

She tossed him a smile, hoping to soften him somewhat. "I need coffee and food. Can I make you something?" A little bribe might go a long way.

"I already ate." He was in a sour, dour mood.

He was such a liar. There were no dishes in the sink. While she fixed something for herself, she needed to convince Kane she needed answers as much as he did. "I know you're upset with what went down last night, but all I wanted was to find out if Randall's swipe card gave me access to any of the buildings on the perfume factory property." Her breath came out fast. "I tried each of the greenhouse doors, but that didn't work. If the card hadn't opened the shed, I would have left. Besides, I knew you were there."

He stood so fast the chair nearly tipped over. "Do you understand they could have shot you for trespassing?"

"You're overreacting. I became a cop with the understanding there would be risks." Her statement was made with as much calm as she could muster.

He stepped closer, and her breath caught. For some unexplained reason, she was angry and in lust at the same time. Stupid hormones.

"Reasonable risks? No, they were too-stupid-to-live risks. I can't let you do something like that again."

I can't let you do something like that again. Like he was her guardian? "I took precautions—going at night, sneaking along the side of the building, having the swipe card in my possession." He stared at her. Now she could see that having him on the case wasn't such a good idea. "Like it was safe for *you* to go there?" It didn't matter if he was a super hero in his former life.

Kane didn't respond. He turned and paced, acting like he was trying to decide how to punish her or if he should tie her up for the rest of her life—as if that would work.

She wiped down the counters, straightened the canisters, and filled the saltshaker. The adrenaline still hadn't left her system because of that damned fall. She shut her eyes tight, but the images remained.

"Can you stop fussing and sit?" That was the best he could come up with? He was practically admitting it wasn't safe for him either.

She gritted her teeth at him and sat. "Fine." Somehow, it was okay for him to pace and wear off his excess energy, but she couldn't?

He stabbed a hand through his short, thick hair and walked up to the table then leaned over real close. "How did you know I was there?"

She leaned back in her seat and smiled—albeit one that didn't come from her heart. A shame he'd underestimated her deductive reasoning powers. "Your backpack wasn't in the bedroom, and your Jeep wasn't in front of the house." She lifted her chin, daring him to find fault with her logic.

His brows pinched. "I could have gone to Page or into town."

"At midnight?" She gulped some of her coffee, nearly burning her tongue. "You wouldn't have left me alone unless it was important. The only place you would have gone was to the factory."

His face softened. "You're right this time, but that doesn't excuse your behavior." He held her gaze longer than usual as if he wanted to say something but wasn't sure how to phrase it. "Listen, I need to be someplace in a few minutes. We can continue this discussion later."

"I can't wait." She was surprised he'd leave her alone.

He placed a hand on the table and leaned over. "Please don't..." He shook his head and straightened. "Just be careful. If anything happened to you, I'd feel... responsible."

That was all? Just responsible? He wouldn't be upset?

His shoulders sagged, and her sympathy heightened. "I promise I won't even drive on 89 today. I'll go straight to work and stay there." She looked up through her lashes and turned her mouth into a pout in an attempt to lighten his mood. "Where ya goin'?"

That almost got a smile out of him. "It's a secret."

She rolled her eyes. The man had been put on this earth to infuriate her. He wasn't a detective, yet he acted like he knew everything. The least he could do was have the decency to discuss his plans and theories with her.

"Be that way. The next time I learn something important about the case, I just might keep that info to myself." Unless it benefited her to tell him.

He leaned over and kissed the top of her head, suddenly acting as if they were some married couple who'd just made up after a fight. As if. However, she did soak in the comfortable act for a brief moment, despite not being ready to forgive his holier-than-though attitude.

Once Kane left on his ever-so-special mission, she poured a second cup of coffee, needing the caffeine to help her through the day. Despite rushing through the chore of pouring her drink, getting the cream, and locating the sugar, her mind wouldn't let go of the fact that Kane had been right in not divulging his plan. If he had told her, she would have wanted to go with him. In which case, he'd be saddled with having to keep her safe.

As for today's plan, she absolutely didn't have the time to follow Kane Cornell all over town. She dressed in her uniform, but this time the house seemed emptier than before Kane had stepped foot in her place—colder even, in more ways than the temperature. It might not be healthy for her to dwell on their indefinable relationship, which had started flirtatiously, then after one disastrous kiss, had turned a little contentious, but she couldn't help it. If only she could stop her mind from running through what had happened in the past few days—especially the night at the Senator's RV when they'd kissed.

Because of the kidnapping, and the almost capture at the factory, she needed Kane to stay around, which meant she had to try to be more cooperative.

After downing the coffee, Sky headed into work, looking forward to a calm day where no one would accuse her of doing something wrong or stupid.

Upon her arrival, the first thing she did was to return the swipe card to the evidence locker. She had no intention of using it again that was for sure. Once at her desk, Sky read over the information she'd entered into the murder book to find some overlooked clue.

Harriet traipsed over to Sky's desk with a plateful of the best smelling food. "A croissant?"

Sky grabbed one. "You are my hero."

She smiled. "Have two then."

"Don't mind if I do." She usually didn't give into the fattening foods, but after Kane's inquisition, she needed some comfort.

The phone rang at Harriet's desk. "I need to get that." The receptionist waddled back to her station and answered the phone.

Sky devoured the first croissant and was halfway through the second when the light on her phone lit up. "Sky Nash." It better not be Kane. She didn't want to see or hear from him for a while —or at least until she got home.

"It's Earl." His voice sounded raw.

She dropped the croissant onto the napkin. "What's wrong?"

"I need you." He coughed and wheezed. "Someone broke into my house."

"Dear God. Are you hurt? Do you need an ambulance?"

"No-oo. Come. Hurry." He disconnected.

Sky told Harriet where she was headed but didn't take the time to speculate about what had happened. The man sounded scared, and that troubled her, since nothing ever bothered Earl.

The VW didn't have nearly the power as the cruiser, but she arrived at Earl's in a little under twenty-five minutes. As she scooted out of the car, she waited to see if he'd roll down the plank to greet her—but he didn't, and her flesh rippled with apprehension for what she might find. Nothing appeared disturbed on the outside, but clearly something bad had happened or he wouldn't have called. She ran up to the door and pounded.

"It's open." The weak call came from inside.

Sky rushed in and stopped in her tracks. Earl sat in his wheel-chair, the right side of his face bruised and his lip bleeding. She raced over to him. "Dear God, Earl. What happened?"

"Sit, please." He waved her to the sofa, but all the cushions were on the floor.

"Can I get you some ice for your lip and face?"

He nodded.

In the kitchen, she placed ice cubes in a dishtowel and returned. The shelves lining the living room walls were torn apart and much of the furniture had been flipped over.

"Here," she said.

As soon as he placed the cold pack on his face, Earl winced. "They wanted Crandall Thompson's swipe card—or whatever you said his name was."

Her heart dropped to her stomach. "Those bastards. I used the card last night. I was able to enter the first level of the underground Base, which by the way was right next to the perfume factory."

He started to smile, winced, and then stopped. "So you were right when you said the hologram symbol meant something."

"Yes." She chastised herself. She should have thought what might happen when she took the card.

"I told the two men that I gave the card to the police, but they didn't believe me." He dropped his head in his hand, his back heaving. Poor Earl.

She wanted to console him but wasn't sure he wanted to be touched. Feeling helpless to stop his pain, she scanned the living room for her cone and the alien fuel cell, but couldn't find them in the mess. "Where are the things that were on your shelf?" She held her breath.

He lifted his head. "They took them."

She dropped onto the chair opposite him, and her breath shortened. "They must have recognized those objects. Maybe that's what they were really after."

"No one knew you'd brought me your cone."

True, but she bet the men didn't care where Earl had found the items. They saw something they liked and stole them. "When were they here?"

"'Bout an hour ago. As soon as they left, I called you. I was worried they'd go after you next."

"Because you gave me the card?"

"Yes."

"You had to turn it over to the police. It was evidence in a crime, but just so you know, the ID tag is safe in the evidence room at the station. Kane is staying with me so you don't have to worry about them coming after me." Assuming Kane came back tonight. "I'll call Harvey to photograph the scene. When he's done documenting the break-in, I'll ask Phyllis to stop over. She'll have this place spic and span in no time. Don't you worry; we'll find them and our stuff too." She knew he didn't care how messy his place looked only that someone had stolen what he valued most. He removed the icepack from his face and her heart broke at the purpling. "You sure you don't need me to send the doc here? I bet he could give you some good pain meds."

"No. I got me enough liquor to put me out of my misery. You go and find those bastards." He slowly shook his head. "Sometimes I wish I'd never come back from Serpo."

He couldn't really mean that. "Can you give me a description of the men?"

"They wore masks and gloves."

They were probably the same ones who broke into her place. "Damn, no prints then."

Earl did the best he could at guessing their height and weight, but the two men sounded like most of the young men around there—fit and strong. They could be military, but they also could be a couple of hired thugs.

"I'll call as soon as I have anything." She wanted to stay and care for him, but the more time the men had to escape, the harder it would be to find them—assuming they weren't holed up in the underground military base.

She returned to the station ready to make some calls when Chief Lapahe came out of his office and crossed his arms. "Nash. In my office. Now."

What now? She needed to file the report about Earl's break-in. There was no way he could have found out about her escapade last night since she hadn't been caught. Sky straightened her back and strode in head high. "Yes?"

"What were you doing at Fleur to Paris in the middle of the goddamn night?" He slid a photo across his desk, and her breath caught. It was a blurry picture of her at the factory, but there was no mistaking her identity.

Her hands trembled, barely able to hold the photo. When the hell had the guard taken the shot? Sky glanced up, not sure how to respond. "Who gave this to you?"

He slapped his palm on the desk, and she jumped. "That doesn't matter."

Her knees locked. "It sure does." She firmed her lips. "If you must know, I was on police duty. I had reason to believe Randall Tyler worked there."

"Why?"

From the jut of his jaw and the harsh delivery, she wasn't going to get off easy. "Earl found a swipe card buried in the sand near the headless man that had the imprint of a perfume bottle on it. I was just trying to see which door it opened." All of that information was in the murder book.

He whipped back his chair and dropped onto the seat. The air seemed to rush from his lungs; he was acting as if he was afraid of something. "That was dangerous."

"I know, but I wanted to find the secret base below the perfume factory. Someone else must have wanted to check this out, which might have been why they broke into Earl's house looking for it."

"When did this break-in happen?"

"About an hour or two ago, but they didn't find it because we have it here."

"Why didn't you tell me your plan to check it out?"

Because I don't trust you. "It was a last minute decision. Besides, you'd mentioned that I shouldn't waste my time on my alien fantasies, and I considered this to be one." That was lame, especially since she'd told him most likely the government had abducted and drugged her.

"I thought you just said you were investigating Randall Tyler?"

Caught. "I was, along with the aliens." Her voice trailed off at the last four words.

He worked his jaw as if he was trying to decide his next move. "Why did you have to go at night?" His voice wavered as he gripped the arms of the chair.

The truth seemed like the only answer. "I didn't want anyone to see me, which they surely would have if I'd gone during the day. According to what I read, the Base gets activity only after the perfume factory closes. In hindsight, maybe going in the day would have been better."

"Uh-huh." He cleared his throat. "Why didn't you sign out that piece of evidence?"

Oh, shit. Large claws scraped the inside of her gut. "I meant to. I was so excited, I must have forgotten."

"You never forget procedure."

"With my temporary capture, and everything else that was going on, I was distracted. It's back there now." The chief never checked her procedure before, and she wondered if the government had spoken to him.

He took a bite out of a half-eaten croissant. "Did the card open a particular door?" He acted as if the answer didn't matter, but from the way he averted his gaze and held his breath, this might be the most important question in the lot.

She debated how much to tell him. "Yes. A tool shed, or at least what looked like a shed from the outside."

He swallowed. "Why would a factory need a swipe card to get into a shed?" She couldn't tell from his tone if he had a hidden agenda.

"I don't know, which was why I was curious. I didn't stay long enough to investigate. There was a guard circling the building, and I only had seconds to get in and out."

"You mentioned there was an underground military Base somewhere around there. Is that what you were looking for?"

"I didn't know what I would find." She hoped he'd be satisfied with her evasive answer, but she doubted it.

He pulled out a pad and wrote something then looked up. "Who was your accomplice?" His tone had lightened, almost to the point of being friendly.

The hair on her skin prickled. Surely, he couldn't know Kane was there. "No one."

"The guard said a man was with you, and that he called you, Doll. Was it that Kane fellow who's been hanging around here, looking for the Senator?"

Think fast. "It was just someone who caught me right before I made it to the door. I don't think he wanted to get caught coming in late either, so he told some crazy story about showing me some military maneuvers."

His jaw clenched, and his brows furrowed. "You aren't a good liar. Who was he?" The last question was said at shout level that no doubt Harriet and Harvey could hear.

"Tony something. I didn't ask his last name." She shrugged, but she doubted he believed her. The lies were compounding faster than she could come up with answers.

"And you let him kiss you?" He pounded a fist on the desk.

Dear Lord. Had cameras caught their every move? "I didn't *let* him. He just kissed me." That was true. She never expected Kane to plant one on her. "Look at the video." Assuming there was one. "You'll see I tried to get away from him, but he kept me pinned against him." If they had good surveillance, they'd have identified Kane by now.

Lapahe stood and walked around his desk. "Sky Nash, you are under arrest for breaking and entering, taking evidence without the proper authority, and for stealing government property." He dragged her hands behind her and cuffed her.

CHAPTER TWENTY-ONE

"Stealing Government property? What the hell?" Sky tugged on the cuffs that bit into her skin.

Both crimes against her were bullshit. Sky might be guilty of breaking and entering as well as removing evidence without signing it out, but she certainly hadn't stolen anything. All she'd done was enter a stupid tool shed. Okay, it was with a lifted key card. That was the truth, but the Chief didn't believe her.

Lapahe's face remained hard, cold, and unfeeling. What had she ever done to him?

"Tell me exactly what I theoretically stole."

"I'm not at liberty to discuss it. You're a suspect now."

Suspect? She stood as straight as possible. "That's not fair. I have a right to know what I'm accused of stealing and you know it." She shouldn't have rubbed the law in his face.

"We need to process you." He flipped her around and waved a hand as if he was swatting a bug.

Kicking the desk would have helped her emotionally but wouldn't have aided her case. "You can't do this to me."

"You want to bet?" He led her to the holding cells and undid her cuffs. Lapahe stuck out his bulbous chest as if he'd succeeded in nabbing someone on the Most Wanted list.

Talk about embarrassing. She'd been in cuffs—in uniform! Luck intervened because the cell area was vacant. What hurt the most was that her own boss didn't believe her mostly true story. "I want my one call."

"I can arrange that." He almost sounded happy he'd tossed her in jail.

She wanted her one call to be to Kane, but Mr. Honest would say he'd been at the Base with her, and that would land him in jail too. Clearly, *they* wanted to get her off the case, whoever *they* were. Apparently, she was close to exposing their secret, and they weren't happy about it. Aliens or alien technology had to be involved or the government wouldn't have been so paranoid.

Instead of contacting Kane or her father, she called the only defense attorney in town, which seemed like the smartest choice at the moment. She could have looked up a name in neighboring Page, but she doubted they'd let her surf the net for his number.

Three hours later, Harvey showed up with keys in hand. "Your lawyer will see you in the interrogation room." He didn't smile or act as if he cared that one of Savory's finest was in trouble.

"Great. Does my dad know I'm here?" Since her father was on the city council, maybe he'd pull some strings for her, though he'd never had to do that before.

"If you didn't call him, no."

Harriet might have. If not her father, Sky bet her friend would have contacted Kane, though she wasn't sure what he could do. Hell, he was probably still angry with her for putting herself in danger.

He'd better not have decided to go back to the underground base in broad daylight to ask questions. An act like that could get a guy killed, and the thought of Kane being held captive or injured, sent shivers tripping up her spine.

"You okay, Sky? You look, I don't know, shaky."

She didn't believe he really cared. "I'm good."

She entered the small room containing a table and two chairs that smelled of potato chips and some other foul odor she didn't dare identify. The department needed Phyllis to come and give the place a good cleaning. Once she was released, she'd make the recommendation.

Her lawyer, Mr. Pritchard, had a pencil thin nose, a chin that barely held his teeth in place, and eyes the size of peas. His suit looked expensive, but she'd never liked him. He represented the scum she arrested, not to mention that she and Pritchard had had run-in's before. It was ironic that she now had to depend on him to save her.

Mr. Pritchard sat. "I'm sorry I'm late. I was tied up. There's a lot of case work in town."

She didn't buy his story since the criminals would have had to come through the station first, but it wouldn't serve her cause to accuse her lawyer of lying. Most likely, he was delayed because either Lapahe or the military were grilling Pritchard to see if they'd allow him to take the case, wanting to ensure he'd bend to their will.

As she sat at the rather unsanitary table, Harvey planted himself in the corner. She turned toward her fellow worker. "Come on, Harv. I'm not a flight risk for God's sake. Let me talk to my lawyer in private." The man probably never read the law to know she had this right.

"I'll be outside," he said to Pritchard. What was stuck up his butt? Maybe he'd asked for the headless man case and the Chief had told him no.

When Harvey's footsteps receded, she leaned her elbows on the table and clasped her hands. "So how bad is it?" Her teeth nearly cracked from pressing her jaw together so tightly.

"Bad."

She wanted to have everything out in the open. "I'll cut to the chase. I did remove the swipe card I'd put in the evidence room. I was in a hurry and just forgot to sign it out. I drove to the factory by myself. I tried the card in a few doors and found it opened a shed door, the width of a two-car garage and maybe twice as long. It was empty. That's it. I didn't steal anything."

He lifted a photo from his front pocket and placed it on the table. It showed a man in a suit standing in front of her house holding the silver pineapple-shaped treasure. "You recognize this?"

"That's my cone!" Frustration beat anger to the punch.

"So you admit you stole it."

She slapped the table with her palm. "First off. You're my attorney. A real one would never ask me that. Furthermore, did I say I stole it?" He dropped his gaze. "Didn't think so." She leaned forward. "I was in the caves on the edge of town searching for a missing Senator. It was on the radio for God's sake. Call Senator Overton, or Kane Cornell, for confirmation. Kane, who's from Phoenix, will confirm the Senator was missing for a few days, and that I was helping to find him. In the process, I unearthed this treasure. I have a picture of me holding this object taken days ago. It's on my phone, which is at my desk."

"You could have stolen the object then taken the shot."

Her stomach turned raw, and she had to work at getting her mouth to form the words. "Go look at the picture. It's time stamped. For the record, the cone wasn't even at my house, so how the hell did this dude find it there?"

"I have no idea."

"Look, I took this object to Earl Chee to see if he recognized it."

"That old coot? Why would he know anything about it?" She stared at Pritchard. Surely, he could put two and two together. Pritchard's mouth opened. "Oh, crap. You think it broke off an alien spaceship?"

"Maybe."

"You have proof you gave it to Earl?"

"No, but his place was ransacked this morning. They took the cone and something else of his—the fuel cell off a spacecraft engine."

He shook his head, clearly not believing her story. "Earl will corroborate this?"

"Drive to his house, and you can see for yourself. They beat him up and wrecked his house. I called Phyllis Tucker this morning to help clean up." She lifted a finger. "Afterward, I asked Harvey to photograph the scene and write up the report." She forgot to ask him if he'd done what she'd asked. The lazy slug probably hadn't.

"I'll check it out." Pritchard took notes then flipped through some pages. "It says here you had an accomplice when you broke into the factory."

Not that again. No good could come from giving up Kane. "I went alone." That wasn't a lie since she and Kane had driven separately. "I didn't break into the factory. I entered the shed at the side of the property with the key card."

"Did you procure a warrant?"

"No. There wouldn't have been enough for probable cause."

"I see." He pulled out the other photo Chief Lapahe had shown her. Kane stood off to her right, but all one could see was a silhouette of a tall man and her face brightly lit by a flashlight. Pritchard tapped the photo. "Who's that?"

She crossed her arms. "He was there when I arrived." That also was not a lie.

"If you don't come clean with me, I'm finished." Pritchard stood.

"What do you mean you're finished? We need to find out who's framing me."

"It's your word against theirs about the artifact. As for the B&E, you'll plead guilty."

This wasn't what she expected to hear. Her heart palpitated. "I can't go to jail." She pushed back her chair. "Come on, Ted. You've known me forever. I'm as upstanding as they come. I was doing my job, investigating a murder, and the clues led me to the factory—a factory that I believe is really a secret underground military base."

He jerked as if she'd punched him. "You have proof?"

"No, which is why I was there. Only I didn't see anything." Kane did, but she wouldn't break that confidence. "Who's claiming I stole their property?"

"I'm not at liberty to say."

"That's bull. You're my lawyer. You have to tell me."

The air seemed to escape his lungs. "I don't know, and that's the truth."

"Do I have to wait until I'm in court to learn who's out to get me?"

"Perhaps." He closed his briefcase. His cheeks sagged, and his tilted head told her he seemed to feel sorry for her. "Let me check out the photo of you holding the silver object, and we'll take it from there."

"Remember to check the time stamp. Did my accusers say *when* I stole this object?" She was gaining speed, creating her own case.

"The papers weren't specific."

"Well, ask them to be specific. I can prove I had that object in my possession over two weeks ago. Do they have any pictures of the object in their insurance papers to prove they owned it?"

His smile came out weak. "You have a point. Don't worry. We'll work this out."

If not, she'd spend the better part of her life in jail.

Two hours later, Lapahe finally took her back into his office where the light through the Chief's office window was brighter than the light eking through the bars in the holding cell. The air smelled a hell of a lot fresher too, helping to release the tension squeezing her temples.

He waved the grainy download. "This photo is time stamped, so for now, you're off the hook for the theft. I wish I'd known you had this sooner."

She was about to say she wished he'd told her what she'd been accused of stealing a lot sooner too, but she bit back the sarcastic retort. "That's okay. I didn't think of it until my lawyer showed me the picture." She inhaled the clean air and dragged her palms down her pants. "Who was trying to frame me?" She tried to sound casual, but her voice turned raspy.

"The U.S. Government."

Her chest caved. This was her worst fear. Stopping some crazed maniac was one thing, but taking on the government was an entirely different matter. "Did they say why they targeted me?"

"Sky, please sit."

Dear God. Her stomach tumbled again. Doing anything wrong tore her apart. "What is it?" His clenched hands implied she wasn't going to like what he said.

"I've suspected for a while there was something funny going on at that perfume factory."

"Bowl me over with a steamroller." She wanted to ask why he'd withheld that piece of important information, but maybe he thought it was on a need to know basis.

"I saw no reason to mention my concern until this mess with your B&E came up." He avoided eye contact this time, but if she'd been in his position, she probably wouldn't have told her either. He drained the coffee from his mug. "An hour ago, I spoke with someone who works there and learned there were deep ruts in the ground leading behind the factory. These ruts could only have been made by a lot of heavy machinery going back and forth on a day-to-day basis."

She picked up the paperweight at the edge of his desk and twirled the object in her hands. The cool glass felt good in her palm. "Did these people you spoke to ever *see* the military come or go or witness any odd happenings at night?" Maybe she could pick up a good piece of intel.

"I checked. The Fleur de Paris is locked tight at six p.m. and no one is allowed back after that time. The factory has a high level of security. Even the people who take care of the flowers have a strict schedule."

"That aligns with what Mr. LeFloch, the owner, told me. He's afraid someone will learn his secret formula."

"Given the plant is in the middle of nowhere, I think that's a cover."

"I agree." The military was a sneaky bunch. "Now what do we do?"

His eyes widened. "*You* aren't going to do anything." She was pretty darn tired of hearing that phrase. "There is still the issue of the B&E and taking evidence from the property room without permission."

"Come on, Chief. Those are trumped up charges, and we both know it. I forgot to sign it out. I didn't do it with any intention of breaking the law." Okay, so she had planned to look inside the factory. "What do they really want from me?"

He tucked his cheek into his mouth. "You won't like it."

"Tell me."

"They want to know who you were with the night you were caught sneaking around." If only they didn't have that damned photo. "The government doesn't consider you a threat, but they believe your accomplice is dangerous. They want him."

Mr. Military-I'm-a-security-guard Kane was dangerous? She was positive her heart was beating so fast, her shirt was moving. "I went there alone."

"That's not what I was told. They're serious, Sky. Deadly serious, if you get my drift."

Her insides turned soft. If she'd been standing, she wasn't sure she'd be upright at this point. "I'm sorry to have brought you into this mess."

He folded his arms over his chest again. Man, did she hate that stance. "If you tell me his name, I'll drop all charges against you."

He was resorting to blackmail now? She held up her hands, palms up. "Why won't you believe me? I drove there with me, myself, and I."

"So you swear the man who called you *doll* was a stranger?"

"Absolutely." She said it with conviction because in reality Kane practically was a stranger. She didn't know his favorite food, which side of the bed he slept on, or how he liked to make love. He was as much of an enigma to her as she was to him.

"Go home. You're suspended until I figure out what to do." His blustery attitude had dampened somewhat. The military clearly had gotten to him. That was a shame, but she wouldn't throw Kane under the bus. She'd let him decide how to proceed.

"Thanks." *I think.*

On her way out, she told Harriet everything—okay, not everything. Not that Kane had been with her. Even though she trusted Harriet more than anyone in world, she didn't want to put her friend in a position to lie. She contemplated telling her dad the whole truth, but he'd grill her more than the Chief had, and she wasn't ready for that confrontation until she'd had time to figure out a few things.

Sky kept her voice low and her back to the Chief's office as she spoke to Harriet. "Did you get a hold of Kane?"

"I called, but he didn't answer. His cell went straight to voicemail."

Meaning he'd turned off his phone. "If he stops by or calls, tell him I'm home."

Sky wasn't sure if she wanted to lock herself in her house, especially since some military or FBI suit had possibly gone inside, but until she regrouped, she had no place else to go. She thought about seeing how Earl was doing, but if someone followed her there, no telling what they'd do to them. She firmly believed the military had ordered one or two of their snipers to scare her and Earl off after they killed Randall Tyler. Add in trashing Earl's house and she had to stay away from him before they seriously hurt the old man.

So home it was. The idea of a hot bath and a glass of wine in the middle of the day appealed to her decadent side.

As soon as she arrived, she headed straight to the bathroom, not even wanting to know if the intruders had messed with anything else in her house. She filled the bath with steaming water and then dumped in a ton of lavender salts. The tangy aroma eased her senses, and while she didn't normally drink at two in the afternoon, she figured a nice glass of Merlot would help calm her frayed nerves.

In the kitchen, she removed the bottle of wine from the rack and was about to get a glass from the cabinet, when the front door clicked open. Her hand stilled, her pulse raced, and her muscles froze. She could have sworn she'd locked the door. The image of two men in black garb trying to either plant something that would incriminate her for real this time, or kidnap her once more, nearly paralyzed her.

Gun. Where was it? Crap. The Chief had confiscated her badge and weapon. Damn, damn, double damn. Her spare was in the glove compartment of her car.

CHAPTER TWENTY-TWO

"Sky?" The deep, gravelly voice that heated her blood came from Kane, and she set down the bottle and sank back against the kitchen wall.

She glanced at the ceiling and exhaled the anxiety she'd been holding in her lungs.

He leaned against the doorjamb. "You okay? You look pale."

Only pale? She'd been petrified. "I thought you were someone else."

He edged toward her, acting as if she were some feral animal ready to attack. When he reached her, he slowly raised his hands, cupped her face, and kissed her forehead. "You're safe now."

My God, he acted like he really cared for her and that did wonders for her heart. "Thank goodness it was you." No lie there. Even with the new locks Kane had installed, a sense of danger lurked behind every closed door.

"You thought it was the boogie man, huh? Or maybe an alien?" His smile made her chuckle.

She punched him in the arm. "Maybe." She didn't say which one.

"I'm sorry I scared you. I just spoke to Harriet, and I can't believe your boss tossed you in jail." Before she had a chance to respond, he enveloped her in his strong grasp, and his hug was way better than any bath or glass of wine, though she wasn't sure why he'd had a sudden change of heart. It didn't matter though. She was in his strong, protective arms now, and she was going to enjoy it.

He smelled like sunshine and clean wind, and she wrapped her arms around his waist, loving what that muscular torso did to her body. She'd never been given the chance to get this close without danger pounding at them.

With her face against his chest, she remembered why she'd been so scared and worked hard not to let the flood of tears flow. She sniffled and stepped out of his grasp, wanting nothing more than to drag him to bed. Too bad, he wasn't ready for that type of commitment. "I guess I should tell you what happened."

She clasped his warm, palm-calloused hand and led him over to the living room sofa. She dropped down at one end and he scooted next to her then wrapped both her hands in his.

"Tell me everything and leave nothing out," he said.

"I thought you were mad at me."

"I am."

"Why are you being nice then?"

"Sky, hon, it scares the crap out of me whenever you're in danger. I'm nice now because I can only imagine how scared you were sitting all alone in jail."

How sweet was that? "I was scared." She told him about the harsh way Chief Lapahe treated her, about Earl's beating, and the depressingly dingy holding cell.

He squeezed her hand tight. "Why didn't you tell them you were with me?"

Because I'm falling in love with you and I didn't want to see you in jail. "We're a team, remember? Black face paint and all. Oo-rah?" The instant flashback of him picking her up by the waist when she'd stumbled in front of the Senator's RV caused her to nearly lose it. She withdrew her hands from his grasp, since touching him messed with her train of thought. "The military wants you for something—something that could get you locked up for a long time, or worse, killed."

He dragged a finger down her cheek and shot her a puppy dog look. "Don't tell me you're turning soft about me?"

She jerked back, almost as if he'd gently pushed her. Yes, dammit, she was crazy about him, but she wasn't ready to reveal her feelings. If she spoke the words out loud, he'd feel more responsible for her—or just plain guilty because he couldn't return the sentiment in the truest sense.

Sky straightened her shoulders, refusing to jeopardize their mission. When this case was closed, she'd reevaluate her decision.

"Me, getting soft? Not Sky Nash." She threaded her fingers together, not sure what to do with her hands that wouldn't give away her feelings. "Listen, I didn't tell them because there's no logic to their demand. They tried to frame me for that metal sculpture, but then backed down when I showed them I'd found the cone days before. They should have just said they found some secret documents at my house, or else planted an alien artifact or a lab report on my desk and said I'd stolen that."

"They'd have to doctor their logs to say you'd snuck inside their Base."

"They'd have to do that with the cone too. I can't see them admitting they broke into Earl's house."

He frowned. "I wish I had all the answers to your questions, but I don't." He glanced at the ceiling for a moment. "If their surveillance is so good that they saw you with me, why didn't they stop us before we made it to the shed?"

"Perhaps the guard saw me waving the white key card."

"Maybe. At first, I thought the military might have had facial recognition for every employee so they didn't need to ask for our ID. I guess it took them a while to realize our pictures weren't in their system."

She dragged a hand through her tangled hair. "How sure are you of the General's honesty?"

He cocked a brow, looking like she'd asked if the Pope was Catholic. "General Stentfield is on the up and up. He'd never betray me if that's what you're thinking."

"Just thinking out loud." She closed her eyes and leaned her head against the cushion, feeling truly safe next to Kane.

He snapped his fingers. "We need to beat them at their own game by finding out what they're up to and telling the world before they succeed in silencing us." Kane's voice came out hard.

She sat up straighter. "How do you propose we do that? We can't go back there without getting into deep trouble." She held up a finger. "Didn't Harriet tell you I'm on suspension until further notice?"

"Yes. That's why you need to tell them I was with you."

She was impressed he was willing to sacrifice himself for her, but she wouldn't do it. "They'll arrest you. You can't find anything out from jail." *And you can't protect me from there either.*

"True." He placed his hand on her thigh, and her leg tingled. "I guess one good thing about being on suspension is that you won't have to spend time at the office." There was a gleam in his eye.

"Meaning what?"

"You won't have to lie about your whereabouts, and I'm betting they won't be checking up on you." He lifted a lock of her hair and twirled it around his fingers, and the sensation ignited her body.

"Good point," she said, trying to keep her breathing under control.

"What if we contact Whistleblower2 and find out what he knows about getting inside the Base undetected?"

Her pulse shot up. "Are you kidding? You must not be well versed in conspiracy theories. From what I've read, the government kills whistleblowers or harms their families. The real whistleblower wouldn't chance coming out of the cold for us.

Even if he were willing, how do you propose we find him? If the military can't find him, I doubt we can."

Kane leaned in closer, his face having a predatory look. "Ah, my pretty. You underestimate the power of the computer."

"Don't tell me you're a hacker?" Kane was bright and strong, but she didn't picture him as the computer geek type.

He laughed, and the sound lightened her mood, almost to the point of excitement. "No, but the General has the best talent in the world at his fingertips."

"Wow. You're going to use the military to fight the military." She kissed his cheek. "You truly are a superhero."

***

After Kane's bright idea of trying to find the whistleblower, she'd spent most of the day contacting more than ten people who she considered diehard conspiracy theorists, but they had no idea about how to reach him despite the fact he was well known in the alien believer community.

Exhausted, Sky and Kane headed over to EBE's for a mental break and some food. Cathy, the waitress, glanced over at her and sent her an, I'm sorry smile. Either she was still remembering what happened to Sky when she was in the bathroom, or she'd somehow found out about the jail time. It didn't seem to matter that both she and Harriet had agreed not to mention anything to anyone about Sky's suspension or her arrest. The notoriety would have made asking questions about secret underground facilities difficult.

Sky polished off her now cold coffee just as Kane's cell rang.

"It's the General." Kane answered but didn't say much. "Thanks."

She leaned close to him. "So?"

"Nothing. He's completely frustrated. All of a sudden, the well of information seems to have dried up."

Typical government stonewalling or else the General was

lying. "What about hacking into the whistleblower's IP address?" Though, if it had been that easy, the Base would have done it by now.

"It didn't work. They thought they had a lead, but the guy's smart. Apparently, he uploaded his information to a cloud computer whose IP address isn't static."

"Too bad." She finished her last French fry. "I'm at a dead end too. While everyone I've spoken to has heard of him, they have no idea how to contact him either."

"That sucks. We need him." Kane bit into his hamburger. How eating a hamburger could be sexy, she didn't know, but Kane pulled it off.

Cathy came over. "More coffee?"

Sky held her hand over her cup. "I'm about to float away as it is, but thanks."

Cathy set the white carafe on the table and leaned over. "I stopped by Earl's this afternoon with some food. I'd heard he was under the weather."

"That was nice of you." She hoped his *under the weather* referred to the beating and not from some bug he'd caught. He was prone to infections due to a weak immune system. Maybe he hadn't contacted Sky because he felt she was dangerous to his health, or else he was angry because he lost his prized fuel cell because of her.

Nothing she could do about it now. She hoped Pearl had stopped by Earl's to give him some loving.

Kane pushed his plate to the side indicating he was finished with his meal. "Thanks, Cathy." He turned to Sky. "Speaking of Earl, when was the last time you spoke with him?" Cathy picked up the coffee and went over to another table.

She shrugged. "Why?"

"I bet if anyone knows about the whistleblower, it would be him."

"If he knows, he won't tell me. I seem to cause him problems." She pushed back her chair.

"You sure?"

"Not a hundred percent."

"Do you think it's too late to visit?"

Sky stood. "Maybe, but it's not too late to call. I don't want to talk in here though."

Kane stood and dropped a twenty on the table, enough to cover their meals and a large tip. "Let's go."

Outside, dark clouds obscured the moon, and the chill in the air had intensified, forcing her to draw her jacket close around her shoulders. Once in Kane's Jeep, she pulled out her phone. Earl answered on the second ring.

"Hey, Sky. I heard you ran into some bad luck." His voice sounded strong.

So much for anyone in this town keeping quiet. Harriet just couldn't keep from spreading gossip, or in this case, the truth. Good thing the whistleblower didn't live in Savory, or he'd have been found in an instant.

"How are you feeling?" she asked.

"I'm okay. The headache's still bouncing around in my head from that pounding those guys gave me."

"You aren't really sick then?"

"Nothing the medics need to come for."

Good. "Remember I told you about an article that detailed the existence of a deep underground military base on 89?"

"Sure do."

"You ever hear of someone called Whistleblower2 or know about his claim?" Other than some heavy breathing, Earl didn't respond. "Earl? You okay?"

"You know how I hate to break a promise."

She pumped her free hand. Earl knew this person. "Okay, here's what we'll do. You contact this guy and tell him about the theft, about me missing for a day, and how the men stole your stuff. Confess anything you want then ask if he'd be willing to meet with me, or rather Kane and me." She held her breath. When he didn't answer, she gave one last plea. "We're on the same side here, you know. I was arrested for entering the Base."

"Oh, Sky. I didn't know that. You should have told me."

She thought the fact he knew she'd run into bad luck implied he'd learned she'd been arrested. "It's not something I'm proud of. Will you help me out here, Earl?"

"For you, I'll ask, but no promises. This whistleblower can be slipperier than a greased pig. But since they took you and tried to frame you, not to mention arrest you, I'm thinking he might be willing to cooperate."

She smiled at Kane. "Tell him I won't tell anyone about him. I don't even need to know his name. I want to expose what the government is doing as much as he does. I think whoever is behind this wants me dead too."

"If I find him, I'll give you a holler."

"Sweet. You are a true treasure." She disconnected, leaned back against the Jeep's passenger door, and smiled. "Now, we wait."

* * *

Sunlight streamed through Sky's kitchen window and bounced off her long, dark hair. She looked extra pretty today despite the circles under her eyes. Kane inhaled, and the rich aroma of bacon, eggs, and strong coffee made his stomach yearn for food. He barely remembered the hamburger from last night, and he certainly needed more nutrients than that piece of meat provided.

The eggs crackled, and she maneuvered from one part of the kitchen to the other. Sky had to be the bravest woman he'd ever met. If they could meet with the whistleblower, Kane might be able to learn how to get into and out of the Base—alone—and without being caught on any surveillance camera.

He leaned back in his chair and had to remind himself why he was still in this Podunk town. He'd be lucky if he even got paid for his protection detail since the Senator had returned home, safe and sound. Overton had asked that Kane keep trying to find out who'd abducted him, so maybe a paycheck would be forthcoming. Regardless, it was his sense of Marine honor to see this through to completion.

Who was he kidding? His protective instinct was strong, but with Sky it was, no pun intended, sky high. Another reason he was around was because he wanted to see if he and Sky could have a meaningful relationship—assuming she'd give him half a chance.

The scrape of a pan on the kitchen stove returned his attention to her. Kane rose from the table and walked behind her. Watching her cook and swinging her hips back and forth while she hummed a little tune, turned him on. He spun her around. With one hand holding a spatula and the other a fork, he leaned around her, turned off the stove, and removed the utensils from her hands.

"What are you doing?" she asked. "The food's still cooking."

"This." He drew her close and kissed her. Sure, he was still pissed that she'd run to the factory after he'd ordered her not to, and she never seemed to be able to stay out of trouble, but, dammit, she meant something to him. If he didn't taste her, his body would go crazy.

She broke the kiss, her eyes wide, from either the surprise of him kissing her, or because she felt his erection pressed against her. He wanted to make love to her. Now. It didn't matter that it was barely daybreak. Last night, he'd had erotic dreams of them together, convincing him they'd make a great pair. She was all fire and passion and strong enough to match his needs. Kane wanted her all right and should have made love with her last night, but even though Harriet told him Sky had dumped Chris, he wanted to hear her say the words.

"What was that about?" she asked.

He wasn't ready to explain his erratic behavior. "Just felt like it."

She studied him for a moment. "Well, I liked it."

Her cell rang, but she didn't move. "You going to answer it?" Part of him wished, she'd say no because she wanted to continue what he'd started.

Sky huffed out a breath. "Yes." She grabbed her cell. "It's Earl. Uh-huh. Sure. We'll be right there." She faced him. "Earl has something for us."

***

Once in the bedroom, she closed the door and plastered her back against the wall. Why did Earl have to call at that exact moment—just when things were getting good? That kiss had shot spears of lust straight through her. What that man did to her.

After splashing some water on her face and brushing her teeth, she rushed out. Kane drove and they arrived at Earl's half an hour later.

As they pulled in front of his house, a car she didn't recognize sat in the drive and Sky reached for her gun only to realize her spare was in her car. Crap. Being on suspension sucked. She hoped those two men hadn't come back demanding Earl give them that stupid card.

"Let me go first," Kane said.

She nodded for him to lead the way. As soon as they stepped from the Jeep, Earl wheeled out the door, and when no men in masks followed him out, she blew out a breath. He was safe. Thankfully, the bruising on his cheek and around his eyes had receded.

"Did the Chief return my cone or maybe your fuel cell?" she asked.

"Better than that."

The door behind him opened, and someone she thought she'd never see again stepped out.

CHAPTER TWENTY-THREE

"Mr. Morris?" Sky ran up the ramp and practically threw herself in the arms of her former high school science teacher.

She stepped back and lifted her hand to her heart to quell its rapid tattoo. His face was rather pasty and his hair thin, making him look closer to a vagrant than a respected member of the academic community, but the fact he was alive thrilled her—especially since she thought he'd died ten years ago.

"Yes, it's me. I know it's a bit of a shock."

Her mouth dropped open. "A bit? I went to your funeral and cried for days. You were my favorite teacher." He'd had a closed casket because of the fiery nature of his death.

"I'm sorry to have put you all through that." He wrapped an arm around her shoulders. "Come inside, and I'll tell you what happened."

She glanced back at Kane who appeared a bit perplexed and for good reason. Once inside, she looked around the now cleaned up living room. "Your place looks great."

"Smells good too," Kane added as he stepped in behind her.

Earl smiled. Thank goodness, he had his dentures in this time. "That Phyllis sure is a miracle worker, but I could do with a pinch less cinnamon."

She chuckled. She and Kane sat on the couch, and Mr. Morris pulled up a chair.

He cleared his throat. "I'll bring your friend up to speed first, Sky. After I left the military, I took a job teaching at Savory High where I taught Sky here."

She smiled. "I was a terrible student. I always wanted to thank you for putting up with me."

He waved a dismissive hand. "Nonsense. You were a joy. Three years after you graduated, the military recruited me to work at an underground military base nearby."

Sky swore her heart nearly stopped. "Blackthorn Base?"

"Yes. Earl told me you'd discovered the government's little secret." A corner of his mouth turned up, and he acted as if she'd figured something out no one else had. He seemed proud of her intelligence.

No way. "Don't tell me you're whistleblower2?"

"I am." He didn't look happy about it.

Oh my God. "I'm so sorry about your family. You never got them back, did you?" According to the Internet article, he'd stolen artifacts from the Base and was told unless he returned the items, they would hold his wife and child hostage.

"No. I know the government. They either killed them right away or did experiments on them." He squeezed his eyes shut for a moment. "It was a tragedy, and that's why I need your help to expose the murdering military."

"You have my word I will do my best." If her family had been taken, she would have tried to save them no matter what. "You never went back in?" Her tone must have been harsh because he flinched.

Mr. Morris gritted his teeth. "You don't understand. It wouldn't have mattered if I had been able to get in. I had friends who worked there at the time who looked for them but to no avail, so I assumed they were already dead."

"I'm sorry. I can't imagine anything so terrible." She glanced at Kane whose gaze was off to the side, as if he might be reliving his wife's death. She wanted to hold his hand to give him comfort, but now wasn't the right time.

"I feared they'd come after me next." For the next hour, Morris explained why he had to convince the government that he'd died in a car accident.

"Did you work with any alien technology?" She'd been dying to ask.

"Not personally, but I always believed it existed in other parts of the lab. In fact, I was trying to understand the scope of the place, when I found evidence of a book that appeared to contain alien technology. That's one of the things I took."

She glanced from Earl back to Mr. Morris. "Do you still have this book?"

"Not anymore."

"What happened to it?"

His lip curled. "As soon as I stole the book, I went to Washington and spoke with a General Richard Habberd, along with a panel of men who claimed they were interested in investigating alien life. I gave them what I thought was proof that aliens existed, but they called me a crackpot, booted me out, and then refused to return the book. You don't know what it's like to attempt to expose them. The government is too powerful."

That didn't surprise her.

Kane leaned forward. "How can I get into the Base and look around without being caught?"

"You can't."

"We have a key card that's in the evidence locker back at the station that gives us access to the first level." As soon as Sky opened her mouth, Kane's hand tightened on her knee.

Morris inhaled. "Oh, that's different. There might be a way if..."

All four bounced ideas around, but in the end, there was no clear-cut solution. The ones that might work, Kane nixed, saying it was too dangerous and that he had to go alone.

Mr. Morris stood. "I'm sorry I couldn't help you more, but I need to leave. I never stay in any one place for long."

"You think after all this time the government wants to kill you?"

"Yes. I've had several, obviously failed attempts on my life in the last few months alone."

She didn't want this fount of information to slip out of her fingertips. "How can I reach you?"

"Ask Earl. He has his ways."

Without even waiting for a hug goodbye, Mr. Morris slipped out.

Sky stepped over to Earl, leaned over, and gave him a peck on the cheek. "Thank you for contacting him."

Earl nodded, but from the grim expression, he didn't seem certain he should have exposed his friend, especially since they weren't any further ahead than when she'd arrived.

Kane grabbed her hand. "Let's go." He led her to the Jeep and held open the door. "How about we stop at the grocery store and pick up some steak. I'm not in the mood to run into anyone else if we go to EBE's."

"Great." Now that sounded like a plan. For a second, she wanted to suggest marshmallows for dessert, but given how the event fizzled last time, she decided against it.

While she wanted to continue brainstorming a way in which she, Kane, and maybe a few others could sneak into the Base, she'd let it go for tonight. Not arguing for a change would be a wonderful reward for Kane's heroics. He deserved it.

Once at the store, she let him pick out the cut of meat and the wine, while she chose some asparagus to go with the steak, and then picked up a box of chocolate chip cookies for dessert.

The temperature was a little chilly outside for cooking, but Kane didn't seem to mind grilling in the near dark even with the wind blowing. Inside, while the asparagus was cooking in the oven in a lemon butter sauce, she put on music, set the table, and poured the wine. Sky had picked up a bouquet of flowers at the store and placed them in a glass vase on the table, admitting the setting was very romantic.

"Steaks are done," Kane announced as he entered with the sizzling plate of food. The door banged shut behind him.

"They smell sooooo wonderful."

"I agree. I'm starved. I used a lot of energy the other day saving a damsel in distress." He winked and smiled, causing his dimples to sink deep into his cheeks, which made him look so sexy.

She laughed. "I can only imagine." Pulling their combined weight up a thin rope had to have taken a tremendous effort.

Because the food tasted so good, they ate fast—probably too fast for their own good. They drank their wine and talked about what they wanted in life.

"So why don't you leave Savory?" he asked as he tossed his napkin on top of his plate.

"I understand that if I want to be a detective in a big city I'll need to leave at some point, but I haven't because I'm a little afraid to be on my own." That might have been the first time she'd been honest with herself.

"You're what? Thirty?"

She planted a hand on the table in an attempt to look affronted. "Twenty-nine, but enough about me. Tell me what you want out of life?" She might as well toss the uncomfortable line of questioning back at him.

He cocked a brow. "Adventure."

"You get adventure every day." She expected something along the line of a family, children, and a white picket fence.

"I know, but I want a different kind of adventure now. I'm feeling restless, but I can't put my finger on what it is I want."

He sipped the wine then swirled the remaining liquid around in the glass. She might not be an expert on reading people, but there was something he wasn't telling her. *Be that way*. Sky poured herself a third glass of wine.

"You sure you should be drinking like that?" A hint of smile crossed his lips, probably remembering her low tolerance level.

"Yes." Like she'd ever tell him she was drinking because she wanted to be uninhibited when she ripped off his clothes and had her way with him.

"How's Chris these days? Hear much from him?"

Her hand stilled. That came out of left field. Talk about a mood killer. "I broke up with him a while back."

"Nice."

Now she regretted not telling Kane before.

He set down his glass and plucked a rose from the vase. "Come on."

She swigged down the rest of her wine. "Where to?"

"Trust me." He winked.

"What are you planning?" she asked, wanting confirmation before she obeyed.

"I think you know," he said, dragging a knuckle down her cheek.

As much as she wanted to jump his bones, she wanted to be sure that he truly was interested. She'd just told him she and Chris were through. "Are you sure you're ready to move on?"

He slipped his hands down her shoulders. "If you're asking me if I will forget my wife, the answer is no, but it's time that I move on. It's what she would have wanted."

He grabbed Sky's hand and slowly led her over to the sofa, probably to give her time to tell him no—only she wouldn't. The music filled the whole room, and the essence of steak and wine mingled with the sweet aroma of the flower he'd plucked from the centerpiece. He set the rose on the coffee table.

"Lie down." Without saying a word, he unlaced her right boot, keeping his eyes on her face the whole time. As he pulled off the first one, along with her sock, he let one finger drag across the bare skin of her ankle so lightly that she had to glance down to see if he was actually touching her or if it was just the sudden rush of hormones causing her skin to tingle. He repeated the divine movement on the other side.

Kane stepped over to each of the lamps and flicked them off. Had it not been for the light filtering in from the kitchen, she wouldn't have been able to see at all. "I want you to close your eyes and not move, no matter what I do," he said.

"Why?"

He held up a hand. "Sky."

Because she trusted him with her life and with her heart, she bit her lip and pressed her legs together so as not to appear too eager. Then she did as he asked.

With her eyes shut, she listened to his feet move across the wood floor and tried to figure out what he was doing. A match struck the side of a box and that tangy smell of phosphorus wafted over to her. Even through her closed lids, light danced. She'd had the dang candle for over two years and had never lit it.

She had no idea what was in store, but whatever it was, it would be memorable. With her head on a throw pillow and her feet extended, she should be almost asleep, but the tingling that raced up her legs and the wetness building between them made her heart pound.

Kane scooted her legs closer to the back of the sofa and sat next to her waist. He smelled of charcoal and smoke, and she wanted to reach up and touch him, but decided that for once in her life, she'd follow directions and not move. His breathing was even, but his thigh against her tensed. Something velvety soft touched her forehead, and it took her a moment to realize it was the rose!

He dragged the flower over the bridge of her nose and down her lips before caressing her throat. The scent of sweetness teased her nostrils, and she inhaled deeply. He brushed the petal over her eyes, lingering there before returning it to its downward path. Around and around, the soft swirls relaxed every muscle, and she couldn't help but smile.

"No moving," he warned.

He wanted her not to react at all? That wasn't possible when every nerve in her body fired off electrical pulses of pleasure, making her toes curl.

"I won't lie. I want you, Sky." His hand rested on her zipper.

"I want you just as much."

He exhaled on a large huff and then unzipped her jeans, the metal teeth clicking open one by one. Remaining still when he was doing such wondrous things to her body was one of the hardest things she'd ever been asked to do.

"Keep your eyes closed. Promise?"

She nodded and moaned in anticipation. The rose returned to kiss her lips, and he moved it back and forth until her mouth was swollen with desire. She wanted to yank the flower away from him to stop the intense sensations, but the lazy movement held such caring and sensuality, she didn't dare interrupt his dance.

"Lift your hips."

Once again, she followed his command, and after a few tugs, he slipped off her jeans, the material slowly dragging over her thighs and across her calves. The flower of torture found a new location. It traveled over her belly, then made its way between her legs for what seemed like an eternity, before he dragged it over her hips, thighs, and calves, the touch so light it tickled the small hairs on her legs. He treated the bottom of her feet to the delightful petal touch, but each brush of the flower wreaked havoc with her senses. Each caress was so sweet and soft, it ratcheted up the need for him to be on her and then in her. She was pulsing with desire.

The pressure on the sofa disappeared. What? The legs of the coffee table scraped on the floor, and then his breath cascaded across her belly, even though his lips didn't touch her.

"I want you." Each of his words caressed the hairs on her stomach.

The flower suddenly landed on her lips as if he was forbidding her to respond. The lack of his touch drove her crazy. She wanted to feel his hands on her body and willed his lips to her mouth. Damn him for withholding the pleasure. His plan must be to drive her over the edge.

"Be right back." The sound was so low she almost didn't catch what he said.

A moment later, cool liquid pooled in her belly button then overflowed onto her stomach. The shock of the cold made her suck in her breath, and she fisted her hands to keep from grabbing him. This torture was too much. From the tangy, rich scent, it was wine. When his tongue licked her navel, she inhaled, the throbbing between her legs intensifying at his mere touch. A groan escaped. She elevated her hips and slipped her hands underneath her butt, her willpower having evaporated. She could almost taste him on her tongue even though she hadn't licked him—yet. And lick him she would.

He slid his fingers under her shirt, and the rough pads of his fingertips prickled her skin. "Sit up a bit," he commanded.

She didn't mind following any of his instructions. Off went her shirt, and a few seconds later, her bra followed. She waited for his tongue, but apparently, he had more frustration in mind. One by one, he dropped rose petals on her breasts then blew air across each once so that they fluttered over her chest up to her neck. Her core ached. Hell, she ached all over. How much more did he expect her to withstand?

The tips of his thumb danced over each nipple, and no doubt they were standing erect, worshiping him. He tweaked one nipple, and then the next, sending erotic messages to every inch of her. From the way his breath skated across his skin, he was close to losing control.

Her inner walls contracted, again and again, her climax brimming. She bucked her hips up and down and fisted her hands, wanting him to see that this wasn't fair, but he didn't seem to notice. She moaned loudly, and as her orgasm claimed her, she let out a yell.

Breaths rapid, she collapsed back onto the sofa. She defied

him and opened her eyes. She'd never come before with so few touches.

Kane leaned back grinning. "You liked that?"

She swatted at him. "You bastard. If you ever do that again, I'll have to arrest you for torturing an officer of the law." Her glance went from his face straight to his crotch where his huge cock was peeking out from the top of his low-rise jeans. "I see I wasn't the only one turned on."

"That you weren't."

Without another word, he stood and stripped off his jeans and shirt that showcased muscles and sinew bulging everywhere. "Wow."

"You're the wow in this duo."

"Can you just shut up and kiss me?" she begged.

And then he did—after he donned a condom he just happened to have nearby. Kane obeyed very well when he wanted to. The kisses weren't soft either. He devoured her lips while his hands plied her body. In a flash, her panties were gone and he eased inside her, each inch stretching her wide, and taking her higher and higher.

"You feel so damned good, girl."

"So do you." Joining with Kane was better than she could have ever imagined.

He pumped and thrust, acting as if this might be his last moment on Earth. Heat built inside her as her inner walls clamped down on his hard shaft, wanting to keep him inside her forever.

Between the blood rushing to her brain, pounding against her skull, and her screams of ecstasy, she barely heard the grunts and groans of his pleasure. His fingers tightened on her shoulders as he dipped his head and kissed her again, their tongues trying to possess each other.

Time flew as their passion soared, and finally, their time together ended with a shattering release. She was spent, never having experienced anything so remarkable in her life.

Kane lay on top of her, and as much as she wanted to say something, no words came out. Kane too seemed speechless. Once he caught his breath, he stood and carried her into his bedroom. As he placed her under the sheets, she'd never been so happy in her life.

***

The sound of wind buffeting the windows woke her, forcing Sky to crack open an eye. The glowing clock read 7:00 a.m. and Kane was no longer in the bed. She sat up quickly but immediately regretted the movement. Her head pounded, but not so bad she couldn't function. They'd made love—twice! Once in the living room earlier, and then last night in his bed. She fell back onto the pillow and nearly giggled. The room smelled of their hot, passionate sex.

As she exhaled, his voice filtered in through the door. Kane was speaking to someone in the kitchen, or else he was on the phone.

Sky slipped out of bed. Not wanting to walk into the kitchen naked, she pulled on the shirt he'd worn last night and inhaled his scent. Without panties, she managed to tiptoe out of the guestroom and into her own bedroom without him noticing.

She drew on jeans without underwear and planned to eavesdrop just in case Kane was speaking to the General. She stood by the kitchen entrance out of his sight and leaned against the doorjamb.

"Her only choice is to quit being a cop, and she'll never do that." Her heart dropped to her stomach. He was talking about her? "She's great. I agree, but it isn't going to work, I'm telling you." He paused. "We just don't have the kind of relationship we would need for things to work out in the long run." This was followed by a long silence. "We got along in the beginning and had great times working together, but I don't have that strong of an attachment to make a go of it."

Sky's knees almost buckled. He never said he loved her last night, but she assumed he at least liked her a lot. For starters, he had taken such care to make her happy before he sought his release. True, she anticipated he'd leave someday, just not now. Dear God, she'd been a fool.

CHAPTER TWENTY-FOUR

"Sky?" Kane had his hand around her arm helping her to remain upright as he pressed the phone closer. "Listen. I gotta go. Talk to you later." He swiped off his cell and stuffed it in his top pocket. "Why are you hiding?" His voice came out soft and not accusatory. He must have realized she'd overheard his conversation.

Sky pasted on a smile. "I wanted to surprise you."

"You did." He tapped her nose. "Listen. I need to take care of some business this morning. Promise me one thing?"

"Sure." How she managed to smile with her broken heart barely managing to beat she didn't know. Inside, her stomach was devouring itself, probably eating the heart that had dropped into her gut.

"Please stay in the house."

She refrained from tossing out a retort, mostly because she wasn't in the mood to listen to his bluster this morning. "No problem. I've got lots to keep me busy around here." He had to see she was lying.

"Good."

Guess not, or else he didn't care enough to question her. He kissed her quickly and then practically ran out the door, acting like he hadn't just told the person on the phone that he didn't give a shit about her.

She didn't move until the sound of his engine disappeared down the road.

In an attempt to keep from breaking down, Sky went through the motions of fixing breakfast. Too bad the eggs tasted like rubber, and the coffee did nothing to help the headache that fully blasted her. She wanted to cry and beat something, but her energy had disappeared. How dare he say there wasn't a strong attachment between them? There was, dammit. She slapped the table, and the coffee sloshed out of the cup. The tears trickled out at first, before the sobs came in full force.

She'd been abandoned again. What was wrong with her? Her rational side screamed, nothing, but her emotional side said she was just plain unlovable. She bet Kane would say she was too stubborn, didn't listen, and was too afraid to open her heart.

"That's not true," she announced to the air.

Hoping a hot shower might help shed some light on this mess, she placed her dishes in the sink, and then disappeared into the bathroom. While the hot water and lavender scented body wash soothed her skin, her heart wouldn't stop crumbling. Not in the mood to enjoy the shower, she finished and dressed in her fanciest outfit, hoping her new blue top would cheer her up —and it did somewhat. She put on makeup and even curled her hair, but then decided she looked dumb all dressed up with no place to go.

Sky stared in the mirror at a person she barely recognized. Anger, frustration, and depression nearly swallowed her. Her life was in shambles, plain and simple. Not only was she on suspension from a job she'd worked her ass off for, the man she was falling in love with had rejected her.

Follow your dream.

That little person in her head screamed at her to do something positive with her life instead of wallowing in despair. With the military out to frame her, it might be smarter to just leave town, because, knowing her, if she stayed, she'd be tempted to go back to the Base.

Hell, she'd been wanting to visit her cousin, Jessie, is West Virginia, for quite some time, and a few days of rest might help clear her head. If she recalled correctly, Jessie's man used to commute to Kerry, West Virginia from Baltimore. Perhaps he could even help her find a job in the big city.

Sure, Harriet and Earl would miss her, as would her dad, but that would be all. Harvey, Elmer, and the Chief would forget about her in a week. Sky would catch the next flight out east and call Harriet when she was safely with Jessie.

Happy with her decision to start living her dream, she tossed a few things into a suitcase, wrote a note to Kane about why she was leaving, and then headed out. For the first time in hours, Sky had pep in her step.

Once in her car, she headed toward the Page Airport. The windy day had calmed, and the sun was shining brightly. She tried not to think about Earl, Pearl, or the good citizens of Savory. She'd miss them for sure, but they'd survive. She hoped Kane was successful in learning something about the Base and was able to expose them.

Her thoughts were filled with regret, but this was the best thing for her. A light reflecting off something in front of her startled her. She reached up to shield her eyes from the glare when suddenly a trailer carrying cows entered the roadway directly in front of her car.

"No, no, no. Shit." She slammed on her brakes but couldn't stop in time to prevent the collision. The airbag deployed and her whole body jerked forward. Her first thought was that this couldn't be happening again. Then she mentally thanked her dad for insisting she have airbags installed in her old VW. It had cost a mint, but now she was happy she had them.

Instantly, the bag deflated, and she let out a big breath. Other than the blood pounding in her head, only the mooing of the cows reached her brain. She slumped forward, not willing to assess the potential damage to her body or her precious car.

A few seconds later, a knock sounded on her window. "Hey, lady, you okay?"

***

The moment Sky's house came into view, and Kane saw her car was missing, he slapped the wheel. "Goddammit."

That pig-headed woman would never listen. He should have taken her with him, but if he had her by his side, he would have ended up kissing her endlessly and never would have been able to do any work.

He let himself in, and in case she'd loaned her car to someone, called her name. "Damn it, Sky. Couldn't you follow orders just this once?" he mumbled.

She'd done a bang up job lasting as long as she had on that sofa, doing an amazing job of withstanding his brand of torture a lot better than he ever could. She'd followed his orders then, so what had changed?

A note sat on the table next to her phone, and his gut churned. She always kept her cell with her. She must not want him to be able to contact her. He read her note: *When I heard what you said on the phone this morning, I realized you didn't want me the way I wanted you. With things being so heavy in town, together with my suspension, I'm going to follow my dream and be a detective in the big city.*

He had to read the message twice, and each time he did, the pain was like a saber through his heart. He let the paper float back to the table. What had he said on the phone to make her think that? Kane replayed his discussion and realized what had happened. "Oh, shit."

She was wrong, so very wrong.

The worst part was that he had no way to contact her. He'd seen her standing there when he called his friend, but damn it, he wasn't talking about Sky. Kane wanted to go after her, but he had no idea which big city she was talking about.

Harriet. He bet she knew what was going on. He dialed the police station, but no one answered. Okay, that wasn't good.

Kane rushed out to his Jeep, jammed the engine into gear, and raced toward Savory, not caring if he broke every goddamn speed limit. He parked in the NO PARKING ZONE and marched up the steps to the police station, but when he stepped inside, the place was deserted.

Well, shit.

***

"I'm good."

The farmer eased Sky out of the car. "You sure? You don't look so good."

She wasn't going to complain about a little neck injury. "How are the animals?"

"They're scared, but okay." The cows were standing on the side of the road watching her.

The metal trailer seemed to have protected them, but the impact must have broken the lock allowing the animals to escape.

"That's good. I need to get to the airport. I have a plane to catch. Let me see if I can drive my car." Thankfully, the engine sat in back. She turned the key and the engine fired up. For once, something seemed to be going her way. Sky waved, but as she edged forward, the grill scraped against the tire. Damn. She wouldn't be able to drive it like this.

Slumping against her seat, she blew out a breath.

The farmer tapped on her window. "I can give you a lift once I round up my animals."

Other than her plane crashing on the way to West Virginia, the day couldn't get any worse. At least this wasn't the government's doing. "Thanks." She got out and checked the damage. "I'm hoping my mechanic can fix it."

"I'm sure of it. You want to call him? How about I push your car to the side of the road and then drive you to Page?"

That was so sweet of him, but in all honesty, her hair must be a sight and she smelled of perspiration from the trauma. She needed to head on home and fly out later. Hell, she hadn't even called Jessie to see if the timing worked for her.

"Can I borrow your phone? I'd like to call the mechanic."

"Here ya go. Take your time. I need to gather my animals."

"Thanks." She called Richie at Morton's garage, knowing he'd give her grief.

While the farmer coaxed his animals back into the trailer, she slid into the passenger side of the VW and closed her eyes. She ached—ached for Kane and ached for what could have been. She probably shouldn't have run away without talking to him. It was one of her many flaws. She sucked at confrontation, but what could he say? He didn't believe things could work out between them anyway.

Forty-five minutes later, Richie pulled up and whistled. "Man, girl. You sure are hard on your cars. You should marry Ole man Jespers." He owned the used car lot.

"Funny. Just tow the car, please."

He saluted. She waited by the side of the road, and while he put her car up on the back of his truck, she exchanged her insurance card and information with the farmer.

"I'll drop you back home on my way to town," Richie said.

Home. She wasn't ready to face Kane, but maybe he was still out doing his errands. If there was any luck in the world, he hadn't read her note. If he had, she didn't know if he would be furious or happy that she would be out of his hair for good.

"Can you drive me to Jespers instead? I'll need a loaner."

"The cruiser's nearly fixed. You want that?"

She laughed. "I couldn't afford the repair bill if anyone else ran me off the road." Besides, she wasn't technically with the department.

"You got it."

Once she picked up a loaner, she decided she deserved an Area 51 coffee from EBE's before going home. Not only that, she needed to see some friendly faces. She parked in front, checked the mirror, and gasped. Her forehead and cheek were black and blue. The seatbelt had cut into her shoulder, and a few flecks of blood had seeped through her shirt. The crowd might stare, but at this point, she didn't care.

As she walked in, she didn't look around as she headed to the side of the café where she always sat. Chair legs scraped, and she looked up.

Oh, shit. Her dad was sitting with Kane. Both faced her. Kane's eyes widened, but her dad's brows were pinched. She straightened, winced, and then slouched again. Taking a full breath, she marched up to their table and faced Kane. It didn't matter that the note said it all. "I can explain."

The entire café seemed to come to a screeching halt. Blood pounded in her ears as sweat pooled under her arms. She was about to bear her soul in front of the entire town—a town that used to care about her. A strong chance existed that after her confession, they wouldn't. Kane pushed back his chair and stood, but she held up her hand.

"I take it you read the note?" He nodded. "Let me tell you why I really left." She sucked in a big breath, hoping for the courage to tell him.

Before she was able to say she loved him and that she'd made a big mistake, someone slammed open the café door, and both Kane and her dad faced the newcomer. She turned too. It was the Chief. Really? He was the last person she wanted to see. Now, it might have been better to be on some crashing plane.

The Chief looked straight at her. "Thank God, I found you. Harriet's missing."

CHAPTER TWENTY-FIVE

Panic ripping through her veins, Sky, Kane, her dad, and the Chief quickly returned to the station to regroup. Harvey and Elmer joined them as they sat in a circle to come up with a plan to find their beloved Harriet. Sky shoved her confession as to why she'd run off, to the back burner for the moment. Finding Harriet was all that mattered now.

Kane kept looking over at her, sympathy in his eyes, but he must have understood that now wasn't the time to talk. Dixie, Harriet's sister, wanted to be in on the discussion, insisting they call in the FBI, but the Chief and her dad told her they would do everything they could to find her sister.

"Ms. Dixie," Sky said. "It would be best if you went home and waited for any word from Harriet. We're doing our best to locate her. I promise we'll let you know if we discover anything."

When she hesitated, Kane moved in front of her and took hold of Dixie's hand. "You know how you can really help us?"

"How?" she sniffled.

"Keep the coffee coming. You make the best stuff at the diner."

Her eyes sparkled. "If you're sure it'll help, Mr. Kane, I'll do it."

The man seemed to be able to sway every female around. Dixie hurried back to the cafe to do his bidding.

"I know I'm on suspension, but I want to help too," she said.

"Thank you," the Chief replied.

As if Kane was in charge, he made eye contact with each person in the circle. "No holds barred. Everyone with me?"

In unison, they chanted, "Yes."

After they batted around what they were going to do and when, Kane asked that they go through the facts one more time to make sure they hadn't missed anything. "Chief, you start."

"Last I remember, Harriet was dishing up a batch of her fresh chocolate chip cookies right here in the office and left work at her usual time, happy and helpful like always."

Harvey piped up. "Dot said she saw Harriet at EBE's around five thirty, grabbing her usual chicken salad sandwich and then poof, she vanished."

Kane leaned forward, his hands dangling over his knees. "Poof?"

Harvey nodded. "Apparently, Harriet paid and left, but forgot her glasses on the table. When Dot went out to return them, Harriet was gone. Poof. Couldn't have been more than ten seconds, she said."

"Okay, poof it is."

The Chief spoke up again. "Maybe we should wait to see if they return her, like they did Sky and Dan Joe."

"It's Harriet," Sky said. "She's no spring chicken. She'll be scared. We need to help her now."

The Chief nodded. "You're right."

Elmer held up his hand, as if he still thought he was in school. "I'm not sure they will return her, like they did with Sky. They know we know about them now. Maybe they're trying to lure us, and once we get inside the Base, they'll show us there is nothing in there but military stuff—no aliens and no hostages."

She didn't buy it. "If that's true, we need to strike before they bail and hide any evidence."

They went through their options. In the end, they chose the "Wookie Gambit" trick, the device used in the *Star Wars* movie, in which Sky would pose as a prisoner, and Kane would be a sentry and escort her back in. Sky wasn't sure it would work, but with Kane at her side, they might have a chance.

Kane finally spoke directly to her. "Sky, I need you to see if Dr. Williams will agree to our plan."

"I'm on it."

The Chief puffed out his chest. "Harvey, how about we do a little reconnaissance?"

Harvey looked like he'd been asked to wear a purple tutu and dance around town. "Of what?"

"The military Base, you idiot."

"Isn't that dangerous?" Harvey sounded scared.

"It can be."

"Take some night vision goggles," Kane said.

The chief's chin sunk. "You got some?"

"In my Jeep." Kane slapped his thighs and stood. "If you find out anything, Chief, let us know."

They all agreed that when Sky reached Dr. Williams in Page, they would reconvene in the morning, as they needed Dr. Williams's assistance before undertaking the operation. As they walked out, Kane suggested they drive to Page tonight.

"The morgue closed at five." It was after that now.

"He might open up shop once he knows this is a matter of national security."

Kane had a point. "Doc Williams might believe us more if the General called him."

Kane pulled open the door for her, something she'd come to expect. "You're good, I'll hand that to you." She thought she caught a wink.

She stopped. "Wait. I almost forgot. I have my car, or rather my loaner here. I'd rather not leave it on the street. Why don't I meet you at the house and you can call your friend?"

He stood over her and looked down. "What happened to

your car? I saw the bruises and the spot of blood on your shoulder at the restaurant but then the Chief rushed in and everything went crazy." His shoulders slumped. "Don't tell me you totaled the VW too."

Sky looked to the side and shuffled her feet. "Um, I was in a bit of an accident."

She went into a shortened version of how a farmer pulled out in front of her on the way to the airport.

His chest seemed to cave. "You didn't end up leaving. Was it because you had a change of heart or because you wrecked your car and couldn't get a ride to the airport?" His mouth firmed.

Now wasn't the time to go into detail, but she wanted to come clean. "I changed my mind. The farmer offered me a ride to Page, but I was too beat up and looked a mess." From the way his eyes darkened, she might have made things worse.

"Oh."

Now why hadn't she told him the truth? *Chicken, chicken, chicken.* She could have sworn Harriet was right behind her, whispering in her ear.

"In light of your third wrecked car in as many weeks, I don't think you should be behind the wheel," Kane said.

"That's not fair. The last accident wasn't my fault."

His brows rose. "I'm sure. How about you ask Elmer to have the rental place pick up the car?"

Sometimes, Kane could be the most infuriating man in the world. "Fine."

They headed back inside the station and gave Elmer the rental car key. He seemed happy to have something useful to do and was out before she had a chance to snap her seatbelt or figure out why her stomach was in turmoil.

Once they arrived at her house, she wanted to lock herself in the bathroom and never come out, but she was hungry and didn't want Kane to think she was some psycho case. Sky walked out in the cleanest pair of jeans she could find and a fresh top.

She still looked like hell, but at least she didn't have bloodstains on her anymore.

Kane glanced up at her, his cell phone to his ear. She could have sworn his eyes sparkled when he noticed her. "Thank you, sir. I'll keep you in the loop." Kane pocketed his phone. "All set. You have the swipe card, right?" He was very matter of fact. She could handle him acting all military. It was the sweet, kind man she could do without right now.

"Yes. The Chief reluctantly let me have it, and then said he was sorry he had accused me of taking evidence without permission."

"I'm glad he noted the error of his ways. Let's go."

Sky wanted to talk about the note and why she'd left, but it wouldn't do to distract Kane now. There'd be time later. Besides, she wasn't in the mood to listen to his excuses about why he wasn't interested. Because it was better to let it go, they discussed their plan to free Harriet.

Dr. Williams was waiting outside the morgue when they pulled up, and from the way he shifted from foot to foot, he wasn't anxious to help, but a command from a top military official was probably hard to turn down.

"Sky. Mr. Cornell." Williams unlocked the door. "You'll have to tell me which finger you want." From the way his voice was high, he wasn't pleased to be doing this.

Putting him in this bad position almost made her sick, but they needed to get into the military base.

"Index," she and Kane said in unison.

"You do know this is illegal." The doc's lips pinched, and his cheeks were paler than usual.

"The military needs this."

He nodded and Sky cringed. She was already one step from losing her badge, and could only hope that what they were about to do was never found out. It didn't matter someone in the military had sanctioned it.

In silence, they followed the doctor to his room. After the

morgue door closed, the air was heavy and filled with a sickly sweet odor of death. He pulled out the drawer containing Randall Tyler. "A cousin came forward to claim the body, but I wasn't sure if I should release him. I was waiting for you to get back to me."

The doc was a saint. "Thank you."

"This will take a minute."

Sky didn't want to watch him cut off the man's index finger. It shouldn't matter the guy was dead and didn't have a head; it was still dismemberment to her. The sawing noise grated on her nerves, but from Kane's calm expression, he didn't seem to mind. Good thing he'd be the one wearing the dead man's finger and not her.

***

The drive back to her place involved Kane rehashing the details of what was going to happen when they attempted to find Harriet. The whole time, her stomach remained in knots. To keep from fidgeting too much, she played with her straggly hair.

Tell him.

She couldn't—not yet. As soon as they rescued Harriet, Sky would tell Kane how much he meant to her, since holding out on Kane was eating her alive.

Once home, he ordered her to sit in the kitchen while he found a pen and paper. It was after ten p.m., and while she wanted nothing more than to crash, Kane insisted on drawing a few diagrams. She understood full well the need to be on the same page, but come on. It wasn't rocket science to have him drag her to the entryway and claim one of their prisoners had gotten loose.

Mr. Morris, Mr. whistleblower himself, had detailed what the area looked like and how to get to the lower levels. His intel would be invaluable.

"It's 22:25. Let's go."

Her stomach tumbled, her nerves raw. "You said we'd go tomorrow night. We're supposed to meet up with everyone tomorrow morning, remember?"

"I wanted them to think that."

Her heart hammered in her chest. "So you don't trust them either?"

"No."

"Who do you think is the traitor?"

"I'm not sure."

"Me, neither. I trust Elmer and that's about it."

"Ready? You can say no if you want."

As brave as she'd been throughout her career, right now, she wasn't so sure she was emotionally ready to break into a military base and risk it all. She could end up in the prison underground forever. "We don't even know they're holding Harriet prisoner there."

He stepped so close she could feel his breath on her face. "Are you saying you don't want to do this? Because if you don't, we won't go in."

He was giving her the option to say no, but Kane needed her, and so did Harriet. "No. I'm in."

"Good. Remember the whistleblower said prisoners escaped periodically but were always caught. The numbering system he gave us might not be exact, but it should allow us to gain access. We won't have a lot of time to find her, so you do understand we can't search every room or every level?"

"Yes. Men will be patrolling and checking everywhere." She made sure her phone, with its camera, was charged, and then inhaled deeply. "I'm as ready as I'll ever be."

"Then let's put on our costumes."

She hurried as fast as she could, carefully applying the makeup. A few minutes later, she stepped into the living room where Kane was dressed in fatigues, like the kind the guards wore.

He tapped her nose. "You look cute."

Where had that cheer come from? She gave him a defiant stance. "My hair is all ratted, I have brown streaks all over my face, and I'm wearing horribly tattered clothes. I can't possibly look cute with fake blood on my cheek and arm. At least the purple bruises are real. It saved me makeup time."

He seemed to be fighting a smile. "It's mission time."

Without saying another word, she followed him to the Jeep. He went over the details one more time as they headed to their lot a mile from the base. They parked there because it had to look like she'd escaped.

It was chilly, so they jogged to keep warm. A coat would only prove she hadn't escaped from the DUMB. As they drew near, he pulled up. "I need to put the cuffs on you." His tone implied he didn't relish the idea.

She nodded. This was the uncomfortable part, and the memory of her boss slapping them on her wrists returned. Kane issued some orders loudly, and in less than thirty seconds, four men with guns arrived. Her pulse was racing so fast, she didn't need to fake the fear.

"Halt. Where are you going?"

Kane stepped forward and held up his badge. "I found prisoner 45813 wandering about a mile from here. I'm just returning her."

Silence.

She tried to jerk out of Kane's grasp, as a real prisoner would do, but it was fifty-fifty whether they'd believe the story. They leaned close to each other and conferred. Sky improvised. She doubled over and pretended to vomit. In the dark, they wouldn't be able to see if she was spewing her guts or was dry heaving.

"Take her inside."

Kane saluted and trotted her toward the shed. She stumbled, and this time she wasn't faking it.

He swiped the card and the door clicked open. The moment she stopped to look around, he jerked her arm and dragged her toward the ramp. From here on out, she had to act like his prisoner, and that meant no whispering and no improvising. She hoped Harriet appreciated their sacrifice.

The shed had been a new addition since Whistleblower2 had been there, and they had no idea if there would be stairs or not. They took the paved pathway downward, and as they reached the end of the long ramp, there were two doors. One required a fingerprint scan and the other an eye scan. Guess that answered the question why the killers took Randall Tyler's head. The eye scan must be for more secure area.

Kane pressed the dead man's finger over the scanner and tossed her an evil glance. Because cameras were probably watching their every move, she hung her head. The extra makeup she applied was to make her look like she'd been beaten.

The door clicked and they slipped in. She couldn't help but take in the bizarre surroundings. "Oh, my God."

"Silence," Kane said, acting super tough.

The entryway looked like a subway station, only instead of tiled walls, the rounded sides were reinforced with steel girders. A train track ran as far as she could see, rounded a bend, and then disappeared to who knew where. While there was a walkway along the side of the track for human or alien traffic, there appeared to be no doors or windows. The place smelled of grease, dirt, and sweat. Gross.

"Move it." Kane gently shoved her.

"Can't you uncuff me, now? I ain't going anywhere."

He tossed the key a few feet in front of her to make it look like he was in charge. She knew he was acting tough for all the watchful eyes. Playing along, she dropped to her knees and picked up the key. With much deliberation, she unlocked her cuffs, and the relief was considerable. Regardless of the circumstances, cuffs hurt.

Whistleblower had told them that once they were through the main doors, the way to the prison was down four levels. First, they had to walk several hundred yards to get to a second doorway. They re-scanned and entered an area that looked similar to the one they'd just crossed, except this one had no train tracks. This air was stale and seemed to be a mixture of oil and cement dust. It wouldn't be a nice place to work, especially since lung disease had to be prevalent. Sky wondered if they'd brought her here when they'd taken her. Unfortunately, she couldn't remember.

"Keep moving." Kane's tone sounded gruff, but she could tell he didn't like issuing the orders any more than she liked hearing them.

After a good three minutes, the path rounded a bend. What she wouldn't give to take photos and document this place, but that would land them both in a cell.

Once they passed the parking garage, they came to a large room off to the side that was filled with huge tubs of what looked like grass or some kind of thin green vegetable. Six-foot diameter heat lamps sat overhead and workers tended to the plants' care. It appeared the Base made some of its own food, unless the grass was there to help with oxygen production or feed animals.

Kane shoved her again. "Stop gawking."

She kept walking until the *sidewalk* turned to dirt, and the walls became rock. So far, Whistleblower hadn't steered them wrong. They rounded another curve and were faced with a fifteen-foot tall door that was twelve-feet wide. Given the size, it had to be at least three feet thick, reinforced again with steel bars. It wasn't something anyone could escape from. So how had she supposedly gotten away? Dear God. If they were caught, no one would find them—FBI or no FBI.

Kane must have sensed her despair, because he grabbed her neck. She bet he made it look rough to any onlookers, but when he massaged her muscles, she almost sank against him. She wondered how he had gone on missions where he could have been blown to smithereens at any moment or tortured and held captive when he didn't have anyone around to rub his neck or give him comfort. She shivered at the thought.

They entered the big doorway. Behind glass windows were science labs run by humans. The typical equipment was there, ranging from computers with large screens to machines that probably did tests on different materials or on humans. It wasn't something she wanted to think about.

If they couldn't find Harriet, she and Kane needed some evidence to show what the military was up to—whatever that was. Several armed men in uniform strode by. A few saluted, but they mostly ignored Kane and his prisoner. They then passed what she guessed was a cafeteria next to an empty library. She darted inside.

"Prisoner. Stand down."

When no alarm sounded, Kane ducked in behind her. This looked like a small high school library with maybe twenty rows of books, fifteen-feet tall. She was surprised they had any books, unless they figured electronic files were too easy to hack into. Four tables housed artifacts that could have been alien or pieces from a space shuttle. On the second table were several large books. She flipped through a couple of them, noting all were in foreign languages she didn't recognize, and the paper felt old. Then there was a sealed glass container that held the first two pages of some kind of legal document. She quickly scanned the contents.

"Holy crap."

This time she didn't wait for Kane to come over. She pulled out her camera phone and snapped two pictures of the contents.

"Sir, what is the prisoner doing in here?"

She froze.

CHAPTER TWENTY-SIX

Sky straightened and slipped the phone in her pocket before facing the too tall man in a well-fitting uniform. She hoped Kane wouldn't have to take him down, as the adversary's chiseled jaw and broad shoulders indicated he would be a formidable enemy.

"At ease, sergeant," Kane said. "I was taking the prisoner back to her cell when she dashed in here." Kane grabbed hold of her arm. "I won't let her get away again." His lip curled.

The military man hesitated for a second, firmed his mouth, and then saluted. "Yes, sir."

Thank goodness Kane wore a high ranking uniform. He dragged her from the room and leaned over close to her ear. "Don't do that again." He wasn't playing this time. She scrunched up her nose and debated spitting at him for effect, but then decided not to.

An exit door was off to the side, which hopefully led to the other levels. She prayed no one was coming up who would stop and question them. According to Mr. Morris, not only was the prison below, so might be the aliens.

They skipped level 2, 3, and 4 and went straight to level 5. Damn. She really wanted to take a quick look at level 3 to see if she could spot the extra-terrestrials, but they didn't possess

Randall's eye, which they would have needed for the security scanner.

Now came the hard part—checking out the jail. Kane didn't plan to hand Sky over; they merely wanted to see if Harriet was there.

At the end of the stairwell sat a door. He faced her. "Stay here. If I'm not back in five minutes, get the hell out of here."

She'd assumed she'd be by his side throughout the mission, but with her palms sweating and terror kneading her gut, perhaps this was for the best. "I won't move." The five-foot wide steps ended four feet from the door. She flattened her back against the wall and tried to be as invisible as possible, though if anyone entered the stairwell, he would see her.

Kane stared at her for a second. "You have to leave if they catch me. Promise?"

"They won't. You're too good."

She thought she caught a small upturn to his lips. "Then I guess I'll be back soon." He kissed her quick and disappeared into Level 5 before she had a chance to say more.

The next few minutes drove nails into her heart, as the narrow space closed in on her. The stairway turned twice before reaching the next level, and she was constantly on alert for foot-steps. She was a professional for God's sake and shouldn't be afraid, yet she was, not only for herself, but for Harriet, for Kane, and for all of the other people held captive against their will.

A noise sounded on the stairs above her. Shit. She dropped to her haunches and waited, blood pounding in her ears. She counted silently to sixty, and then again and then once more.

The door to Level 5 eased open and when Kane stepped out, she was so relieved that her feet almost slid out from under her. He shook his head implying no Harriet then motioned with his hands to go.

She pushed off the wall and stood on trembling legs and mouthed, "Right behind you."

They made it as far as the library when two men in uniform stopped them. The first was squat, the second thin, but both appeared fit. "Where are you taking the prisoner?"

Her heart flipped, and she could barely breathe, sucking in air in short raspy spurts.

With no hesitation, Kane stepped forward and cold cocked the first guard, stepped back and dropkicked the second. She'd never seen anything like it. The two men collapsed to the ground without a word. Next thing she knew, Kane grabbed her hand, and they were racing toward another door. Her lungs burned, and the soles of her feet hurt.

"I can't run...any...faster."

"You have to."

She knew the alarm would sound the moment anyone saw Kane running toward the exit with a prisoner. They'd be caught and maybe killed. Her heart squeezed until the physical pain was almost unbearable.

When they reached the final door, Kane had to scan the dead man's finger once more to exit. For a long second, the door didn't send out the familiar click, and a tight band squeezed her chest. Dear Lord, they could be locked in for life.

Then the door mercifully opened, and she and Kane entered the final stage of their journey. If she could have stopped to catch her breath, she would have, but there was no place to hide and take the needed break. The train tracks had a third rail that probably carried the electricity, so there was no way she'd be jumping down into that pit to hide. Touching the rail would kill them.

Kane pulled her along with him, their pounding feet echoing in the cavernous room. Finally, they made it to the shed without being stopped, and while the cameras probably caught their whole departure, no one had shot them. She found that odd but good.

Kane drew to a stop just outside the door to freedom, and before he pushed it open, the big garage door slid opened.

"Shit." Using hand signals, Kane motioned her toward the outside, knowing a guard was out there somewhere with a big gun. She went first, and was met with nothing but blackness. Even the moon must have decided it was best to hide.

Kane came up behind her, and they headed north, in the opposite direction from the ledge where she'd nearly fallen to her death. Several hundred yards later, he held up a hand for her to stop. It was probably because her breaths were too rapid, and he feared she might not make it.

He clasped her hand, and they slowly inched along the top of the canyon wall. One misstep and they'd tumble. There'd be no rope to save them this time. Kane must have deemed it safe, because he lowered them to the ground and pulled her onto his lap. He rubbed her arms. Only then did she realize the temperature had dropped to near freezing. Fear had a way of disguising certain discomforts.

"You okay?" he whispered in her ear.

At that moment, she loved him more than she ever had. He'd risked his life for her friend. She nodded. "I'm dreaming of a hot bath."

The moon made its appearance and glinted off his smile. "I say, let's do it."

**

Kane paced outside Sky's bathroom, angry with himself for going ahead with the plan. They hadn't found Harriet after all. He'd also found no evidence of foul play, which meant the FBI wouldn't have enough reason to charge in and see who was kept below. In fact, Kane saw no prisoners at all. Perhaps they'd learned he and Sky were coming and had moved the captives to a different level, one that required higher security.

He slapped the wall. The fuckers knew he and Sky had been there the whole time, and allowed them to see that nothing was amiss. Smart bastards. He'd put Sky through hell for nothing.

Someone had to have betrayed them. Was it the Chief, Harold, Elmer, or someone else?

Chief Lapahe had told him to call him no matter the hour if Kane learned anything about Harriet's whereabouts, but that was when he believed they were searching for her tomorrow. Kane had to trust someone, and he believed the Chief was clean. When he called, it took a moment to tell the Chief about the change of plans.

"You and Sky went in? Does that mean you freed Harriet?" From the anxiety in his tone, Lapahe wasn't in bed at this late hour. Most likely, he was refining the plan for tomorrow.

"No, sir. I found no evidence of any prisoners."

"Shit. Then where is she?"

From that question, Kane assumed there'd been no ransom demand. "I don't know, sir."

"Is Sky okay?"

"Yes. We can debrief in the morning."

The moment Kane hung up, the bathroom door opened, and Sky appeared. She was a vision with her hair wrapped in a towel and her body encased in a fluffy pink robe. "Next." She smiled, and his groin ached.

He wanted to grab her and kiss her, but he needed Sky to explain the note—when she was ready. He wouldn't feel right taking advantage of her in her fragile emotional state. She had to be reeling—one minute she was about to realize her dream of living in a big city, and the next, she was on a dangerous mission with him.

Kane took longer in the shower than usual, partly because he kept going through the details of the Base fiasco in his mind. They should have been caught and questioned. He'd seen the cameras mounted on the ceiling and didn't think the military would have fake security cams. As for Harriet, he had no idea where she was being held.

After he shaved and changed into jeans and a T-shirt, he had every intention of grabbing a beer and dropping into bed, but Sky was in the kitchen on her computer.

"You've got to see this." The excitement in her voice surprised him.

He pulled up a chair and sat next to her as she downloaded photos. He leaned closer. "What is it?"

She clicked to one of the pages she'd photographed in the library. "This is some kind of contract between the human race and the aliens."

"You can't believe that garbage. If it meant anything, a ton of MPs would have been down our throats."

"I hid the camera in front of my stomach. Unless they had cameras every few feet, they might not have seen me take the shot." She lowered her chin. "If this was junk, why keep it in an underground secret Base, under glass, where no one can steal it?"

From her bloodshot eyes and the way she slumped in her chair, she was barely holding on. He wouldn't be surprised if the military planted the evidence there—assuming they'd been tipped off about their break-in. What they hoped to gain, he didn't know. "Okay. Tell me what it says."

"I'll need to read it a couple more times as the whole concept is a real paradigm shift for me." He cocked a brow. "Basically, it says the aliens made an agreement with the human race a long time ago as they passed from one life to another."

His Christian upbringing wouldn't allow him to buy into the existence of past lives, but he'd let her have her opinion. She was entitled. "What did the agreement say?"

"The aliens are our custodians. They don't want to interfere in our lives, but when they saw how we were struggling, they changed our DNA—like a mutation that helped us adapt." She sat back and smiled. "This is so cool. This is why the aliens fly by but don't visit. They're checking up on us to make sure we're okay."

It was beneath him to roll his eyes, but he sure felt like it. "I think we both need some sleep. You can reread it in the morning."

She blew out a breath. "You might be right. This is mind-boggling. I can see why the government wants to keep this under wraps."

He pushed back his chair, grabbed the beer he'd come in the kitchen for and headed to his bedroom. If she followed because she wanted to talk about the letter, fine. If not, he'd have a rest-less night sleep.

***

A pounding at the front door jarred Sky awake. At first, she thought she was dreaming, but then the fists pummeling her door stopped and voices sounded—angry ones. Sky pulled on her robe and dashed down the hall to the living room where her breath evaporated. Five military men, in full uniform, had cuffed Kane.

Her tongue wouldn't work.

"Ma'am. I'm sorry, but we had a break-in at one of our facili-ties, and Mr. Cornell's name showed up."

That made no sense. She was with him, so why not take her too? Kane's glare sealed her lips but only for a moment.

"Where are you taking him?" She glanced at Kane, and between his narrowed eyes and hard jaw, he wanted her to say nothing more.

"To a safe place."

She had a thousand questions, but the men disappeared before she had her chance. Poor Kane. She raced to the window and watched two Hummers leave. *No, no, no.* They'd take him into the bowels of that terrible place, and no one would be able to free him.

Her knees weakened, and she wanted to vomit, but she had to stay strong—for him.

It was close to four in the morning, and she wasn't sure

where to turn. One thing was a must; she needed coffee—and lots of it. After three cups, she was no closer to coming up with a plan than when she'd been startled awake. The military had to have been aware both she and Kane had been there last night, so why only arrest him?

Sky pushed back her chair and paced. Maybe the Save Harriet team could help her come up with a plan. While it was early, she dressed and rushed outside, thinking it would be better if she were at work. Crap. She didn't have her car—but Kane's Jeep was there. Back inside, she located his wallet, keys, and phone.

Since she hadn't driven a stick in a long time, she drove with great care. At first, the car jerked and sputtered as she accelerated, but the feeling of the stick came back to her after a few minutes. With no traffic on the road, she made it into work in record time. As soon as she stepped inside, Harriet's empty desk tore at her insides, and Sky ran a hand over her seat, her heart breaking.

Elmer was the only one there. He looked up. "What are you doing here? The Chief called in and said the operation already took place."

"The military arrested Kane."

Elmer came over and took her hand. "Tell me everything."

There wasn't much she could tell, other than how they'd barged in.

"I'm sorry. What are you going to do?" he asked.

Like she had any idea? "The Chief's not in?"

"No, but he called less than fifteen minutes ago."

"I need to speak with him." she dialed her boss's home phone.

"Lapahe." He sounded on edge and very wide-awake.

She told him about the abrupt arrest.

"I'm sorry, but I had to do it."

Sky's stomach nearly revolted. "What do you mean you had to do it? Why?" She dropped onto her seat.

"I had to call in the FBI. I couldn't lose Harriet."

He wasn't making any sense. Sky had no idea he cared that much for their receptionist. And then it hit her. They were involved. "Wait a minute. The FBI didn't come to my door, the military did."

"Once I explained to the FBI what happened, they were obligated to call the military."

The Chief was an officer of the law and had to uphold his oath, but it should count that Kane risked his life, and hers, to find Harriet. "Thanks for not having them haul me off as well."

He didn't answer.

"Tell me how having Kane arrested helps get Harriet back," she demanded.

"I'm not sure, but I was grasping at straws."

"Sure." She disconnected then dropped her forehead on her desk, closed her eyes, and watched her world turn black.

"Sky?"

She jerked her head up. Elmer was standing next to a stocky, erect older gentleman in uniform who had more medals on his chest than she could count. He wasn't smiling.

She slowly rose, fearing he'd tell her Kane was being shipped to Washington to stand trial. At least that would be preferable to being hidden in the bowels of the Base. She swallowed hard and went over to learn more. She stuck out her hand. "I'm Sky Nash. How can I help you?"

"I'm General Stentfield, Kane's former CO."

Okay, that wasn't who she'd expected to show up here—especially at five in the morning—but the fact he was there had the joy in her heart nearly colliding with the spasm in her stomach. "Did Kane call you?"

"Yes, he was allowed one call."

"You made it here fast."

"Kane asked me to come yesterday, so I was staying nearby when he called."

"Please, have a seat." She pulled back Harriet's chair.

"I'd rather go for a drive." His warm blue eyes lessened her fears.

"I'll grab my coat." Kane probably told her he didn't trust someone at the station, and he'd been right. Chief Lapahe was a traitor as far as she was concerned. Arresting Kane wouldn't help anyone.

Once inside the General's rented car, he pulled out of town and then stopped by the side of the road. "Tell me everything, and leave nothing out."

By the time she finished, her mouth was dry. "You think letting us escape was a set-up?"

"I'm not sure what to think, but it looks like it. Military operations are well-run, especially secret ones."

"You have to get Kane out of jail. He was only trying to help a friend."

"I know, but you two did break the law, and I'm afraid it doesn't matter if it was for the better good."

It always seemed to come down to that. "I know, but does that mean you can't help in anyway?"

"Tell you what. I'll see what strings I can pull, but in the meantime, since you said you were on suspension, why don't you stay put in your house."

He sounded like Kane, but this time she'd listen. "I'm okay with that." He took her back to the station to pick up Kane's Jeep. She pulled a card from her purse, scribbled her cell number on the back, and then handed it to him. "Here's my number. Please let me know what you find out."

As soon as she slipped out, he took off. Not wanting to be around when the Chief arrived, she took the General's advice and drove home. No sooner had she walked in the door than her phone rang. The General couldn't have pulled strings that fast.

She lifted her home phone receiver. "Hello?"

"It's Earl. I have someone I think you want to see."

She had no idea what he was talking about. "Who? The whistleblower?" She didn't see how he could help.

"Just get your fanny out here and find out." He laughed.

She was so not in the mood for humor this early in the morning. Hell, the crows weren't even up. She had told the General she'd stay put, but she assumed he meant for her not to go snooping at the Base.

"Sure."

When she arrived, there wasn't a car in Earl's driveway, which implied Mr. Morris hadn't made an appearance. She knocked on the door and entered. Earl wasn't big on locking doors.

When she stepped inside, she nearly fainted.

CHAPTER TWENTY-SEVEN

The moment Sky recovered, she raced across the room and hugged Harriet. "How did you get free? What happened?"

Harriet hung her head. "I'm sorry about Kane's arrest and everything."

"How did you hear that? You've been gone."

"I called Bill, and he told me. In fact, he's on his way here now."

Bill? "The Chief is coming here?" She definitely didn't need to be here when he arrived. He might accuse her of kidnapping Harriet herself.

Harriet nodded.

"I can't stay." Sky studied the dreamy look on Harriet's face. "So it's true. You and the Chief are having an affair?"

She nodded. "For the last year."

Now wasn't the time to ask Harriet why she'd kept that nasty secret from her. No wait. It made sense; it was because Sky would try to talk her out of it. "So where have you been?"

Earl piped up. "Mr. Morris thought the only way to get you to go inside the DUMB was if you thought Harriet was in there."

"Why did he want me inside?" She couldn't connect the dots.

"He thought you'd find evidence of aliens, and then you'd bring in the FBI or something to shut them down. He's never forgiven them for what they did to his family or to the other people when he was working there."

"That was a rotten trick." It didn't matter that it worked. She had planned on sharing the alien-human pact document with him, but after that stunt, she just might keep it to herself. "I gotta go."

Neither attempted to stop her, which was a good thing since she made it to her turn off without passing the Chief. She wasn't even sure if she could be in the same room as those two again. She'd believed she and Harriet had no secrets.

Tears leaked out of her eyes, and she decided she couldn't trust anyone.

By the time she arrived home, all she could think of was a hot shower and a nap, though she doubted she'd sleep. It might be days or weeks before the General could spring Kane—if he could at all. She passed his bedroom and stopped. His gear was gone, and her heart hammered against her chest. Either the military broke in and nabbed it, or by some miracle, Kane had been released and he'd come for his stuff.

No. He couldn't have left since she had his Jeep.

She raced into his room and when she pulled open the drawers, they were all empty.

Numb, she headed back to the kitchen in search of a note and found it on the table in neat, block letters.

"Dear Sky. The General was able to pull strings and have me released. If I ever go back to the DUMB, it will be permanently. Listen, what we had was real. I'm sorry you didn't see it that way. Take care."

His signature came out stiff, as if he was controlling his emotions. For a split second she thought perhaps someone had made him write the note to make sure she didn't come looking for him, but then decided he wouldn't have penned something so personal.

Sky had to read the note five times before she was ready to believe that something had changed since his conversation. Her hands shook and she sat at the table and cried.

She thought about calling Harriet for advice, but Sky was peeved at her for the stunt she pulled. Besides, her former friend was probably in bed with the worst jerk she'd ever known.

Her cell rang and when she checked the caller ID, she debated not answering. It was the gossip queen, Rosalie, who owned the B&B where Kane had stayed. She was probably calling to see how Sky was doing after being dumped. News traveled really fast in this town.

"Hi Rose."

"You'll never guess who just stopped by with a rather handsome older man."

"Kane?" Her heart sputtered saying his name. Perhaps the General was staying there too.

"Yes."

"Are they there now?"

"They headed over to the café. Kind of had a feeling you just might want to know that tidbit."

Suddenly, things were looking up. "You're a wonder. Thanks." Sky disconnected. If she hurried, she might be able to find Kane before he headed back to Phoenix. After all, she did have his Jeep.

Before she left, she printed off the evidence that aliens existed—assuming the document she'd photographed at the Base was real.

She pushed the Jeep to its limits and practically skidded to a stop in front of the café. Few cars were parked there, and she slid right into her lucky spot. Hands sweaty and slightly out of breath, she straightened her shoulders and walked in. Her heart nearly stopped when she spotted Kane—handsome, strong, and looking oh so confident in deep conversation with the General. This probably wasn't the right time to tell him how she felt, but it was now or never. She wasn't going to lose Kane.

She strode up to his table. "General." Both men looked up, but she returned her focus to Kane, who looked a bit guilty.

"Can we speak in private?" she asked.

"The General and I are in the middle of a negotiation."

She pleaded with him with her eyes, having too much pride to beg. She glanced at the General, half expecting Stentfield to excuse himself out of politeness, but instead he leaned back in his chair. Okay, she hadn't planned to do this in front of the entire restaurant, which had suddenly quieted, but she wasn't ashamed of what she had to say. Thankfully, it was early and the place wasn't very crowded.

"I came here to tell you something." Her breath caught in her throat. She'd tell him about locating Harriet in a moment.

"I'm listening," he said.

"I shouldn't have left and only written a note. I imagine that hurt your feelings, and for that I am sorry."

"Apology accepted, but I don't think——."

She didn't want him to interrupt or she might lose her courage. "I need to finish. When I overheard you on the phone the other morning, I was devastated. You said, and I quote, *She would never quit being a cop, and I just didn't have that strong of an attachment to go through with it.* I realized then that you never intended to be with me." Her voice quivered, and she glanced over at Cathy, who was smiling, trying to give her some moral support. *Bless you.* "Because you didn't think we had a future, I went in search of mine."

Kane pushed back his chair and stood. He hesitated as if he wasn't sure what she wanted, but the look on his face caused more pain in her gut.

"Are you done?" He reached out and slid an errant strand of ear behind her ear. That one touch caused her insides to rejoice.

"No." She had more to say. "It's because of *you* that I found passion in my life. You've shown me how to be free and how to love." She took off her sunglasses and placed them on the table. "What I'm trying to say is that I love you and I want to be in——"

"Shh. You don't need to say anything else." He cupped her face and kissed her forehead. "When I saw the love in your eyes, I saw everything I needed to know." He leaned in close and when he kissed her, all of EBE's exploded with applause.

Now, she was totally embarrassed, but she didn't care. She had Kane in her arms.

He tapped her nose. "That conversation wasn't about *you* by the way."

She stilled. "It wasn't?"

"No, my little eavesdropping friend. One of my buddies wanted me to hire his sister. We've worked together before, and there was no way I wanted a repeat of that fiasco."

"Why didn't you tell me?"

"Why didn't you ask?"

Because my heart was breaking. "Good question."

"You know, Nash, you look like crap. How about something to eat?"

She sniffled and nodded.

The General smiled as she sat down. "That was quite a speech."

"Thanks. I've been rehearsing it for a while." She faced Kane. "In fact, I was about to tell you when the Chief rushed in and told us Harriet went missing." She snapped her fingers. "I almost forgot. Harriet is safe." She told him how the Whistleblower had taken her and why.

"That little shit."

She wasn't sure if he was referring to the Whistleblower or to Harriet, but she didn't want to ask. "Maybe it's for the best. You're out of jail, and I'm betting the Chief will drop the charges now that the Base knows who you are."

"That would be nice." His tone didn't sound happy, but she was too excited to read anything into what he said.

Sky slapped a hand on her chest. "I can't seem to remember anything." She pulled out the two pieces of paper she'd printed that showed the alien-human pact. "General, Kane and I found something at the Base."

He pulled out his glasses. "What is it?"

She detailed how the item was secured under glass. "The flash reflected off a few words, but you can make out most of it."

While the General took about ten minutes to read the document, Sky's heart nearly burst. Perhaps now she'd finally get confirmation that aliens existed.

The waitress came over. "I'm so happy for you." From the way Cathy's antennae were bobbing, she was telling the truth. "You want to order something?"

"Oh, yeah. I'm going all the way today, baby. I'll have the Nebula crab cakes with Anti-matter hot sauce and a double Black Hole espresso."

"You got it."

The General put down the paper. "This is incredible, but I don't think we can let this get out." Too bad Sky couldn't tell if he was stringing her along or not.

Like a popped balloon, she sank into her chair. "Why not?"

"People would be scared shitless, excuse my expression, if they thought someone was manipulating their DNA from up above. The stock market would go crazy and people might try to kill themselves before letting aliens touch them."

Kane leaned back, legs stretched out, and arms across his chest. He kept his expression shuttered, so she couldn't tell if he thought the General was pulling her leg or not.

"I'll tell you what I'll do," the General continued. "I'll take this to Washington and see what the government wants to do."

She smiled. "Thank you for taking me seriously."

The General nodded and Kane looked, well disgusted, as if she was being played by his former CO. Hell, maybe she was.

Her food arrived. While she ate, they polished off a few cups of coffee as the General regaled her with stories of Kane's heroics in his FAST team. She loved hearing about how selfless Kane was and how much his men respected him.

Kane cupped her hand. "The General is very fond of telling tales. Don't believe half of what he says."

Stentfield acted affronted, but it was clear the two were very fond of each other.

Once she finished eating and paid, the General pushed his chair back and turned to Kane. "I need to head back to the airport. You might want to grab your stuff out of my rental."

Sky dug into her pocket and handed Kane the keys to his Jeep. "You'll need these."

Once he transferred his gear from the rental to his Jeep, he slipped a hand around her waist. "You look like you could use a nap. I know I sure could use one." Then he winked.

"Need a place to stay for a bit?" He'd packed up his things from her place as if he planned to head to Phoenix right away, but perhaps she could convince him to stay now that they no longer had the misunderstanding. She cocked a brow trying to look as sexy and appealing as possible.

"I wouldn't mind hanging out a bit."

She did a mental fist pump. "Great."

Actually, it was more than great, but she didn't want to act desperate to get him into bed.

CHAPTER TWENTY-EIGHT

Kane held open the Jeep door for her. "Thanks for not wrecking my car."

She jabbed him on the shoulder. "I don't wreck cars. People run into me."

"Whatever you say." He smiled and nodded. She climbed in.

Once home, Sky unlocked the front door, her mind abuzz with all the things she wanted to do to Kane Cornell—like strip him naked, run her hands down his rippled chest, and kiss him silly, just to name a few things. She dropped her purse on the floor near the entrance, and the next thing she knew, Kane's lips were on hers, and her back was flat against the wall. Whoa. She swore the man had a hundred hands as he touched and caressed her body, sending her into sensory overload. This ferocious beast was not what she'd expected. Her seducing him had been the plan.

Sky let out a groan and took hold of his face to return his passionate kisses, drinking him in.

Kane dragged a hand down her face. "You have no idea how much I've been dreaming of this."

"Me too."

He stepped back, retrieved his wallet, and then plucked out a condom. "You want to do the honors?"

She'd been dreaming of taking him into her mouth and driving him wild. "Mind if I suck on it first?"

He groaned and then clenched his jaw. "Be quick. This will push my resolve to the max."

She unbuttoned his jeans, pulled open his fly, and lowered his pants over his taut butt. The man was solid muscle. Sky inhaled, grabbed his rigid cock, and dropped to her knees. When she licked his length to test the waters, he hissed, grabbed her hair, and tugged.

"I'm on edge. Be careful."

From the way his voice wavered, he was serious. The need to taste him drove her to engulf his cock and suck hard. The pressure on her scalp increased, almost to the point of pain, but she loved his passion. Twirling her tongue around his cock, she pumped her fist up and down while she sucked on him hard.

"Enough." Kane grabbed her wrist and pulled her upright. "I want you."

"Oh, yeah? What happened to the man who liked to take his time, who was capable of tormenting me with a flower?"

"He's so gone. The moment you told me how you felt, all bets were off."

He ripped open the condom and donned it, fire and lust pooling in his eyes, and she'd never been more turned on. Wanting to torture him like he had her, she pressed her chest against him, loving how his pecs flexed as his hands explored her body. He parted his lips. Taking advantage of the invitation, she delved in.

Love, heat, passion, and pure joy filled her. Each thrust stole her breath and made her wetter. She tried to push away from the wall, but Kane managed to keep contact with her as he removed her jacket, all the while kissing her lips, her eyes, and her throat. He only stepped back when he lifted off his shirt and helped her out of her top. The touching increased, and throughout it all, she wasn't aware when he'd kicked off his shoes and managed to rid himself of his jeans, but she wasn't complaining.

"You're way ahead of me." She giggled, so happy that she could be with the man she loved.

Sky unhooked her bra and stripped off her panties, waiting to see what he wanted to do next.

Kane sucked in a breath. "I have to have you. Now."

His eyes were mostly closed, and his lips were soft and open. God, what he did to her. He cupped her butt and lifted her up against his big, hard cock. Sky wrapped her legs around his waist then drew his head to hers and kissed him again. The moment their tongues tangled, he slipped his hard dick into her wet folds, and drove upward, her inner walls screaming from the friction.

Kane was raw power, in control, and oh, so heavenly to look at. He slowly withdrew, as if he wanted to give her a moment to accommodate his size. She didn't want to wait and tried to lower her hips, but he held on.

"Hurry," she begged.

He grinned. "You don't really want that." His Adam's apple bobbed.

Instead of returning to the kiss, he lowered his head and swirled his tongue around her nipple, never actually touching the tip. She was convinced he truly wanted to drive her wild—and he succeeded. His cock remained still, and her desperation grew. To let him know she needed him, she clamped down on his hard shaft.

He stopped stroking her nipple to let out something akin to a growl. "Don't do that." His gaze lowered as if she'd committed a crime.

She might have responded had he not captured her mouth again. This time, his tongue darted in and out furiously, while he slowly eased his cock inside her. He pressed her harder against the wall, his hands holding her up by her ass. Using his teeth, he tugged on each nipple, creating a welcoming pain. Rapid bliss shot down to her belly as he pistoned into her again. He twirled his tongue around the tips repeatedly until the heat built inside her to a point where she was ready to come.

Kane hung on tight and thrust into her hard. He grunted and moaned, saying her name over and over again as if he were possessed. The harder and faster he went, the higher he took her, until she could no longer stop the overwhelming climax from claiming her.

"Kane!" Waves of powerful glory slammed into her as the contractions rippled down her body, and her orgasm tore through her at a furious pace.

She yelled once more as his cock expanded, his climax rippling through her so violently she could only imagine what he must be feeling.

"Sky. Oh, Sky." His eyes closed as his hot cum filled the protective barrier.

With his arms wrapped tightly around her, his breath poured over her shoulder, and she wished she never had to unwrap her legs.

"Wow." She'd never had such an amazing experience in her life, though the flower seduction was something she'd never ever forget.

"A little different from the last time, huh?"

Sky grinned. "You can say that again."

He lifted her off of him. "I wanted to take my time, I really did, but the moment I started kissing you, I just— "

She held a finger over his lips. "I'm happy."

"Yeah. Me too. What do you say we take a shower? Together."

"You are full of such good ideas."

***

Kane insisted on fixing the coffee and treating her to one of his dinner specials. "I think I could become accustomed to this pampering," she said.

He looked over his shoulder and smiled. They'd been skirting the issue about how long he planned to stay or even why he was staying, though she wasn't going to broach the subject until necessary. His cell rang, and he took the pan off the burner and answered. "Yes, General." Kane paced while he listened. "I understand. Thanks for trying."

From the slight slump of his shoulders, the news wasn't good. "What did he say?"

"The FBI won't investigate the Base. They said there is no reason for them to interfere in a military operation. To be honest, I'm not surprised."

"Neither am I, but where does that leave us in exposing them? I believe they abducted me, the Senator, and possibly Dan Joe. They shouldn't be able to get away with that."

"I know, but I think Savory is stuck with a secret base miles from town."

"It's hardly secret anymore. Maybe I should write an article about them."

"If you did, you'd have to admit you broke in and trespassed."

She finished off her coffee. "True, but losing my freedom might be worth it if no one was abducted again, or killed, like Randall Tyler." She leaned back in her chair, her mind sorting through her options. "There is something I might be able to do."

Kane returned the pan to the burner and stirred. "Is it legal?"

"Yes, and the best part about it is that the military won't like it."

His hand tightened on the pan. "What is it?"

"I have a friend in Page who's a news reporter. What if they go in at night, using lots of lights, a couple of cameras, and a truck on the road doing live feed to investigate? It would make great press if the station showed up and they were stopped by an armed guard."

"What do you hope to accomplish?" He sounded more curious than cautious.

"If the Base knows they're being watched, maybe they'll be

more careful about taking our residents."

Kane shrugged. "I don't see any harm in letting them try, but this time, let's tell Lapahe and get his permission. If you want your job back, you'll need to be on his good side."

She didn't trust her boss after the stunt he'd pulled, but what Kane said made sense. "He'll need to promise not to call the FBI and turn us in before we take the news crew there."

"You're right about that."

"I'll set it up with the Chief, but first I want to see if my friend in Page, Lauren Sanchez, is interested."

Sky was able to reach Lauren on the first ring and explained the situation, making sure to mention there was a possibility the Base housed aliens. Her friend had a strong interest in the topic.

"Are you shitting me? There's a secret base miles from my house? Are you sure?"

"Let's just say I have first-hand knowledge and leave it at that."

"You got it. George, my cameraman is also a big conspiracy theorist. He'll be up for it, I'm sure. I can have a truck by the road to transmit live, and if I bring in a second cameraman and two guys with lights, there are sure to be fireworks."

Excitement raced through her. "I love it. When can you be ready?"

"Is tonight soon enough?"

"Perfect. Lauren, let me put you on speaker phone so Kane, my friend, and you can hash out the details."

Kane turned off the stove and returned to her side. "Hey, Lauren. Both Sky and I have been inside the Base, so I'd like to be there when you approach them."

Yikes, why did he have to tell her that? Sky didn't need the world to know what they'd done.

"No problem."

"I also think we need some police back up. The Savory PD has no jurisdiction there, so can you ask the Page police to help us out?"

"I'll try but..." Lauren hesitated for a moment. "I have another idea. How about if I bring in a group from MUFON?"

Kane's brows pinched. "Who are they?"

"You've never heard of them? You must live under a rock."

Her friend had stepped over the line. "Lauren."

"Sorry. MUFON stands for Mutual UFO Network. They are a group of volunteers who are resolved to study UFO's and everything related to possible aliens. They're a very respected and widespread agency. They'll want to expose this Base if aliens are being held captive."

"Yes! The military wouldn't be able to hide anymore," Sky said.

Kane leaned closer to the phone. "How about we convene at the intersection of 98 and 89 to discuss the details? Say 2300 hours?"

"We'll be there."

Sky was happy Lauren sounded so excited. Five hours wasn't very long to plan the major coup of her life, but she was up for it. With Kane to guide her, she was sure everything would go well. "I'll sign out the swipe card again, since I think we might need it."

"Assuming Chief Lapahe goes along with your little plan."

"How can he not?"

"You are kind of persona non grata, remember?"

"I'm still a cop. Maybe I should have Elmer sign it out for me."

"Do whatever you need to, but make sure it's legal and that you have the chief's permission." Kane walked over to the refrigerator and pulled out the box sealed in plastic that contained the finger.

"That thing is just gross." She winced. Thinking about keeping the nasty appendage next to the food disgusted her, but Kane assured her he'd sealed it tight.

He pulled up a chair. "Now, we plan. Here's how it's going to go down."

CHAPTER TWENTY-NINE

When they arrived at the designated intersection, the KWLP van was stationed on the road next to the perfume factory drive. "I wonder if the Hummers will run us off again." Sky zipped up her jacket, ready for the confrontation of her life.

Kane pulled behind the news truck and cut the engine to his Jeep. "We'll find out soon enough."

She wished she understood how he could remain so calm. It would be easy for the military to grab everyone and shove them in cells for the rest of their lives. Even though Lapahe knew where she'd be, she wondered if he'd bother to save them.

Two more cars pulled up behind them. From the way they rolled to a stop instead of sliding to a halt, Sky figured they were part of the station's team. If not, they all were in trouble. Lauren exited the passenger's side of the van, and Sky jumped out of the Jeep. She met her friend halfway and they hugged.

"Everything ready?" Sky asked. Despite the dry, cold air, she began perspiring. She used to be so cool under fire, but her abductors must have removed her nerves of steel.

Lauren nodded to the cars behind the Jeep. "We have Rick and Phil from MUFON, along with Joe, who's a big UFO fan, in the other car. He's an off-duty cop from Page. I called his precinct, but they didn't want anything to do with this."

"That works for me. My chief and one of the deputies know where we are, but they won't be here—not that they have any jurisdiction anyway."

Kane handed Sky a bulletproof flak jacket. "Put this on." From his stern tone, she figured it was better not to argue.

All the people assembled in a circle. Rick blew into his hands, while Phil rocked back and forth. Besides Kane, only Joe seemed in control.

Huddling near because voices traveled far in the clear night, Kane addressed the group, giving them the instructions and what to expect. "Let me go first. You're going live, right?" Kane asked.

"Yes." This came from the cameraman.

"Okay. Let's do this."

Sky was relegated to bringing up the rear. While she didn't like the end position, she understood why Kane put her there. With a deep breath, she followed the group along the road and up the drive to the factory. To her surprise, no Hummers were parked in the lot. Most likely, they'd stationed themselves around back. Kane motioned with his hand for the group to proceed.

Sky glanced around, expecting a guard to walk around the corner at any moment and stop them. Only no one appeared. In fact, no one seemed to be about. Even the light above the shed was off, and her belly tingled. Something was definitely not right.

Lights from the camera lit up, and Lauren stepped in front. With a microphone in hand, she faced the camera. "We are in the back of the Fleur de Paris perfume factory where it is reported a secret underground military base exists."

Using a red filtered flashlight, Kane trotted toward the shed door, swiped the card, and pulled it open. Sky expected a siren or some shouts, but nothing other than the gurgling of the river below reached her, along with a few birds squawking overhead. Kane motioned them inside. As previously agreed, one cameraman would stay outside in case military personnel appeared. The KWLP employees had walkie-talkies to warn those inside should they be spotted.

The air was still inside the shed, and no noise came from below. Kane motioned they follow him down the ramp. A camera was mounted in the corner where she was sure none had been before. Those in charge had to know they were there, so why was there no resistance? The bad feeling in her stomach worsened, but she followed the group downward, keeping an eye out for anything else suspicious. Kane pressed the dead man's finger against the door and the familiar click sounded.

"We're inside the military base," Lauren announced with the camera rolling. "So far, we've not seen anyone."

When they reached the long walkway next to the rails, their footsteps echoed off the walls, but no one said a word. Lauren motioned the cameraman to keep filming. At the doorway to the stairs, Kane halted.

"From here on out, no talking. Be vigilant. Let's go."

While they didn't speak, their footsteps sounded like a hundred high school students racing down the steps. When they made it to level 2, the door was propped open. Kane raised his hand and caught Sky's eye. Something was going on. This was where they did human experiments, like mind control.

"Stay here." He whispered the command, but she suspected their stealth wasn't required.

Kane ducked inside while they all waited in silence. A minute later, he returned. "They're gone."

"Gone? Can we go in?" Lauren asked.

"I see no reason why not."

For the next half hour, the crew explored the levels. Other than the kitchen, where plates and dirty dishes sat on the counter, there was no evidence of humans or aliens.

"Kane?" Sky ran a hand down his back to get his attention. "I want to check the library."

"We go together."

She didn't argue. Deflated, they made their way up from level 2 and then back to the level where the library was housed. Only a few books remained on the shelves, most of which were physics books. The treaty that had been encased in plastic and housed under glass was also gone.

Lauren stepped next to Sky. "Do you think the Savory PD tipped them off?"

"I'm not sure. Could it have been the Page PD?"

She shrugged. "I have no idea." She turned to Joe, the off-duty cop. "Do you think your boss would have called this in?"

"No. We've discussed the possibility of a Base existing somewhere around here, but he's not a believer. Besides, he wouldn't know who to call."

"Well, someone let them know."

General Stentfield might have been pressured by some higher up to tell them if another breach was about to occur, but Sky wasn't about to suggest Kane's boss betrayed them.

Kane turned to Lauren. "You have enough footage?"

"Yes. I might be able to use some of this to show the Base existed, but this is not a big story."

"I'm sorry to have dragged you all out," Sky said, working hard not to let defeat color her tone.

The group was quiet as they left. The cameraman outside told them no one had shown up. Kane wrapped an arm around Sky's shoulder. "With the Base abandoned, at least Savory should be safe from any more abductions."

That was some consolation. "I feel like I'm in the middle of that television show The X-Files where we never really know for sure whether aliens were responsible for what happened."

"I think we can be assured it was the government in this case."

"Maybe. I want to know who exposed our plan. It had to be the Chief, Harvey, Elmer, or the Page PD."

"Or it could have been Harriet, Dan Joe, or any of the family members of the TV station crew who wanted to make sure they stayed safe."

"It still sucks."

***

The next morning, she half expected Kane to say he was heading out, but instead he suggested that they go to town for a good breakfast at EBE's. She wasn't sure of his agenda, but since she wasn't in the mood to cook, she agreed. Being in town would give her a chance to tell the Chief about the closed Base. Whether he agreed to let her come back to work was anyone's guess. There probably wouldn't be a trial as those prosecuting her had left town and wouldn't want to admit they existed.

Sky wanted to suggest to Kane they search for the Base's new location, but she understood he'd be heading back to Phoenix soon since he wasn't getting paid to stay in Savory. To add to her depression, Lauren had called this morning to say she wasn't going to air her piece since they'd found nothing. Sky said she totally understood.

Sky twisted in the front seat to face him. "You know what sucks the most?"

"What?"

"We never did figure out who killed Randall Tyler."

"You probably never will. I think you'll agree that he was killed because his murderers needed access to the Base."

"It's gross to think they killed him for his eyes."

"It could have been two workers from the Base who wanted more secure access, but they'd have to be pretty desperate if they were willing to kill a man for it."

"I agree. Those men are probably long gone, and until they commit another murder, they're going to get away with it," she said.

"True."

Kane parked in front to the restaurant. As she slipped out, her cell rang. "Uh-oh. It's the Chief."

"Sky. Where are you right now?"

"I'm about to go into EBE's." What did he care?

"I'm glad I caught you." She hoped he didn't think she'd flee town.

"What's up?"

"A couple of things. Harriet told me what happened, and I wanted to thank you for risking your life to look for her. I also received a call from some General explaining everything about the Base. You're off suspension. You can start work tomorrow."

"Thanks." Or not. She was enjoying the first vacation she'd had in forever, but if Kane left, she'd want to throw herself into her job.

"One other thing," he said. "Harvey's gone."

"Gone?" Holy shit. Had there been another abduction?

Kane held open the café door, and she headed to her usual spot. The breakfast crowd was particularly noisy this morning, so Sky had to press her palm to her ear.

"Not gone, gone," the Chief explained. "He quit the force. He couldn't live with the lies anymore."

"What lies?"

"You know Harvey's son died several years ago?"

"Yes, he overdosed."

"Harvey knew the drugs came from someone in his son's unit, and ever since, he's had a hate-on for the military. Harvey wanted to drive out their presence before they ruined anyone else."

She tried to connect the dots. "Are you saying Harvey let the Base know we were coming?"

"Yes."

"I would have thought he'd want the Base exposed. It would make the military look bad for hiding secrets."

"I don't think Harvey was thinking clearly. He knew their

presence was bad and wanted them gone. He didn't want anyone else harmed."

"I never would have guessed. Thanks for letting me know." She disconnected.

Kane sat with his back to the café wall. This time, Sky faced him, secure in knowing nothing could harm her with Kane there. "Harvey was the rat." She told him why.

"Maybe he did us a favor."

"Do you really mean that? I wanted to find aliens and help free any prisoners."

"We have no idea if there ever were prisoners or aliens for that matter."

She scrunched up her nose. "You might be right."

Kane chuckled, and Cathy came over to take their order then left. He leaned back in his seat. "I have a proposition for you." He had a twinkle in his eyes and that sexy dimple in his cheek appeared.

"I'm listening."

"I have a feeling with Harvey gone and Carl probably returning to work soon, the Chief will hire someone else new, and your duties will once again be relegated to traffic tickets and bar fights."

"Ouch." She shrugged. "I think you're right. We don't get a lot of crime around here. Well, at least we didn't before the Base stuff started happening."

He grabbed her hands. "What about moving to Phoenix with me and starting a detective agency?"

The wind was knocked out of her lungs. "You want me to move to Phoenix? To start an agency?"

"Yes. There's more. Move in with me."

Her heart pounded so fast, she could barely think. "I'm speechless."

"Can I take that as a yes?"

"Yes! Oh my God. I can't believe it."

Kane's smile nearly made craters in his cheeks. "There is one stipulation."

No way would he make her do something she didn't like. "What?"

"You let me buy you the biggest, heaviest car made."

Sky laughed and loved him even more. "It's a deal."

***

I hope you enjoyed Sky and Kane's story!!

Don't forget to sign up for my newsletter to receive three free books, as well as up-to-date information on my stories. If you prefer to only receive notices regarding my releases, follow me on BookBub.

The End

ABOUT THE AUTHOR

Love it HOT and STEAMY? Sign up for my newsletter and receive MONTANA DESIRE for FREE. Click here

OR Are you a fan of quirky PARANORMAL COZY MYSTERIES? Sign up for this newsletter. Click Here

Not only do I love to read, write, and dream, I'm an extrovert. I enjoy being around people and am always trying to understand what makes them tick. Not only must my romance books have a happily ever after, I need characters I can relate to. My men are wonderful, dynamic, smart, strong, and the best lovers in the world (of course).

My Paranormal Cozy Mysteries are where I let my imagination run wild with witches and a talking pink iguana who believes he's a real sleuth.

I believe I am the luckiest woman. I do what I love and I have a wonderful, supportive husband, who happens to be hot!

Fun facts about me
(1) I'm a math nerd who loves spreadsheets. Give me numbers and I'll find a pattern.
(2) I live on a Costa Rica beach!
(3) I also like to exercise. Yes, I know I'm odd.

I love hearing from readers either on FB or via email (hint, hint).

Social Media Sites

Website: www.velladay.com
FB: www.facebook.com/vella.day.90
Twitter: velladay4
Gmail: velladayauthor@gmail.com
Tiktok: Velladayauthor1
Bookbub: https://www.bookbub.com/authors/vella-day

ALSO BY VELLA DAY

SILVER LAKE SERIES (3 OF THEM)

(1). HIDDEN REALMS OF SILVER LAKE (Paranormal Romance)

Awakened By Flames (book 1)

Seduced By Flames (book 2)

Kissed By Flames (book 3)

Destiny In Flames (book 4)

Box Set (books 1-4)

Passionate Flames (book 5)

Ignited By Flames (book 6)

Touched By Flames (book 7)

Box Set (books 5-7)

Bound By Flames (book 8)

Fueled By Flames (book 9)

Scorched By Flames (book 10)

(2). GODDESSES OF DESTINY Paranormal Romance)

Slade (book 1)

Rafe (book 2)

Will (book 3)

Josh (book 4)

Jace (book 5)

Tanner (book 6)

(3). WERES AND WITCHES OF SILVER LAKE (Paranormal Romance)

A Magical Shift (book 1)

Catching Her Bear (book 2)

Surge of Magic (book 3)

The Bear's Forbidden Wolf (book 4)

Her Reluctant Bear (book 5)

Freeing His Tiger (book 6)

Protecting His Wolf (book 7)

Waking His Bear (book 8)

Melting Her Wolf's Heart (book 9)

Her Wolf's Guarded Heart (book 10)

His Rogue Bear (book 11)

Box Set (books 1-4)

Box Set (books 5-8)

Reawakening Their Bears (book 12)

OTHER PARANORMAL SERIES

PACK WARS (Paranormal Romance)

Training Their Mate (book 1)

Claiming Their Mate (book 2)

Rescuing Their Virgin Mate (book 3)

Box Set (books 1-3)

Loving Their Vixen Mate (book 4)

Fighting For Their Mate (book 5)

Enticing Their Mate (book 6)

Box Set (books 1-4)

Their Huntress Mate (book 7)

Craving Their Mate (book 8)

PACK WARS-THE GRANGERS

Meant for them (book 1)

Meant for wolves (book 2)

Meant for forever (book 3)

Meant for her (book 4)

HIDDEN HILLS SHIFTERS (Paranormal Romance)

An Unexpected Diversion (book 1)

Bare Instincts (book 2)

Shifting Destinies (book 3)

Embracing Fate (book 4)

Promises Unbroken (book 5)

Bare 'N Dirty (book 6)

Hidden Hills Shifters Complete Box Set (books 1-6)

CONTEMPORARY SERIES

MONTANA PROMISES (Full length contemporary Romance)

Promises of Mercy (book 1)

Foundations For Three (book 2)

Montana Fire (book 3)

Montana Promises Box Set (books 1-3)

Hart To Hart (Book 4)

Burning Seduction (Book 5)

Montana Promises Complete Box Set (books 1-5)

Novellas:

Montana Desire (book 1)

Awakening Passions (book 2)

PLEDGED TO PROTECT (contemporary romantic suspense)

From Panic To Passion (book 1)

From Danger To Desire (book 2)

From Terror To Temptation (book 3)

BURIED SERIES (contemporary romantic suspense)

Buried Alive (book 1)

Buried Secrets (book 2)

Buried Deep (book 3)

The Buried Series Complete Box Set (books 1-3)

A NASH MYSTERY (Contemporary Romance)

Sidearms and Silk(book 1)

Black Ops and Lingerie(book 2)

A Nash Mystery Box Set (books 1-2)

STARTER SETS (Romance)

Contemporary

Paranormal

www.ingramcontent.com/pod-product-compliance
Lightning Source LLC
Chambersburg PA
CBHW030238200626
46816CB00002BA/414